BRAVO!

"An unusual _____ if
you think the _____ , it
isn't. She was exactly _____."
—Newgate Callendar,
The New York Times Book Review

"GOOD FUN! Following her entertaining *A
Cadenza for Caruso*, Paul has fashioned another
humorous mystery set in the golden days of the
Metropolitan Opera." —*Publishers Weekly*

"Gerry Farrar, as charming as she is egotistical,
and Caruso romp entertainingly through their
own investigation, to the consternation of the
police. The book is full of interesting details
about . . . the Met on the eve of World War I."
—*Chicago Sun-Times*

"BREEZY ENTERTAINMENT . . . A DE-
LIGHTFUL SLEUTH."
—*Cleveland Plain Dealer*

"Delightful soprano Geraldine Farrar provides
the lively detective work, and behind-the-scenes
vignettes add humor and spice."
—*Library Journal*

SIGNET MYSTERY

Prima Donna at Large

□ □ □

Barbara Paul

A SIGNET BOOK

NEW AMERICAN LIBRARY

PUBLISHED BY
THE NEW AMERICAN LIBRARY
OF CANADA LIMITED

PUBLISHER'S NOTE

This book is a work of fiction. Names, characters, places, and incidents are either the product of the author's imagination or are used fictitiously, and any resemblance to actual persons, living or dead, events, or locales is entirely coincidental.

Copyright © 1985 by Barbara Paul

This is an authorized reprint of a hardcover edition published by St. Martin's Press.

First Signet Printing, May, 1987

2 3 4 5 6 7 8 9

SIGNET TRADEMARK REG. U.S. PAT OFF AND FOREIGN COUNTRIES
REGISTERED TRADEMARK — MARCA REGISTRADA
HECHO EN WINNIPEG, CANADA

SIGNET, SIGNET CLASSIC, MENTOR, ONYX, PLUME, MERIDIAN AND NAL BOOKS are published in Canada by The New American Library of Canada, Limited, 81 Mack Avenue, Scarborough, Ontario, Canada M1L 1M8
PRINTED IN CANADA
COVER PRINTED IN U.S.A.

□ 1 □

It was a mistake, I should never have done it, I should have stood firm, I should have said *no*. Rule number one for sopranos: *Never sing in a world première when you're sick*.

I can't really complain about the reviews, I suppose. The critics were kind for the most part, although not one of them passed up the chance to mention I was still suffering the effects of my "lingering indisposition," as they so prettily put it. (I had a cold—a plain, ordinary *cold*.) The critics all praised my acting, bless them, but *The New York Times* suggested a little more restraint. As usual. Whatever I do, *The New York Times* suggests a little more restraint. They suggest, and I ignore—as I would this time. *Madame Sans-Gêne* is broad comedy; it *has* to be played big, with oversized gestures and the like.

The telephone hadn't stopped ringing all morning—first my manager, then friends and well-wishers, and even a few rivals bent on keeping up appearances. Scotti called twice, dear man. Some fans showed up here at the apartment building and the doorman had to shoo them off, go-away-little-girls, have to speak to him about that. Last night may have been a qualified triumph, but it was a triumph nonetheless.

Geraldine Farrar in Umberto Giordano's new opera, "Madame Sans-Gêne." Has a nice sound to it, don't you think?

Actually, I fared better than the opera itself did. The critics one and all agreed that *Madame Sans-Gêne*, while tuneful and pleasant, is not particularly distinguished or original, tut tut. 'Tis neither grand nor eloquent, those overpaid arbiters of public taste have declared, nor does it contain any real—take a deep breath—*passion*.

Well, I knew that, for heaven's sake! Not every new opera can be a *Tosca* or a *Butterfly*. And besides, there's a real place on the operatic stage for the lighter works. It can get a bit wearying, singing the same standard roles over and over again. I'm always on the lookout for something new, or at least something I myself have never sung before. In fact, it's time I started thinking about my next

5

new role. Perhaps *Thaïs*? I want to get something this time that the critics won't be so quick to dismiss as unworthy of everybody's efforts.

Just the same, last night's glittering audience at the Metropolitan Opera had been excited and uncritically enthusiastic; in the long run, that's what counts. The truth is, I have a large and faithful following that always watches with fascination every new thing I try. The Metropolitan has only two singers who can be relied on to fill every seat in the house every time they appear. Caruso is one, and I am the other. There's no modest way to say it, but my fans *adore* everything I do. Truly. With that kind of support, who wouldn't keep trying new things?

But the fact remains I did not sing well last night; that blasted cold robbed me of all my top notes. I should have refused to sing at all. But that mule-headed Gatti-Casazza had been adamant; and once the Metropolitan's general manager puts his size-eighteen foot down, there's no budging him. He'd postponed the première once because of my illness, from Friday to the following Monday. On Friday Mr. Gatti had hurriedly substituted another opera from the company's repertoire—and most of the audience had asked for its money back. That little item of news hadn't depressed me one bit, ha, nosiree it hadn't. But Mr. Gatti had been appalled at the thought of the same thing happening again, so I had to sing the première performance of *Madame Sans-Gêne* on Monday, January 25, 1915, cold or no cold. Frankly, I was just as glad Giordano, the opera's composer, hadn't been able to come to New York for the première after all. There's nothing more disheartening than an unpraised composer drooping around an opera house.

The telephone rang. It was Caruso, bubbling over with italianate good cheer. "Gerry, *mi amore*, you were magnificent! But then you always are, are you not? Me, I cannot tell from listening that you are sick at all! Not even a little bit sick!"

I appreciated the lie and was quite willing to go along with it. "Why, thank you, Rico—what a nice thing to say!

If you believed the newspapers, you'd think I dragged myself from my deathbed last night.''

"Pooh! What do they know? Just the same, you must take care of yourself,'' Caruso fussed. "No vocalizing today, not even scales. Stay in bed, rest. Do you hear, Gerry?''

"I hear.''

"I send Mario with my special throat spray—you use it, yes? And I send some to Pasquale also.''

"Pasquale? Why?''

"His throat burns like furnace, his eyes they water, his nose does not permit the proper breathing . . .''

I groaned. Pasquale Amato sang the role of Napoleon in *Madame Sans-Gêne*, last night I'd noticed he was looking a bit peaked, but he'd sounded superb and I was so wrapped up in opening-night nerves I hadn't paid much attention to anything else. And now it looked as if I'd passed on my cold to Amato. I asked Caruso, "Will he be all right by tomorrow night?'' The three of us were scheduled to sing *Carmen* on Wednesday.

"Who knows?'' I could hear the shrug in his voice. "This morning, he cannot sing even a nursery tune. But by tomorrow night . . . who is to say? Tomorrow night he may sing his best Escamillo ever!'' Caruso, the eternal optimist.

I had been worrying whether *I* would be ready Wednesday night; Carmen is much more demanding a role than Caterina in *Madame Sans-Gêne*. But I was getting over my cold—Pasquale Amato was just starting his. On impulse I said, "I'll take him some of my medicine.''

"No!'' Caruso commanded with authority. "*I* take care of Pasquale. You stay home and take care of yourself.''

"I feel responsible, Rico. I'm sure he caught his cold from me.''

But my favorite tenor was in a paternalistic mood that morning and kept insisting, so finally I promised to do as he said just to stop his well-meaning badgering. The minute I hung up I called to one of the maids to bring my hat and coat. I started packing a small valise with the various medicines I'd accumulated lately; Caruso's throat spray was good for the ordinary hoarseness that plagues every singer, but it wouldn't do anything for Amato's cold. I checked my appearance in the mirror and ten minutes later was away on my errand of mercy.

The chauffeur drove me from West Seventy-fourth Street down Central Park West, around Columbus Circle, and on to Broadway. Everywhere I looked, bold black-and-white posters were exhorting me to give to the War Relief Fund. Sidewalk billboards proclaimed the day's headlines: *German Submarine Sinks Three Steamers in Irish Channel, Bread Riots in Florence.* I found I was clenching my jaw and had to do a breathing exercise to relax. I *would* not let the European war depress me, even though everyone was saying it was only a matter of time until America joined in.

The limousine pulled up in front of the Hotel Astor in Times Square. I'd decided that if Pasquale Amato was sleeping, I'd quietly leave my valise of nostrums and not disturb him. But Amato's valet assured me that his master was awake and ushered me into the sick man's bedroom.

The first thing I saw was the huge rear end of a woman who was bending over the sickbed straightening the covers. She had all the grace of a Guernsey cow; and when she looked back over her shoulder with enormous cow eyes, I fully expected her to moo. "Hello, Emmy," I said.

"Good morning," Emmy Destinn answered amiably enough. "You have come to visit our ailing baritone?"

No, I'm having an affair with the valet. "Rico telephoned me," I said, figuring that was sufficient explanation. Amato did not look good; he was feverish and had dark shadows under his eyes. "I'm so sorry, Pasquale," I said. "I never dreamed I was making you sick too. I should have been more careful."

Amato gave a gallant little wave of his hand. "Do not blame yourself, *cara* Gerry. These things happen. I—" He broke off, coughing violently.

"I have something here that will help that," I said hurriedly, putting my valise down on a table at the head of the bed. "A special syrup Dr. Curtis mixed up for me—"

"Then perhaps you would be so good as to allow Dr.

Curtis to decide what is best for the patient," a raspy voice said testily.

Whoops. I'd not noticed the older man standing over by the window. "Dr. Curtis! I'm glad you're here. I was going to call you."

"A noble intention, rendered unnecessary by present circumstances. As you see, I am already here."

"I called him," Emmy Destinn said placidly.

"How thoughtful of you," I murmured smoothly. "Well, Doctor? What is the, ah, prognosis?"

"The *prescription*," Dr. Curtis glowered at me, "is bed rest and quiet. So, any time you ladies feel like leaving . . . ?"

Amato started coughing again.

"Don't you have a rehearsal today?" I asked the other soprano pointedly. Emmy just shook her head.

Ever since I'd come into the room I'd been smelling a most peculiar odor. I didn't want to say anything; you know how it is in sickrooms. But the odor was too strong to ignore, and I was about to ask what it was when the door burst open and Enrico Caruso erupted into the room, carrying six atomizer bottles. "Pasquale! I bring you the throat spray myself!" He greeted the rest of us in his usual noisy manner and proceeded to place the bottles neatly on a bureau. "We try some now, yes?"

"We try some now *no*," Dr. Curtis rasped. "I know what's in that spray of yours, Caruso, and it's no good for a cold. Forget about it."

"But it soothes the throat—"

"No, confound it! Later, perhaps, but not now."

Frustrated, Caruso turned on me. "I tell you to stay in bed today!"

Amato sneezed.

By then I'd traced the source of the noxious odor to Amato's bedside table. I picked up a ceramic jar and got a good whiff of the foul-smelling concoction it contained. "What in the name of heaven is this?"

"A salve for rubbing on the chest," Emmy explained. "It is good for colds and coughs."

"May I remind you people that *I* am the doctor here?"

Dr. Curtis growled. "I'm sure Amato appreciates your concern, but *I* decide what medicine he takes, and only I. Is that understood?"

Before anyone could answer, the bedroom door opened again, this time to reveal a bearded, middle-aged man who grew immediately alarmed when he caught sight of three singers hovering over Amato's sickbed. "Stand back! Stand back! Do you *all* want to get sick?" Giulio Gatti-Casazza, the Metropolitan Opera's general manager, looked as if he were envisioning the entire opera company's coming down with colds at the same time.

"What is this place?" Dr. Curtis snarled, exasperated. "Grand Central Station?"

"Enrico, what are you thinking of?" Gatti-Casazza scolded the tenor. "Such a fanatic you are about avoiding infection—yet here you stand, breathing the air of a sickroom! You must be mad to visit Amato now!"

"Mr. Gatti," Caruso said cajolingly, "it is only a *little* visit."

"And Gerry!" the general manager rushed on. "Just getting over a cold—you need to take better care of yourself!"

"You thought I was well enough to sing last night," I reminded him archly.

He glared at me a moment and then turned to Emmy Destinn—who forestalled him by saying, complacently, "I never get sick."

Amato groaned.

Gatti-Casazza threw up his hands and turned his attention to the sick man in the bed. "Pasquale? How do you feel?"

"Not . . . wonderful," Amato whispered.

"Now that's enough," Dr. Curtis snapped. "I want you all out of here. Now."

"Doctor," Gatti-Casazza said, "how long will he be like this? When can he sing?"

"That depends on whether the cold settles into his chest or not. If it stays just a simple head cold, well, he should be back next week."

"Next week!" I cried. "But I need him this Wednesday—for *Carmen*!"

"And I need him Thursday for *Aïda*," Emmy chimed in.

"Out of the question!" Dr. Curtis looked shocked. "Back-to-back performances?" He bent over his patient. "What have I told you about singing two nights in a row? That's the kind of overexertion even healthy vocal cords can't withstand. You should know better, Amato!"

Amato pulled the covers over his head.

"It cannot always be helped," Gatti-Casazza said in what was for him a conciliatory manner. "The schedule—"

"The schedule be damned! Excuse me, ladies. Mr. Gatti, are you trying to ruin your singers? Scheduling Amato two nights in a row, making Gerry sing when she's still hoarse from a cold. And Caruso here you sometimes push out on the stage three times in the same week! The human vocal mechanism simply cannot take such abuse without suffering serious damage!"

They'd had this argument before; Gatti-Casazza merely shrugged and said, "Perhaps he can sing *one* performance this week—yes?"

I made a murmuring sound of agreement and was surprised to hear Emmy Destinn doing the same thing. Surely she wasn't thinking it would be *her* opera Amato would sing in? But it didn't matter anyway; Dr. Curtis quickly vetoed the suggestion. "No chance of that. Next week, perhaps—we'll just have to wait and see. But not this week at all. You'll have to find another baritone."

"But can you not speed up the healing process a little?" Gatti-Casazza hated to give up on Amato. "Isn't there something—"

"Wait a minute," Emmy interrupted. "Look." The bedclothes were heaving spasmodically as Amato tried to fight his way out. Emmy pulled the covers back; Amato looked tousled and disoriented. He closed his eyes and worked his mouth without saying anything. "Pasquale?" Emmy asked with concern. "What is it?"

Amato swallowed with obvious discomfort. "Go away," he whispered. "I love you all—but please, please, *go away.*'' The effort of talking brought on another coughing fit.

"There, you see!" Dr. Curtis snapped. "You have to leave, all of you. If he's allowed to rest quietly and take his medicine, he'll recover faster."

"That reminds me," Gatti-Casazza said, fishing a bottle out of his coat pocket. "This is a tonic my grandmother used to give me when I—"

"Out!" shouted Dr. Curtis while Amato buried his head under a pillow. "I want you out of here right now! Out, out, *out!*"

We were all used to being bullied by Dr. Curtis, but we also knew when he meant business. We left without further ado.

In the elevator on the way down to the Astor lobby, Gatti-Casazza was worrying out loud over whom he could find to substitute for Amato. Suddenly I grew irritated; everyone seemed to have forgotten that I had created a new role only the night before. Singers fell ill and were replaced all the time; why so much fuss? They should have been talking about *me*.

"Aïda is no problem," the general manager was saying. "Scotti can fill in for Amato there, yes? It is *Carmen* that is the trouble—why did Scotti never learn Escamillo?" Pasquale Amato and Antonio Scotti were the two star baritones on the Metropolitan roster for the 1914–1915 season. Since the role of Escamillo, the toreador in *Carmen*, was not one of Scotti's roles, Gatti-Casazza had to start considering various baritones of the second rank. "Bronzelli doesn't sing *any* French roles. The German baritones are out of the question, and Boinville left for London two days ago."

"Use a house baritone," Emmy shrugged.

I shot her a dark look; she wouldn't be quite so casual about it if it were her own opera in need of a baritone. The "house" singers were an undistinguished group of soloists who could always be counted on to fill in at the last moment; their one virtue was their unwavering availability. They were seldom or never assigned roles in the season's regular schedule, because they weren't good enough. Using a house singer was always a last resort.

I made a suggestion. "Why not give Jimmy Freeman a chance? He says he knows the role backwards."

Caruso's face broke into a smile. "Jimmy, yes! What a good idea, Gerry!" He held his hands out before his face, visualizing the billboard: " 'The Metropolitan Opera Company presents Mr. James Freeman making his début appearance as Escamillo in Bizet's *Carmen*.' So, Mr. Gatti, what do you think?"

The elevator had reached the Astor lobby; I quickly stepped out first, as the more *prima* of the two prima donnas—a nicety of distinction I wasn't at all sure Emmy Destinn even noticed. "Well, Mr. Gatti? What about Jimmy Freeman?"

The general manager spread his hands. "He is so young. Twenty-two, twenty-three?"

"*I* was nineteen when I made my début," I pointed out. Marguérite in *Faust*—in Berlin, in happier days.

Unexpected help came from Emmy. "It's not as if it's a real début, Mr. Gatti. You've been listening to him for . . . two seasons now? You know what he can do."

Jimmy Freeman had been singing small roles at the Metropolitan for the last couple of years, learning his art, developing stage presence, growing. The management had visualized easing him gradually into larger and larger roles and eventually, if he proved good enough, into principal parts. To thrust him suddenly into the role of Escamillo did involve a risk, a large one. And Gatti-Casazza was not known for his willingness to take risks.

"Such a good voice!" Caruso smiled. "Give the boy a chance."

But the general manager was not so easily convinced. "I have not even heard him sing the *Toreador Song*!" he cried.

Caruso shrugged. "That is easily remedied, no? Call him in for audition."

At length Gatti-Casazza decided that was exactly what he was going to do, and hurried off to make the arrangements. Caruso invited Emmy to join him for lunch—and made a point of telling me I was not included in the invitation. "Go home and rest," he said gently. "You really must, *cara* Gerry—you do not look too steady on your feet. We escort you home, yes?"

"Thank you, I have my limousine." Caruso was right; I was beginning to feel a bit wobbly. We parted outside the Astor, and this time I did go home to bed.

I slept for one hour and awoke feeling marvelous.

For a while I just lay in the bed thinking about Jimmy Freeman and the unexpected chance that was coming his way. I hoped he was up to it. Jimmy was a nice, fresh-faced American boy who just happened to possess one of the most distinctive baritone voices I'd ever heard. He was still learning how to use it properly; Jimmy had a long way to go before he could be called a first-class musician. But he had a good vocal coach, and he worked hard. The signs were good.

I liked Jimmy and I wanted him to succeed. Young talent needs a lot of encouragement, and I think established stars have an obligation to help when they can. Besides, Jimmy Freeman had one attribute that was bound to work in his favor as far as I was concerned: He didn't care who knew that he was wildly, passionately, head-over-heels in love with Geraldine Farrar.

I didn't mind.

There's no point in affecting a maidenly modesty about all this; ever since I first set foot on the stage, I've had a string of admirers following me about. Opera is a glamorous world; it attracts people. And since most of the sopranos in the business look like Emmy Destinn, a slim brunette with good clothes sense and generally all-round high style is naturally going to receive the bulk of the male attention being lavished about. Some of my admirers were sophisticated men of the world, others were moon-faced boys like Jimmy. But there was always *someone*.

The pleasurable difficulties of dealing with love-sick swains occasionally occupied more of my time than I might have wished, but some things simply cannot be brushed aside lightly. I had a fair idea of how much encouragement to give to the Jimmy Freemans of the world, and I knew exactly how much distance to keep between them and myself. Jimmy was in seventh heaven whenever I allowed him to accompany me on a shopping trip or some such, but I was always careful to appear at important public functions on the arm of Antonio Scotti or another of my older suitors. I tried to treat Jimmy Freeman kindly while making it clear there could never be anything more between us; I know puppy love can hurt. So I never really told him no.

Besides, it didn't exactly damage my image to have a promising young baritone following me about with stars in his eyes.

My thoughts shifted to Pasquale Amato, lying in his sickbed at the Astor. His cold was a bad one; anyone could see that just by looking at him. Perversely, a slight head cold could sometimes enhance a singer's performance; in the early stages the sinuses open up, giving the voice more resonance. Perhaps that was why Amato had sounded especially good in the *Madame Sans-Gêne* première? But a cold that moved down to the chest could spell disaster. Poor Pasquale—that's where he seemed headed now.

Time to get up. I rose, bathed, dressed—how I love the tight sleeves of current fashion! There's no hiding of fat arms in *those*. I went into my music room and tried vocalizing a little but quit the moment I felt myself beginning to strain. I used a little of the throat spray Caruso's valet had dropped off. Suddenly I was ravenous; I told one of the maids to heat up the soup I'd been living on for the past week, and downed two bowls. Then I sat down to do some serious worrying about Wednesday night's performance of *Carmen*.

Gatti-Casazza had dismissed out of hand any possibility of one of the German baritones singing Escamillo, although there were at least two of them who had sung the role in European houses. It was that confounded *categorization* the Metropolitan observed so religiously! One either sang French and Italian roles or one sang German roles, but one never sang both. I'd run into that particular brand of shortsightedness before; it was the reason I had never sung at Covent Garden.

That prestigious London house had made me numerous offers when I was still the leading soprano at the Royal Opera House in Berlin, but they'd wanted me only in German roles. I turned them down. Flat. I didn't want to be known solely as a Wagnerian singer; the Covent Garden offer would have given me no chance to display my versatility. Besides, one can't live exclusively in the larger-than-life world of German romanticism (at least *this* one can't). But here I am caught in that same silly trap at the Metropolitan, only the category is different. Here I sing only French and Italian roles, while the German roles I know so well are denied me. What an idiotic policy. And two qualified baritones were passed over for the role of Escamillo only because they belonged to the German side of the repertoire.

So, by process of elimination, Jimmy Freeman really was our best hope. On impulse I called the Met's general manager in his office to find out what he had decided.

"Freeman is coming in tonight," Gatti-Casazza told me. "I want to hear his *Toreador Song* from the main stage." The Metropolitan was dark on Tuesdays; Jimmy was going to have to sing to that empty, cavernous auditorium to convince Gatti that his voice was big enough for the job.

"What time?" I was thinking my presence might encourage the boy.

"Eight. But another possibility suddenly presents itself," Gatti said with a distinct note of excitement in his voice. "Philippe Duchon may be available."

"Ah!" I understood his excitement. "You mean he's here? In New York?"

"His ship arrives tomorrow morning. If I persuade him to learn the stage movement in the afternoon and sing the role at night—we score a *coup*, yes?"

"Yes, indeed! What a stroke of luck!" I felt a momentary twinge for Jimmy Freeman, but a chance for me to sing with the legendary Philippe Duchon overrode all other considerations, I'm afraid. Jimmy would still get his chance;

it would just come a little later, that was all. One thing worried me. Duchon was no longer a young man; would he have the stamina to undertake the role of Escamillo his very first day in the country? I wished Gatti good luck and hung up.

I'd heard Duchon sing, of course, many times, but our professional paths had never crossed, my bad luck. Duchon was based in Paris, but he'd sung in all the major opera houses in Europe, where he was known as the quintessential French baritone. He sang a few Italian roles—Rigoletto, one or two others; but the bulk of his repertoire was French. No German roles at all. Absolutely and positively no German roles.

For about fifty years the Paris Opéra had been controlled by a powerful group of subscribers who loathed with a passion everything German, especially the work of Richard Wagner. Every time the management attempted to stage Wagner, disaster resulted. Stink bombs were thrown into the theatre during a performance of *Lohengrin*. *Tannhäuser* was booed off the stage. French operagoers evidently took pride in these juvenile goings-on (it was, after all, a Frenchman who gave his name to the word *chauvinism*).

Philippe Duchon was a product of this tradition, and I'd heard it said he'd never even heard a complete performance of any of Wagner's operas. But lately there'd been signs that France's long hostility toward German music was perhaps at last coming to an end; about a year ago the Opéra had staged *Parsifal* for the very first time—successfully, even triumphantly.

But that promising beginning had come to an abrupt end a few months later—in August of 1914. The month Europe blew up.

And now Philippe Duchon was arriving in New York tomorrow morning—the great Duchon, who had never deigned to sing in America before. Was he fleeing? Everyone had said the war would be over by Christmas, but here it was almost February and . . .

Well, no use speculating; Duchon would reveal his reasons for coming when and if it suited him. In the mean-

time, Jimmy Freeman was going to be singing his heart
out to win a role Philippe Duchon could have just by
lifting a finger.

Yes, I would definitely be there tonight. The young man
was going to need all the moral support he could get.

❑ 2 ❑ Even when no performance was scheduled, the Metropolitan Opera House, at the corner of Broadway and Thirty-ninth Street, was never exactly quiet. The stagedoor-keeper told me a rehearsal was going on in the roof theatre; that meant the chorus was probably getting a workout in one of the rehearsal halls. A couple of crewmen were pushing a piano out onto the main stage. One of them threw me a kiss; dear man—what *was* his name? I wandered around backstage until I spotted Jimmy Freeman, listening to some last-minute advice from his vocal coach.

Jimmy's face lit up when he caught sight of me (a nice way to start an encounter). "Miss Farrar!" he called out, unfortunately cutting off his coach in mid-sentence. Then he suddenly became shy. "I, uh, I didn't expect to see you here this evening."

"Why, Jimmy, I wouldn't have missed it for the world! Your big opportunity? Of course I'm here. Good evening, Mr. Springer." The vocal coach smiled quickly and returned my greeting. "How do you feel, Jimmy?"

"Nervous, frankly."

"Good. A little nervousness always sharpens one's performance. Don't you think so, Mr. Springer?"

"Exactly what I was telling him, Miss Farrar. Control your nervousness, James, make it work for you. Look at Caruso—he panics every time he has to go out on the stage. But would you know it to listen to him sing? Never. He *uses* his nervousness. As you must use yours."

"Yes, Mr. Springer," Jimmy said, as he did to everything his coach told him. "I just hope I don't make a fool of myself."

I laughed my favorite laugh, descending thirds. "No chance of that. You'll sing well. I'm not even going to worry about you."

"And remember," Springer added, "you're the only one they asked to come in tonight."

I shot him a startled glance before I could stop myself; was it possible they knew nothing of Philippe Duchon's imminent arrival? Quite possible, I decided. Gatti-Casazza

19

never gave much away. I turned back to Jimmy. "Don't forget, now—I'll be out front cheering for you!"

"Oh, *thank* you, Miss Farrar!" Jimmy gave me a look of such undying gratitude that I began to think I'd overdone it.

A few minutes later Springer and I went out to the dimly lighted auditorium, leaving Jimmy Freeman to face his fate. We took seats close enough to the front that the light from the stage would let the nervous young baritone see us there. "Do you think he's ready?" I asked my companion.

"I do, absolutely," Springer answered without hesitation. "These past six months James has shown enormous improvement. He's begun to understand instinctively the little tricks of phrasing and breath control that earlier he had to learn laboriously. He's ready for a major role. And *Carmen* is a good place for him to start."

It probably was, at that. The role of Escamillo is a flashy one but not particularly demanding. Escamillo doesn't even enter until the second act—when he comes in and sings his one aria, the *Toreador Song,* and exits immediately. He comes on again in the third act, but only long enough to get into a short-lived scuffle with the tenor over the love of Carmen. And then he shows up once more—*very* briefly, only a few measures—in the fourth and final act. A good role for a nervous young baritone.

Something belatedly occurred to me. "Why aren't you accompanying him, Mr. Springer?"

"Maestro Toscanini's choice," he answered tightly. "He wanted to see how well James performed with a stranger. A test of flexibility, he called it."

I should have known; nothing happened in that house without Toscanini's putting in his two cents' worth. But it was a reasonable interference this time, as the Maestro was conducting tomorrow night. "Perhaps it's just as well," I said. "Jimmy will end up looking all the better because of it."

"He shouldn't have to audition at all," Springer muttered angrily. "They need a baritone and James is ready and that should be the end of it."

He was making me uneasy. It didn't seem fair to let

Jimmy go ahead and sing without knowing he was in competition with the great Philippe Duchon. But telling him at the last minute would destroy his confidence, and he was nervous enough already. I slid a glance sideways at the vocal coach; Springer had a big investment in Jimmy Freeman, and he was assuming tonight would be the beginning of a long-awaited payoff.

Osgood Springer was a striking-looking man, in spite of the long scar that ran along his right jawbone. He'd once been a promising young baritone himself, but an accident had put a premature end to his career. Years ago Springer had fallen in the street in front of a carriage, and the startled horse had put one of its feet down right on Springer's face. All the bones in his face had been broken, and he no longer had the resonance one needed to sing opera. A dreadful accident.

Springer had turned to teaching, and he quickly earned the reputation of being a martinet—or so they said; that was all before my time. He certainly had Jimmy Freeman under his thumb, no doubt about that. But Springer knew what he was doing; he'd brought Jimmy along fast, but not too fast. And if he said Jimmy was ready, then Jimmy was ready.

We heard voices behind us and turned to see Arturo Toscanini and Gatti-Casazza taking seats toward the rear of the auditorium. When Toscanini spotted me, he stood up and gave a low, courtly bow in my direction, almost banging his nose on the seat in front of him in the process. I smiled and blew him a kiss. Toscanini and I got along beautifully—whenever we were *not* in rehearsal.

Jimmy Freeman came out on the stage, followed by his new accompanist. I smiled up at him as encouragingly as I could. Jimmy looked a little jittery but not out of control. He nodded to the accompanist; the accompanist played the introduction; Jimmy opened his mouth and sang.

I don't think there's a schoolchild in the Western civilized world who doesn't know the melody of the *Toreador Song*, thump-*thump*-de-thump-thump. One of the most difficult things a singer has to do is reinterpret a tune so familiar that every listener already hears it in his head the way *he* thinks it should be sung. It's very difficult for a singer to take such a tune and make it distinctly his own. Well, Jimmy did it. He sang that old chestnut as if it had never been sung before, his fresh young voice giving it a vigor and excitement I hadn't heard in years. When he finished, I stood up and cried "Bravo!"

Toscanini and Gatti-Casazza were pleased too, I was delighted to see. We all joined Jimmy on the stage, Springer looking understandably proud in the midst of all the congratulations. Jimmy was flushed and happy; he knew he'd sung well.

Then Gatti dropped the bomb. "I'll let you know before noon tomorrow," he told Jimmy.

Jimmy just stared at him, but Springer spoke up. "Excuse me, Mr. Gatti—did you say you would *let him know*? Surely there's no question of James's ability to sing the role?"

"No, no, none at all," Gatti said uncomfortably. "It is just that, ah, you see, the Maestro and I always talk over the casting together, yes?"

Toscanini tried to look innocent.

Springer persisted. "What is there to talk over? Do we use the morning hours to prepare or not?"

"I will let you know before noon," Gatti repeated vaguely.

Jimmy was inclined to accept the delay, but his coach was having none of it. Springer went on pressing for an answer until I couldn't stand it any longer. "If you don't tell them," I said to Gatti, "I will."

Gatti looked daggers at me, but then he told Jimmy and Springer about Philippe Duchon.

They both looked as if they'd been slapped in the face. There was no doubt in anyone's mind that if Duchon said yes, Jimmy's debut as Escamillo would not be taking place the next evening. Jimmy was already slumping in defeat.

I drew Toscanini aside. "Is there any way to divide Amato's roles between them? Dr. Curtis doesn't know how long Amato will be out."

Toscanini took one of my hands in his. "*Cara* Gerry,"

he said gently, "you prefer to sing with the young man
instead of Duchon?"

Ah. Well. Ah.

He nodded. "I think not. We try to persuade Duchon to
sing all of Amato's roles. He is here for perhaps the only
time in his life, yes? The young James has much time left.
His turn will come."

That was true. I went back to the forlorn-looking young
baritone and tried to offer some consolation. "Even if you
don't sing tomorrow, Jimmy, you made your mark here
tonight. The next time there's an opening, you'll be the
one Gatti calls on. You'll see."

His face took on that moony look I knew so well. "Whatever happens tomorrow," Jimmy said, "I will always
remember tonight. Tonight the beautiful Geraldine Farrar
rose to her feet and cried *Bravo* to me!"

Oh dear.

It was getting close to nine o'clock, and I always liked
to be in bed by ten the night before a performance. I told
everyone goodbye and went home.

Things certainly had changed in a hurry. Only that
morning Gatti-Casazza had been worrying about not having a baritone for *Carmen* and now it seemed he had a
choice of two, assuming Duchon would be willing to take
over the role on such short notice. Poor Jimmy—his big
chance had finally come and then he found himself thor-
oughly upstaged. But Toscanini was right; Jimmy's turn
would come. I looked forward to singing with him . . .
someday soon, if not the very next night. I truly did like
Jimmy Freeman.

One reason I liked him was that he reminded me so
much of Willi—dear, sweet Willi whom I had not seen for
years. The two were alike in so many ways: the same
shyness, the same respectful adoration from afar, the same
suffering air of romantic longing. There was one enormous
difference between them, though; Willi was, after all,
Crown Prince Wilhelm of Prussia, son of the Kaiser, and
everything he did was a matter of public interest. By the
time I'd made my debut at the Royal Opera of Berlin, I
was already the object of considerable public attention

myself. So when the Crown Prince, who'd never displayed any noticeable interest in opera before, suddenly began showing up in the royal box every time the new American soprano sang, tongues were bound to wag.

Willi and I were both nineteen then, but he always seemed so much younger—a nice boy, someone you could trust. The Prince and the Opera Singer. Sounds like a fairy tale, doesn't it? Well, for a lot of people it was; operagoers liked to talk about us, and the gossip in Berlin even attributed my success on the opera stage to palace intrigue, thank you very much! But I earned my international reputation legitimately—in Europe I was known as "Die Farrar aus Berlin" (except by jealous rivals; one overripe native prima donna kept calling me "The American Peril"). I didn't sleep my way to the top, I sang my way there. At the same time, I was not unaware of the publicity value of having a royal admirer.

Although I do have to admit that sometimes it got out of hand. I remember receiving letters from total strangers offering to adopt any or all illegitimate semi-royal children I might have! And journalists kept pestering me about our plans to marry. We never did plan to marry. Well, Willi may have had a plan or two, but I didn't. Willi would one day be Kaiser, or so we thought then. When the war is over, who knows? But if I'd married Willi, I'd have had to give up singing and devote my life to helping rule the country. *Give up singing?* Ha, *that* didn't require any hard decision-making. I was an opera star and I liked being an opera star. I still like it.

Eventually Willi realized we would never marry and accepted his parents' choice of a wife for him, a pleasant young woman who turned out to be exactly right for Willi. I stayed friends with both of them. And as for *la grande passion* Willi and I were supposed to have had, it was really nothing more than a sweet romance. As far as I was concerned, Willi went into his marriage as virginal as the day he was born.

It was that innocent quality of Willi's that Jimmy Freeman reflected so exactly. Jimmy's shy and respectful courtship took me back to those happy times in Berlin, before life turned ugly and my European friends started slaughtering one another. But before that happened—oh, those were grand and glittering days! Americans were popular in Imperial Germany at the turn of the century; commercial relations were good, Teddy Roosevelt and the Kaiser were friends, *alles* was *in Ordnung*. As a young American opera star, I was sought after and courted and fussed over. I remember some young lieutenants who would break champagne glasses once my lips had touched them—imagine! And now every time I looked at Jimmy Freeman's unspoiled young face, I thought of those innocent days. Jimmy reminded me of my youth, I suppose. Thirty-three is not old, but it's not nineteen.

It was glorious while it lasted. I sang in other houses, at the Paris Opéra and the Opéra Comique and at Monte Carlo—a gay place, pure froth and frivolity. I sang in Salzburg and Munich and Stockholm, where I made a fan of King Oscar, dear man; he actually presented me with the Order of Merit. I sang in Warsaw, then under Russian supervision and bitterly resentful of it; I saw more than one bloody clash in the streets. I had to cancel singing engagements in Moscow and St. Petersburg because one of their many revolutions was going on at the time. Once I even had trouble getting back to Berlin, there were so many soldiers stopping people everywhere. By the time I left for the Metropolitan Opera in 1906, it was clear that the good times in Europe were over.

But I was back there last year when it started. When the war broke out in August, I was in a Munich sanitarium recovering from a stomach disorder. I wasn't particularly worried at the time; I felt at home in Germany and America didn't seem likely to join in. But by the time I was well enough to travel, Antwerp had fallen and the border was closed. I couldn't arrange passage to America. Everything I tried failed.

I was just beginning to panic when a message arrived from Gatti-Casazza; he was holding a ship at Naples for all the Metropolitan's artists who were having trouble getting out of Europe. With the help of an attentive young officer, I bribed my way through Switzerland, smiling and chatting gaily and pretending that was the way I always traveled. Then I hastened down the length of Italy to the harbor at Naples, where I found a ship full of musicians every bit as frightened as I was. Caruso spent the entire crossing on deck watching out for U-boats.

It's impossible to express the anguish this war has caused me. I have friends and professional associates all over Europe, but Germany has always been a special place to me. My vocal coach who saw me through my early years is still there; I don't even know if she is safe. I don't know if *anybody* is safe. But from the moment the first German soldier set foot on Belgian soil on the march to invade France, Germany placed itself squarely and irredeemably in the wrong.

How could the Kaiser even consider such a thing? I find it hard to reconcile this bloody warmonger with the friendly, laughing man I knew in Berlin. Now every time I think of Germany I get a burning sensation inside. It's a *horrible* feeling. The way you'd feel if you suddenly found out your father was a murderer. What happens then? Do you stop loving him? Can you ever again love him in quite the same way?

But that wasn't the half of it. The anti-German feeling in this country was so strong that I found I was actually suspect because of my long association with Germany and the royal family. My *patriotism* was being questioned, of all things! Why, I was born practically at the foot of Bunker Hill—there's never been the slightest question in my own mind as to where my true allegiance lay! I've sung at war relief benefits, I've sold Liberty bonds, I've done my bit to help. I am *American;* and if America joins the Allies in the war against Germany, then it's the Allied side I'll be on.

Yet numerous unpleasant things kept happening. I was once cut dead by some society women because I did not rise for the few bars of the national anthem that appear in *Madame Butterfly*. A little book I'd written about my early career in Germany was withdrawn from public libraries. When I invited Fritz Kreisler to a party I gave last Christmas, I received a rash of scurrilous letters (all anonymous, of course) reviling me for giving succor to the enemy. Sometimes I actually have to remind people that the United States of America is not at war with anyone.

Not yet, at any rate.

Antonio Scotti kissed the fingers of my right hand one by one. "Gerry, *cara mia*—tell me when we marry. How long do you keep me suffering? Say you marry me."

I laughed. "Now, Toto, I thought we'd settled all that."

He picked up a fork from the table and waved it in the air. "We settle nothing. All you do is keep saying no."

And that, from his point of view, was no answer at all. I never met a man who enjoyed being in love so much as Antonio Scotti. He was in love *all the time*—if not with me, then with someone else. But he was an attentive lover and fun to be with, and I didn't mind the attention.

"You must practice saying maybe," he admonished me gently. "You do not know what joys can be found in marriage."

"And you do?" I smiled. Scotti was a tall, easygoing bachelor whose eyes even now followed an attractive woman as she crossed the room. Scotti was fastidious in his dress and had the natural bearing of an aristocrat. He had a mop of lustrous black hair and a good physique; only a rather long nose kept him from being unbearably handsome. He and Caruso and Pasquale Amato were all from Naples and had been friends for years. I liked all three of them; I liked them a lot.

We were in the dining room of the Hotel Knickerbocker. Caruso was holding court across the room at his usual corner table, surrounded by friends and a few freeloaders. Both Scotti and Caruso lived in the Knickerbocker, and the place had become a sort of gathering place for the opera world. But neither Caruso nor I should have been there right then; the day of an evening performance ought to be spent resting.

Scotti looked over to Caruso's table. "I suppose we should join them."

"I suppose."

I had awakened that morning not knowing which baritone I'd be singing with that night. But now it was settled; Philippe Duchon had said yes. Jimmy Freeman would just have to wait a little longer, poor boy. Caruso and I were to go to the Metropolitan that afternoon to rehearse the stage movements with Duchon. That alone told you in what high regard Gatti-Casazza held the French baritone; normally a substitute singer was taught his stage movements in fifteen minutes by an assistant stage manager and then tossed in to sink or swim. But not Philippe Duchon. For Duchon, the Met's two biggest stars would give up their afternoon of rest and preparation to help the newcomer learn where he was supposed to be on the stage at what time. Some baritones like to leap up on a table to sing the *Toreador Song;* I hoped Philippe Duchon was not one of them.

Just then Gatti-Casazza himself walked in, looking understandably triumphant. Without exchanging a word Scotti and I got up and went over to Caruso's table. When we all had chairs, I found myself sitting opposite Emmy Destinn—who was looking well fed, as usual. "Toto!" Caruso cried. "Gerry, *bellissima*! You hear the news? Duchon may join us permanently!"

"For the duration," Gatti corrected.

"Is that why he came here, then?" I asked. "To join the Metropolitan Opera?"

"Eh, no, as a matter of fact," Gatti said. "He comes to solicit funds for Alsatian war relief. I promise him a benefit performance."

"Which opera?" umpteen voices asked.

Gatti waved a hand. "Details, we work out later. For now, he agrees to sing *Carmen* and *The Huguenots*."

Emmy Destinn put her cup down with a clink. "*The Huguenots*? You promised him *The Huguenots*?" *The Huguenots* was one of Emmy's operas.

"Until Amato is well again," Gatti explained. "There-after—we will see."

Emmy nodded toward Scotti. "Toto can sing it." Scotti and Amato alternated in the role of the villain in the opera.

"And he continues to sing it. Duchon substitutes only for Amato."

"That is encouraging," Scotti said dryly.

"It is decided, then?" Emmy asked.

Gatti nodded. "Duchon sings with you next week."

"No. I want Toto."

Everyone at the table stared at her. "I do not understand," Gatti said, puzzled. "I think you will be pleased with my arrangement."

Emmy thrust out her chin. "I do not wish to sing with Philippe Duchon."

Utter silence fell over the table. Not want to sing with Philippe Duchon? Was the woman out of her mind? I was the first to find a voice. "For heaven's sake *why*, Emmy?"

"I have sung with him before," she said and stopped, as if that explained everything.

"And?" Scotti urged.

Eventually the story came out. According to Emmy, Philippe Duchon had a nasty tendency to take over every production he appeared in. "He wants to conduct, direct, and sing all the parts. He kept telling me—*me!*—how I should sing this or that phrase, what I should do in the duets, where I should stand while he is singing, everything. He is impossible to work with! He completely ignores the conductor."

Everyone at the table was thinking the same thing: *Toscanini*. Maestro Toscanini permitted no disagreement when he was at the podium; he simply *did not permit it*. Toscanini had nothing to do with *The Huguenots*, but he was conducting *Carmen*. Could be trouble.

"We both sing with him, Emmy," Caruso said. "At Covent Garden, at the Opéra. He is difficult, yes, but not impossible. I have no trouble with him. I like him."

"Oh, Rico, you like everybody," Emmy said dismissively.

Caruso thought a moment. "Almost everybody."

Gatti-Casazza had been sitting there in a state of shock. "I do not imagine . . . if you . . . but . . ." He used a table napkin to pat his brow. "I am sorry to hear you are unhappy," he said to Emmy, "but it is settled. This year Duchon sings *The Huguenots* and *Carmen* and one benefit, and for next year we talk about a revival of, uh, muh, umm." He shot a glance at Scotti and finished up mumbling into his beard.

Scotti eyed him suspiciously. "A revival of what?"

Gatti didn't want to say, but did: *"Rigoletto."*

Scotti hit the ceiling. *Rigoletto* was his opera; it was his favorite role. "You say no when *I* ask for a revival this year!" Scotti shouted. "But all this Frenchman has to do is—"

"Now, Toto, be calm, be calm! We only talk about it, you understand?" Gatti spent the next few minutes soothing the irate Neapolitan.

As soon as I could, I asked Gatti, "Have you given any thought to *Madame Sans-Gêne*? You do remember our new opera, don't you? Will the illustrious Monsieur Duchon undertake to learn Amato's part? Or did you ask him?"

"I count on Amato's return to health in time for the next performance of *Madame Sans-Gêne*," he said quickly and changed the subject. So much for my new opera. Well, we'd just see about that.

"He will take over," Emmy repeated stubbornly. "Every opera you put him in, Duchon will take over. He is worse than Toscanini."

Now that was ridiculous. *Nobody* was worse than Toscanini.

"He has wanted to run his own opera company for years," Emmy went on. "He wants to manage and keep on singing at the same time. For years he has been looking for a house where he could be singer-manager. And then he found one."

"Sì, sì," said Caruso, remembering. "At Versailles?"

Emmy nodded. "That old theatre that's stood empty since the French Revolution—L'Opéra Louis Quinze. Duchon got the government to agree to restore it. But then."

But then the war broke out, and government-subsidized plans to restore old opera houses had fallen by the wayside. So Philippe Duchon had instead come to America to raise money for the Alsatian war relief fund and was on the verge of stealing one of Scotti's best roles from him. "Why Alsatian war relief?" I asked. "Is Duchon from Alsace?"

Nobody knew. "His plans are not firm," Gatti said.

"Evidently the fund-raising tour is arranged at the last moment, yes? Everything is done in such haste these days."

It sounded to me as if the French were no longer anticipating a quick end to the fighting. But they'd guessed wrong about almost everything else in connection with the war, so maybe they were wrong again. But this time I didn't think so. It was just beginning to sink in on everybody that this war was going to be a lot bigger than anyone had thought it would be.

"No news in the papers about Prague today," Emmy complained, "again. Alsace, Flanders, Hartmanns-Weiler, St. Mihiel, Le Prêtre—but nothing about Prague." Emmy Destinn was a native of Bohemia who still considered Prague home. She was also an ardent supporter of the Slovakian desire to be free of Austrian rule. "Why do they never write of Prague?"

Scotti offered the traditional comfort. "Perhaps the papers carry no news because nothing happens in Prague, yes? That is *good* news, Emmy."

"Mm, perhaps, but I would feel better knowing for certain that all is well. In Prague we are caught midway between the eastern front and the western front—not a safe place to be. It has been many years since Prague has been safe."

Caruso brought the talk back to the here and now. "Me, I look forward to singing with Duchon again," he smiled happily, thinking no farther ahead than that night's performance. "We fight good at the Opéra." He meant the struggle between the tenor and the baritone in the third act of *Carmen*.

"Watch out for Duchon in the last act, Gerry," Emmy warned me. "He will upstage you."

"He's welcome to try," I said sweetly.

Gatti snorted and turned it into a cough. "Please, I beg all of you. Cooperate, yield stage to him—it is only for a few performances. Right now, all that matters is putting on a good *Carmen* tonight, is that not so?"

"Mr. Gatti-Casazza, I would like to speak with you, please," a new voice said. Osgood Springer had come up to the table without anyone's noticing; when Gatti saw who it was, his face fell. He hadn't exactly double-crossed Springer and his star pupil, but he couldn't have wanted to talk to either of them just then. He invited the vocal coach to sit down with us. Safety in numbers.

Springer didn't like it; he would have preferred a private conversation. But he pulled up a chair and told Gatti what he wanted: a commitment for Jimmy Freeman to sing at least one major role next season.

Gatti went into his vague act, which he does better than anyone else I know. "Later," he told Springer, pulling at his beard in obvious discomfort. "Now is not the time to discuss such matters."

"Excuse me, Mr. Gatti, but now *is* the time," Springer objected. "Only last night you heard what James can do. And you did call him in to audition, remember. You built up his hopes for nothing—you owe him something."

Mistake, I thought. There were ways of handling Gatti, but pressing a moral obligation was not one of them.

"I owe Freeman nothing," Gatti said curtly. "And now if you excuse me, I have matters to attend to." With an abrupt nod at the table in general, he stood up and left.

Caruso broke the silence that followed. "He is preoccupied with other things," he told Springer kindly. "His mind, it is full of tonight's *Carmen*. You ask again later, yes?"

Springer muttered something inaudible.

"I go to the opera house," Caruso announced in a change-the-subject voice. "Gerry? You come too?"

"In a moment," I answered.

"Emmy? Come welcome Duchon. A friendly gesture."

She shook her head. "I think I'll go take a nap."

Caruso grinned. "You have to see him sooner or later, you know."

"Then I'd prefer later."

There followed some vague chitchat and a general pushing back of chairs, and before long only Scotti and I were still at the table with the disconsolate vocal coach. Springer stared unseeing at the Maxfield Parrish mural over the

Knickerbocker bar, depression emanating from him like a tangible thing.

I touched his arm. "Jimmy will get his chance, Mr. Springer. He's far too good a singer for Gatti to pass over. Duchon's arrival just means a temporary delay, nothing more. Jimmy's time will come."

"Will you speak to Gatti-Casazza?" Springer asked me in a rush. "About a major role for James next season?"

"Certainly. With all my heart."

Springer turned to Scotti, as if to ask the same thing— but then hesitated.

Scotti smiled wryly, understanding. "Too many baritones, eh, Mr. Springer? I and Amato and now Duchon." Plus all the second-rank baritones he didn't bother to name. "But do not despair. I too will speak for your protégé. He deserves his chance."

For the first time since he sat down, Springer's expression lightened a little. Having another baritone plead Jimmy's cause would undoubtedly carry weight with Gatti-Casazza, especially a baritone as renowned as Antonio Scotti. "I thank you," Springer said quietly.

"I'm sure Gatti will give him a role next season," I said encouragingly. "Duchon's showing up right at this moment was just a fluke. No one could have anticipated it. All you have to do is wait a little longer."

Scotti made that funny little throat-clearing sound he always makes when he is about to disagree with something I've said. "Perhaps waiting is not enough," he said apologetically. "Perhaps an active campaign is better? Gerry and I speak for Jimmy, but you might want to ask others to speak up too. Caruso, for one. And talk to Toscanini."

A shadow passed over Springer's face. "Do you know something? Is there something going on I don't know about?"

"No, no, nothing like that," Scotti reassured him. "It is just . . . well, it is the war, you see. So far, most of the major singers in the European houses, they simply wait it out. We all think the war is over by the end of the year—*last* year, yes? But the war goes on. Already a few singers flee to America, and now here is Duchon."

"What are you saying, Toto?" I asked him.

"I am saying that right now the European singers who come to America—they make up only a trickle. But if the war goes on, that trickle becomes a steady stream, you see? Then Mr. Gatti has more singers than he can use. He can pick and choose, yes?"

Oh dear, I hadn't thought of that. With that kind of competition, Jimmy might not get his chance after all.

The scar along Springer's jaw stood out whitely against his skin. "You mean if James doesn't get a new contract right away, he might never get one."

Scotti spread his hands, said nothing.

"I'll speak to Gatti tonight," I said hurriedly. "Right after the performance."

Scotti consulted his pocket watch. "Gerry, you are almost late. Rehearsal awaits."

We both got up. "I must go, Mr. Springer. But don't lose heart. We'll all help."

Scotti and I left him sitting there at Caruso's table alone. Very much alone.

□ **3** □ I was excited about finally meeting Philippe Duchon, and wondering at the same time whether his voice had changed any since I'd last heard him; it had been several years. Scotti and I went into the Metropolitan by the Thirty-ninth Street entrance, but Scotti wanted to stay at the back of the auditorium, where he could observe his new rival without being observed himself.

But I couldn't see the great man anywhere. Out on the stage were Caruso and Toscanini, an accompanist waiting patiently by his piano, and four or five chorus members—just enough to give Duchon a sense of where people would be positioned on the stage. I waited in the wings, preferring to make an entrance rather than stand there as part of the welcoming chorus.

Out of the corner of my eye I saw a shadow move among the other shadows backstage. "Who's there?" I said sharply.

A smiling old man shuffled out into the light. "Only me, Miz Zherry," he said in a thick accent. "Me."

"Oh, Uncle Hummy, you gave me a start. What are you doing here?"

"Come for the Duchon."

It couldn't have been more than a few hours since Gatti-Casazza and Duchon had reached agreement. "How did you know he'd be here?"

"I hear," Uncle Hummy grinned broadly, "I hear." Uncle Hummy was one of those characters who are always hanging around opera houses, but with a difference. To say he loved opera would be an understatement; this one lived for opera. The stage-door-keeper would sometimes let him in, and other times he'd sneak in. When I'd given him a copy of the new *Madame Sans-Gêne* score, he'd cried. He was a harmless old man who asked nothing more of life than to be allowed to listen.

"Did someone let you in?" I asked him.

He grinned sheepishly, showing lots of teeth. "No, Miz Zherry. Just self I come."

He'd sneaked in. "Well, don't let Mr. Gatti see you."

He shuffled back into the shadow. Uncle Hummy was

an elderly Italian who'd lived in this country since his young manhood without ever mastering English; some people simply can't learn languages. He was a nice old fellow who lived mostly on hand-outs, and mostly from Caruso; the rest of us gave him a few dollars now and then.

I forgot all about Uncle Hummy when I heard a new voice talking and laughing. Philippe Duchon had arrived, ta-*ta*, making *his* entrance from the other side of the stage and ushered in by a beaming Gatti-Casazza. Duchon was a huge man—big head, big body, big hands. He'd always been a dominating presence on the stage, but up close he was downright intimidating. Gatti was trying to introduce him to Toscanini (oddly, the two had never met) when the French baritone spotted Caruso. "Rico!" he boomed.

"Philippe!" the tenor sang back, and the two men embraced. Everybody liked Caruso.

Gatti finally got his introductions made, and I was delighted to hear Duchon spoke English perfectly (with a good, British accent). Gatti was looking around worriedly. "I suppose we could start . . . but I think it is better if we wait for our prima donna."

Now there was an entrance cue if ever I heard one. "Hello, hello, hello!" I trilled, sweeping onto the stage, flashing my second most dazzling smile (save the good stuff for more important occasions). "I hope I haven't kept you waiting?"

It was Toscanini who stepped forward and bowed gallantly over my hand, playing the courtier to the hilt. "*Cara* Gerry—waiting for you is always a pleasure."

I made some appropriate reply, and Toscanini led me over to Duchon and introduced us. I held out my other hand. "Monsieur Duchon," I smiled. "A great honor."

He did not take my hand. "Ah yes," he said with an icy smile I did not immediately understand, "Miss Geraldine Farrar. The German-lover." He turned his back on me.

You know what that kind of rebuff feels like? As if someone has just slapped you about the head four or five times. I stood there with my hand foolishly extended and felt the shock wave run through the others on the stage.

"Monsieur!" Toscanini said reprovingly.

I withdrew my hand. "I have friends in both Germany and France," I said as evenly as I could. "Am I to be treated rudely for that?"

Caruso and Gatti both jumped in, babbling alternately in Italian and English. Everyone was embarrassed to death, everyone except me; I was *mad*.

Duchon quickly realized that the general sympathy did not lie with him, so he turned to me and in a voice that fooled no one begged my pardon. For the sake of amity, I granted it. But if we'd not had a performance that night, I wouldn't have been quite so obliging, you can be sure. This one was going to require close watching.

A few of the props from Act II had been brought on stage, and we began the scene in which Escamillo makes his first appearance and plunges right into the *Toreador Song*. Toscanini interrupted every few seconds, but both he and Duchon were going out of their way to accommodate the other and no major problems emerged. Duchon did not, I was happy to see, jump up on the table at any time.

After the first walk-through, Duchon started singing. He sang half-voice for most of the aria, but then he opened up and finished full voice, testing the acoustics of the auditorium. It was what we'd all been waiting for, and my resentment of the man's ill-mannered behavior evaporated as if it had never been. When you can sing like that, you can get away with a lot.

And he *could* sing! The voice was undimmed by the years, deep and lustrous and rich. And he sang with a panache that made you forget that the tune was as familiar as your own face. With Duchon's sophisticated singing on one side of me and Caruso's golden tenor on the other, we would make musical history that night! Ha!

Carmen sings one word toward the end of Escamillo's aria—*L'amour*—and without any warm-up I gave it my sultriest reading. Duchon raised an eyebrow at me and finished the aria. Everyone on stage broke into applause.

Now, you'd think a man whose first bit of singing in a new house had been greeted with enthusiasm would at least say *thank you,* wouldn't you? Not Duchon. Instead, he said a very peculiar thing: "Is there someone here who does not wish me to sing?"

We all stared at him. "Monsieur?" Toscanini asked.

"A door is open backstage," the baritone barked. "Someone wants me to catch a chill and lose my voice!"

The Met's backstage *was* a drafty place; at one time or another we'd all complained about it to Gatti, who invariably responded with a what-can-I-do shrug. But for Duchon to claim the drafts were created specifically to get rid of him—oh dear. I hoped Duchon wasn't going to be one of those people who think someone is out to get them all the time.

Gatti tried to apologize for the drafts, but Duchon wouldn't listen. So we all had to stand there and wait while Gatti sent a stagehand around to check the doors. When the man came back with the news that a door had indeed been left open, Duchon trumpeted, "You see? Someone does not wish me to sing!"

Of all the *conceit*! As if he were the only one on the stage! But I held my tongue, and Toscanini called for the rehearsal to resume.

Duchon and Caruso rehearsed the brief fight from the next act, with Toscanini marking the tempo for the piano accompanist. Finally, Duchon and I rehearsed the very brief duet we have in the last act. He sang twelve measures to me, I sang eight and a half measures back to him, and we sang the last three and a half measures together. Those three and a half measures are the only time in the entire opera when soprano and baritone sing simultaneously, so if our voices did not blend that didn't mean the production would be ruined. But it was a nice moment in the opera and Toscanini was such a perfectionist and . . . well, I wanted us to sound good. Duchon and I finished our last *je t'aime* and looked at our conductor.

Toscanini smiled.

It was all right, then; everything was all right. Toscanini was satisfied, Gatti-Casazza was satisfied, and Duchon declared himself satisfied. What he actually said was, "It will do for now."

Toscanini started to bristle but then checked himself. "If you get into trouble," he told Duchon, "do not worry. I follow *you*."

"Now why don't you ever say that to me?" I teased him.

"Because I never know what you are going to do," he replied humorlessly.

The whole rehearsal had taken less than an hour, so there would still be time for a little rest and some vocalizing before the performance began. Duchon and I parted amicably enough; but when Toscanini and Gatti came face to face, they both averted their eyes and passed without speaking.

Oh-oh. Trouble at the top?

I heard a whisper in my ear. "Is good, the Duchon—yes?" I turned to see Uncle Hummy scuttling away.

Scotti was waiting for me by the exit. "Well?" I asked him. "What do you think?"

"I think he is an excellent *French* baritone," the Italian said indifferently, thus consigning Duchon forever to the ranks of the also-ran.

Back to normal.

Carmen was the work that had originally convinced me I was destined to be an opera singer. It was the first opera I ever saw; my parents had taken me to hear the great Emma Calvé sing the role in Boston when I was still a schoolgirl. I left that theatre knowing what I was going to do with the rest of my life.

And now *Carmen* was my opera, exclusively—at least, it was going to be. I hadn't been singing it very long; some things have to be worked up to. The role of Carmen has been sung by sopranos, mezzo-sopranos, and contraltos; and all three voice ranges have had their problems with it. The role really is too high for the lusher-voiced contraltos; half of them end up shouting their top notes. I have the range, and fortunately my soprano has an almost mezzo quality to it (even the know-everything critics say so). So it truly is a good opera for me.

It is one humdinger of a role. The tenor and the baritone have only one aria each, but Carmen has *four*. She also sings in the second-act quintet, in the third-act ensemble, and in the tense and violent duet that ends the opera. In addition, Carmen dances, plays the castanets, gets into a fight with one of the chorus women, gets arrested, escapes, joins a gang of smugglers, flirts with every man in sight, and dies dramatically on stage. Oh, it is a glorious role!

The house was sold out. It always is, whenever Caruso and I sing—or did I mention that? Near curtain time Dr. Curtis came into my dressing room to examine my throat.

"Hm," he said, and waited. He liked to be asked.

"Well?" I obliged. "How am I?"

"Color is normal," he said in that raspy voice that always made *him* sound hoarse, "but that doesn't necessarily mean you're back to full health yet. Hold back tonight, Gerry. Don't strain."

I laughed. "How in the world can I possibly hold back in *Carmen*? I'm on stage more than all the other principals put together, and everything I sing is of such high intensity that—"

"Nevertheless, you must restrain yourself," Dr. Curtis interrupted impatiently. "Gerry, I've known you ever since you were a young girl ready to set the opera world on fire, and even then you pushed too hard. It's understandable in a girl of seventeen, but you don't need to prove yourself now. Hold back. Show some restraint."

I made one of those sounds that can mean anything and started putting on my make-up.

"Besides," he rasped mischievously, "it's Duchon they're coming to hear tonight anyway."

When I threw a powder puff at him he left, chuckling, pleased with himself. While I was warming up I finished my make-up. I made a convincing-looking gypsy, I thought. At least, I looked good.

It never fails to excite me, that moment of waiting offstage for the cue to make the first entrance. Caruso goes to pieces from nervousness, Amato always taps one foot impatiently, and Scotti, blasé creature that he is, lounges about casually as if stepping out on to an opera stage were no more extraordinary than mailing a letter. But as for me, I'm always raring to go. I heard my cue . . . and then the chorus was singing *La voilà! There she is!*

And there I was, vamping my way around the stage, singing the *Habanera*, flirting outrageously with Don José (Caruso) while keeping one eye on Toscanini's baton. I didn't hold back a bit; I gave it everything I had. Two of Carmen's four arias come in Act I, so by the first intermission I should know whether my voice would hold out for the rest of the performance or not. The applause at the end of the *Habanera* was thunderous; a nice way to start. I tossed a rose to Caruso and made my exit.

By the time we were into the second act, I knew I was going to make it. My voice was strong and my energy high. I might pay for it tomorrow, but tonight would be glorious. Toscanini was pleased; he kept smiling and nodding to me from the podium. This was the act where the baritone made his first appearance, and the audience's anticipation was running high; we could all feel it. American audiences had never heard Philippe Duchon, but they'd heard *of* him. I suppose they were wondering whether he would live up to his reputation or not.

He did. He didn't go for the youthful vigor most middle-aged baritones try to infuse into the role of the athletic toreador; instead he was suave and worldly and smooth as silk, and he brought the house down. After Duchon had finished knocking them dead, Caruso got his turn. I don't know why Bizet put both the men's arias into the same act instead of spacing them out, but he did. I was wondering how Caruso could possibly top Duchon, but I needn't have worried.

The way Caruso sang the *Flower Song* that night, it was enough to break your heart. The plaintiveness of his tone, the throb in his voice—they were perfect, neither overdone nor underplayed. When he'd finished I wanted to throw both arms around his neck and give him a big kiss, but of course I couldn't. The action called for me to give him a lot of trouble instead, so I did. The applause at the end of the act was deafening; the audience was actually on its feet cheering *at the end of the second act*. Oh, we had a good one going that night!

Riding high on that wave of audience enthusiasm, I took my courage in hand and went over to the men's side to Duchon's dressing room. I told him his Escamillo was magnificent and I considered it a privilege to sing with him.

He hesitated, and then decided graciousness was the order of the evening. He thanked me and added, "I must say I was impressed by the fieriness of your performance. A strong Carmen, a very strong Carmen."

I've always found that mutual admiration enhances the performance of any opera enormously. So that was all right.

Duchon and Caruso survived their third-act fight without mishap, the opening pageantry of the fourth act played itself out, and suddenly it was time for the final duet. I'd never been completely satisfied with the way Caruso and I did that duet. Oh, the singing was fine; we were both in control of the music. It was the acting that bothered me; I tried, but I didn't get a whole lot of cooperation from my partner. (I dearly love Rico, but he is not the world's greatest actor.) It just seemed to me that in a duologue sung at fever pitch, in which emotions run so high that one of the singers ends up killing the other, we ought to do more than stand there and wave our arms at each other. But the audience liked it; that night we could do no wrong.

We all stood on stage grasping hands for our final curtain call, Caruso and I still sweating buckets from the exertions of the final duet, Duchon cool and immaculate. The *bravas* outnumbered the *bravos* (they always do for *Carmen)*, and from the back of the auditorium I could hear "Ger*ee*, Ger*ee*," chanted in unison.

"The gerryflappers are here," Caruso said out of the side of his mouth.

"I know." Oh, you can be sure I knew! If Duchon noticed my unpaid claque at work, he gave no sign. Tonight was his American début, and he was making the most of it.

Afterward we all wallowed in the good-natured pandemonium that reigns backstage after every successful performance. My maid Bella was waiting in the wings with my robe, protection against drafts and quickly drying perspiration. Duchon was laughing and talking easily with all the strangers who kept coming up to him; it's amazing how quickly instant acceptance can bring a man out of himself. Gatti-Casazza was everywhere, talking a mile a minute. Even after years of both triumph and disaster in the opera world, Gatti could still get as excited as a child with a new toy when things went right.

At that moment I decided to break my promise to Osgood Springer. I'd told him I'd speak to Gatti about a major role for Jimmy Freeman next season, and that I'd do it right after the performance. But the moment wasn't right; Gatti was so full of Philippe Duchon's successful début that broaching the subject of Jimmy's future right then would have been a tactical error. I'd wait until Gatti had come down from his cloud, say another day or two.

"*Bella divina, incantatrice!*" a familiar voice sang out, and Scotti was there, smothering me with hugs and compliments. "Your best Carmen yet!" he cried. "A *perfect* Carmen, Gerry—you must stop this immediately, I cannot tolerate perfection in others! What say you, Maestro? Is she not perfect this evening?"

Toscanini oozed his way through the crowd and lifted my hand to his lips. "Perfect," he said, his eyes glittering. "I can no longer imagine any other singer in the role." Oh, he can be a charmer when he wants to.

Scotti went over to pound Caruso on the back. I asked Toscanini, "What do you think of Duchon?"

"Magnificent resonance," he said. "Like a church bell. And his precision is exquisite. A most interesting Escamillo."

I nodded. "Gatti pulled off a real *coup*, signing him so quickly like that."

Toscanini sniffed. "A matter of luck. Duchon falls into his hands."

Belatedly I remembered how he and Gatti had avoided speaking to each other that afternoon and was about to ask if something was wrong when High Society descended upon us. The *crème* of New York's social world, Mrs. This and Mr. That, half of them tone deaf and all of them wearing enough diamonds and rubies and emeralds to finance several seasons of Met productions. But I was polite and charming to everybody, *de rigueur* for opera singers.

Caruso entertained the crowd by coming over and giving me a big wet kiss. "Is she not glorious tonight?" he asked the world at large. Back to me: "I and you and Scotti, we go eat supper, yes? Del Pezzo's."

Oh dear. Pasta. "Supper, yes," I said, "Del Pezzo's, no."

Toscanini spoke up. "What is wrong with Del Pezzo's?" He turned 'o Caruso. "I invite myself to accompany you."

Caruso was delighted (he almost always is). Scotti was informed of our plans; I wondered if he'd spoken to Duchon but didn't want to ask him in front of the others. The crowd backstage showed no sign of thinning out, so Caruso made the first move by going upstairs to his dressing room. I left Scotti and Toscanini talking together and was about to start up the stairs myself when I saw Emmy Destinn striding purposefully toward me. Emmy! What was she doing here tonight?

"Gerry, I have something I want to say to you," she announced in that alarmingly direct way of speaking she had. "You are the best Carmen I have ever heard. I have heard a lot of Carmens, and you are the best one. There, I've said it."

Oh, how I *hate* it when she does things like that! I have never, never gone backstage after one of her performances and told her she was the best Aïda or whatever that I have ever heard. Prima donnas just don't *say* things like that to each other! And she meant it—she truly meant it, I didn't doubt that for one moment. I was used to handling a barrage of excited and exaggerated compliments, but all this truthful earnestness was another matter altogether.

Someone should teach that woman the value of a little well-timed insincerity.

I thanked her; what else could I do? We chatted about the performance a few minutes, but Emmy's eyes kept straying over to Philippe Duchon. Finally she said, "He is good, isn't he?"

"Yes, he is," I answered. "And Emmy, he didn't even try to upstage me. Not once."

She nodded. "On his good behavior. But now that he's proved himself, he'll start showing his true colors. Watch out for him, Gerry. He's trouble."

I appreciated the warning and took it to heart. On impulse, I invited Emmy to join us for supper. "The men want to go to Del Pezzo's," I added, hoping for an ally.

"Oh good," she smiled. "I like Del Pezzo's."

Grrr. I tried to convince her Sherry's would be a better place to go; there was nothing wrong with Del Pezzo's, but it wasn't very elegant. Besides, Italian food is so fattening. Emmy was wavering—but then an enormous *thud* sounded and at almost the same time someone screamed. We both jumped.

I looked over to see where one end of a roller curtain had come crashing down to the stage. Sprawled out on the stage floor not more than a couple of feet away was Philippe Duchon, a look of absolute terror on his face. We all stood thunderstruck for a moment; then everyone dashed over to Duchon. He was all right, just scared out of his wits. "Someone . . . someone tried to kill me!" he cried.

"Oh no, Monsieur Duchon!" Gatti-Casazza gasped, helping the baritone to his feet. "It is merely accident! You are not hurt?"

Outrage was quickly replacing Duchon's fear. "I could have been killed! Look at that curtain!"

The roller curtain was a sight: one end still hoisted up high over the stage, the other end resting on the stage floor. We all fussed over Duchon, trying to calm him down. "I am devastated that such a thing happens," Gatti apologized. "Are you certain you are not hurt?"

"I tell you someone tried to kill me!" Duchon shouted. "That was no accident! Someone does not want me here!"

I couldn't see any stagehands in the immediate vicinity. The roller curtain was painted blue and was used as a backdrop to represent the sky. The curtain was operated by two ropes that ran from the floor through two overhead pulleys, then down to the points where they were attached at either end of the roller. Stagehands would pull on the free ends of the ropes to raise and turn the roller at the same time, thus winding the curtain material around the roller.

The operating lines were tied off to cleats in the stage floor, and I looked around until I found the one used for the fallen end of the roller. The rope was there, one end firmly lashed about the cleat—but the rest of it lay limply on the stage floor. I picked up the end of the rope and examined it, while Duchon went on insisting that the roller curtain had been dropped deliberately.

"Monsieur Duchon!" I called. "Will you come here, please? There's something here you should see." He came, reluctantly. I showed him the end of the rope. "See, it's old and frayed. The rope should have been replaced long ago. But it has not been *cut*. It simply broke. It was an accident, Monsieur—no one has tried to harm you."

He took the rope from me and examined the end, looking for signs of a knife blade. He found none. He whirled toward Gatti and started lambasting him for allowing unsafe equipment to be used backstage. Gatti apologized.

Duchon's close call had put an end to the festive air backstage. I hurried upstairs and changed, and by the time I got back down the stagehands had attached a new rope to the roller curtain and pulled it back up to its place in the flies.

The others were all ready to go. Caruso, who was a walking advertisement for good eating, announced he was in imminent danger of starving to death. Toscanini, who was thin to the point of emaciation, declared he really wasn't all that hungry and would be satisfied with something to drink. Emmy backed up Caruso but suggested Sherry's instead of Del Pezzo's. Scotti draped a friendly arm about her shoulders and started explaining to her the superior merits of Italian cuisine. We still hadn't reached

an agreement when we went out the stage door, where a
mob of fans greeted us—most of whom were screeching
"Ger*ee*! Ger*ee*!"

Scotti and Caruso got almost as much enjoyment out of
the gerryflappers as I did. For one thing, they were all
girls in their late teens or early twenties, and that alone
was enough to hold the interest of those two Italian lovers.
The girls pushed up against me—not looking for autographs, just wanting to talk, to be a part of what was going
on. In the vanguard, as usual, were Mildredandphoebe.
Since you never saw one without the other, it was hard not
to think of them as one person, Mildredandphoebe. Phoebe
was a sort of lower-case personality anyway; it was Mildred who was the leader.

Those two were my most ardent fans (well, my most
ardent *female* fans). They came to every performance I
gave, kept scrapbooks about my career, wrote a newsletter
about me that they circulated to other fans, collected sou-
venirs, and were always, always *there*. They wanted to
know everything about me. Occasionally I left tickets for
them at the box office, but tonight they'd stood at the back
of the auditorium during the entire performance.

"You were just *wonderful*, Miss Farrar!" Mildred cried.
"I could hardly breathe, you were so wonderful!"

"Just wonderful!" Phoebe echoed.

"I never heard anything like it," Mildred rushed on,
"I've got to tell you, it was, oh, it was an *experience* for
me tonight!"

"An experience," Phoebe nodded.

I really liked this part of it; Mildredandphoebe could
always be counted on to provide me the opportunity to
play Queen Geraldine, graciously acknowledging the adu-
lation of a grateful public. It was fun. I assumed my most
regal manner and chatted with them a while (Scotti says I
put on a British accent for such occasions). One of the
other gerryflappers had cornered Toscanini, who was looking around desperately for an escape route. He was not
very good at small talk.

"Howja like the Frenchman?" Mildred wanted to know.

"Monsieur Duchon?" I said. "I think he made a most

auspicious Metropolitan début and I look forward to singing with him again.'' Mildredandphoebe scribbled in the
notebooks they carried with them everywhere, an item for
the next newsletter.

''I die!'' Caruso cried.

I laughed and told the gerryflappers we had to go.
''Thank you all for coming, all of you, thank you. But
we're tired and we're hungry, and we want to get something to eat.''

''Where are you going?'' Mildredandphoebe asked. They
wanted to know *everything* about me.

That traitorous Emmy Destinn ended up siding with the
men and I was overwhelmingly outvoted. We went to Del
Pezzo's.

□ **4** □ It was my manager, Morris Gest, who brought me the bad news about Pasquale Amato.

"Doc Curtis says bronchitis," Morris told me. "But I think it's pneumonia."

That was Morris, all right—a know-everything. "What makes you think that?" I asked.

"The way the doc talked. He seemed more worried than you'd think he'd be, over just a case of bronchitis."

"There's no such thing as 'just' a case of bronchitis for a singer," I said sharply. But pneumonia or bronchitis, it was still bad news. Amato would be out longer than anyone had counted on. Poor Pasquale. Poor us.

"Gatti-Casazza doesn't have all the schedule worked out yet," Morris went on, "but I think you'd better get used to the idea of singing *Madame Sans-Gêne* with a house baritone. Duchon won't learn the role. Gatti said so himself."

I can't say I was surprised. *Madame Sans-Gêne* is the soprano's opera, with all the other parts more or less orbiting around her role. Amato was amiable enough and secure enough to sing the baritone part without fearing loss of stature, but I didn't think Duchon was cut from the same cloth. He was too used to being center stage; even Escamillo in *Carmen* was a lesser effort for him.

"Sorry I missed your *Carmen* the other night," Morris said sheepishly. "Everybody's saying it was great. But the Old Man had scheduled a family gathering that night and, well, you know how it is."

I knew. Morris was a little intimidated by his father-in-law—whom he never referred to by name, only as the Old Man. Morris Gest had been my manager for some years now; he was an aggressive man who'd started out as a ticket scalper and then gone on to bigger and better things. Morris had one of those rubbery faces that can be absolutely trustworthy one minute and downright conniving the next. But as long as his conniving face was put on in the service of *my* career, I didn't mind. He took a little getting used to, but he was a good manager. I think he was afraid of nothing at all in the world except possibly the aforementioned father-in-law, a soft-spoken man who loved controlling other people, including Morris Gest. Interesting relationship there.

Morris had come to my apartment to work out some details of a Friday morning musicale at the Biltmore he'd scheduled me into, but the mention of Duchon had set him thinking. "What do you know about that tour the Frenchman's come for? Where does he go from here?"

"I have no idea," I said. "I believe Gatti mentioned it was a last-minute thing. Duchon probably doesn't have the details worked out yet."

Morris started grinning, and I could almost see the dollar signs in his eyes. "You mean he doesn't have a manager?"

"Morris, it's a *fund-raising* tour. For Alsatian war relief. There's no profit to be made."

"Sure, sure. But there's such a thing as good will, you know. I help him a little now, he helps me a lot later. Besides, he'll have to sing a few times for himself, won't he? To cover expenses?"

If there was any way to make some money out of Duchon's fund-raising tour, Morris was the one to find it. "Well, good luck," I said, meaning it; Philippe Duchon and Morris Gest should make an interesting combination. "But remember he's committed to stay in New York until Amato is back on his feet."

He shrugged. "It'll take a while to get things set up." He got up to go. "Say, is there a back way out of this building? I had to work my way through a bunch of gerryflappers to get in here."

"Where—out front?"

"Yep. What do they do, just hang around hoping you'll come out?"

I shook my head in amazement; those girls had some sort of sixth sense about these things. "As a matter of fact, I'm going to be leaving for a luncheon engagement in a few minutes. But I don't know how they knew about it."

"Yeah? Who you having lunch with?" Morris was never shy.

"No one you know," I lied. I told him how to find the

tradesmen's entrance and ushered him out. I didn't want him to know I was meeting Philippe Duchon; Morris would pester me to put in a good word for him, or—even worse—invite himself along.

The invitation from Duchon had been a complete surprise; it arrived in the form of a note carried by a handsome young valet who spoke no English. I wondered what the baritone wanted. We had a rehearsal scheduled that afternoon, and Duchon had timed the luncheon so we'd have about half an hour to talk after eating. So whatever it was couldn't be too important; nothing of significance ever gets said in thirty minutes.

I wrapped up warm against the cold. Out front were a dozen or so girls shivering in the winter weather. Mildred-andphoebe were not among them; these girls turned out to be neophyte gerryflappers because they asked for autographs, something the old-timers no longer did. These new girls had a tendency to hang back, too unsure of themselves to start a conversation with an opera star. So I started the conversation, chatting a few minutes before I got into the limousine. Never neglect your public. *Never*.

Duchon had selected Delmonico's, on East Forty-fourth Street, probably the most famous restaurant in New York City. (Right across the street was Sherry's, which I would have preferred.) My host was already there, rising quickly from the table when he saw me come in. Duchon was a new celebrity in town and I was a well-established one, and between the two of us we captured every eye in the place. I followed the smiling maître d' across the room (not too fast), and this time Duchon did take my hand. When he gave a low Gallic bow, a most satisfying murmur ran through the restaurant.

We ordered, both of us eating light because we had several hours of hard singing ahead of us. Toscanini had called a brush-up rehearsal of the middle two acts of *Carmen* with full orchestra. The Maestro had made it clear that the rehearsal was not solely for the benefit of Duchon; the rest of us, he said, were getting a bit ragged. Hmph.

When we'd finished eating and were lingering over coffee, Duchon finally got to the point. "I want to apologize," he said, "for my boorish behavior when first we met. I hope you can find it in your heart to forgive me, Miss Farrar."

"Call me Gerry."

"And you must call me Philippe. I can only plead ignorance as an excuse. I did not understand how distinguished a colleague I was speaking to. I hope you will forgive me."

Meaning that if I were a nobody, rudeness was permissible? "Of course I forgive you, Philippe. Think no more about it." There, wasn't that gracious of me?

"Ah, *merci,* Gerry," he smiled. He had a nice smile. "Nevertheless, I feel I owe you some explanation."

"You don't have to explain anything."

"But I wish to explain. I can't have the beautiful and gifted Geraldine Farrar telling everyone what a boor Philippe Duchon is."

Protecting himself. "Very well, I'm listening."

"You must understand that I have had experiences you have never been through—experience with the Germans, I mean to say. Americans are wonderfully innocent people. Your country has never been invaded, for instance. Your childhood was not destroyed by soldiers killing and burning and destroying everything in their path, is this not true? You cannot understand the suffering of those who lost everything because of *Germans.*"

He made the word sound obscene. I also got the impression that he was sneering at *me,* because I had not been subjected to the same abuses he had. Tactless he might be, but his anguish was real so I merely said, "Tell me what happened."

"You may know that Alsace is my homeland. That is, it was my homeland, when I was a boy. The Germans came when I was fourteen, during something the politicians dignified by calling it the Franco-Prussian War. It was a rape. They killed my father and took our land. They violated my mother and my sister, and the only reason I was allowed to live was that they wanted someone to take care of their horses for them. My mother and I eventually escaped to Paris, but to this day I do not know what happened to my sister. The Germans simply *stole* Alsace from France. And the rest of the world stood by and let it happen.''

Oh, the poor man! No wonder he was so unforgiving toward anything German. Who wouldn't be, after that? I thought of saying something about soldiers in wartime turning into beasts or that to forgive was divine, but it was so embarrassingly inadequate that I ended up saying nothing.

''And now they're doing it again,'' he continued bitterly. ''Only this time they will be content with nothing less than all of France. It is happening again, but on an even bigger scale than before.''

''But this time the rest of the world isn't just standing by and watching. The English—''

''The English are helping, yes. But they are not enough. Only the Americans are strong enough to tip the scales. But you shillyshally, you hold back! Does the war have to be fought on your own soil before it means anything to you?''

I was slightly taken aback. ''Well, everyone is saying it's only a matter of time—''

''Time, time! There is no time! How many Frenchmen must die while you take the *time* to make up your minds?'' Suddenly he recollected himself and made a visible effort to calm down. He sat in silence for a few moments and then said, ''*Ma chère* Gerry—again I beg your forgiveness. I know you still have ties to Germany and must feel torn by what is happening. But you must understand that where the Germans are concerned, I am incapable of objectivity. I beg your indulgence.''

I reassured him the best I could. It occurred to me that a lot of Europeans must see us the way Duchon did—fat, rich Americans unwilling to exert themselves to help people in trouble. On impulse I said, ''Your fund-raising tour—would a joint concert help, do you think? You and I together?''

His eyes gleamed. ''You volunteer to help? The Alsatian war relief?''

''Certainly. I'd be glad to help. What do you think?''

He laughed in relief. ''I did not quite dare to ask . . . I

was hoping . . . ah, yes, yes! I think a joint concert will be most helpful, and an exquisite experience for me as well. I thank you from the bottom of my heart, lovely Gerry. You are a very generous lady.''

Yes I was, wasn't I? "I'll have Morris come see you, then. Morris Gest, my manager. He can arrange matters for us, if that's satisfactory with you.'' There, I'd come up with a legitimate reason for Morris to meet with Duchon; he should love me for that.

"I am certain that will be most satisfactory.'' For the last few minutes Duchon had kept glancing over my right shoulder at someone or something behind me. "Excuse me, Gerry, but do you know that young man over there?''

I turned and looked. And there was Jimmy Freeman, sitting at a table by the wall and looking like an earthquake about to happen. He was tensed up and sitting sideways to his table with his fists pressing against his knees. He glowered openly at our table. I told Duchon he was a member of the opera company.

"Ah.'' Duchon looked amused. "And a young admirer, no doubt? He is coming over.''

Then Jimmy was standing by our table, and before I could make any introductions he said to Duchon, "So, it's not enough that you steal my role! Now you steal my girl as well!''

Duchon's eyebrows shot up. "Your *girl*?''

"Your *girl*!'' I echoed. *Don't laugh*, I told myself. *Don't laugh at him*.

"That's right, my girl,'' Jimmy persisted with slightly shaky bravado. "You come here and you take whatever you want—first Escamillo and now Gerry. You have your nerve!'' I was astonished; Jimmy *never* called me by my first name.

"Just a minute, young man.'' Duchon stood up. "In the first place, I do not even know who you are. Your name is . . . ?''

"Freeman,'' the younger man said loudly. "James Freeman. Remember it, old man!''

Oh dear. This was my shy, stammering, insecure young

Jimmy Freeman? Duchon was in his late fifties; I wondered how he liked being called *old man*.

He didn't like it at all. "You forget yourself, sir," he bristled. "We are in a public place, and you are embarrassing the lady."

"She doesn't look embarrassed to me. Go home, Duchon. It's time you stepped aside and made room for younger men."

Duchon's face darkened. "How dare you talk to me like that, you impudent young wh, wh, wh . . . ?"

"Whippersnapper?" I suggested.

"Whippersnapper, *oui*, thank you. I suggest you leave, young man, before I forget I am a gentleman. Or shall I summon the maître d'hôtel and have you escorted out?"

The two of them stood there glaring at each other. In addition to the authority of his years, Duchon towered over Jimmy, his big head and body dwarfing his adversary. Jimmy was of normal size, but he'd never looked younger or more insubstantial. It occurred to me that everyone in Delmonico's could tell what was going on just by looking at our little tableau. I placed my hand at the base of my throat and raised my head; thank God for a good profile.

By then the maître d' was there, and he quickly hustled Jimmy out of the restaurant. Actually Jimmy let himself be hustled out; I suspect he didn't know how to resolve the little drama he'd started. Before Duchon could sit back down, I said, "We might as well leave too. It's almost time for rehearsal."

He nodded agreement, still miffed. "What did he mean, I stole his role from him? It was my understanding I was replacing Pasquale Amato."

"I'll explain when we get out of here. Shall we go?" I led the way, being careful not to hurry. We were the injured party; why should we beat a hasty retreat? Poor Jimmy, whatever could have gotten into him? Every eye in the place was on Duchon and me as we left; I couldn't see Duchon because he was behind me, but I know I was the very picture of dignified innocence.

Nothing like a lively little scene to brighten up the day.

*   *   *

About an hour later, I was seriously thinking of murder.

"The tempo is wrong, wrong, *wrong*!" I screamed for about the hundredth time.

"The tempo is right, right, *right*!" Toscanini screamed back. "It is you who are wrong, Miss all-American prima donna!"

I took a deep breath. "Now you listen to me, you musical Napoleon. It's. Too. Fast. Do you understand? *It's too fast!*"

"Oh, I see." The Maestro put down his baton and folded his arms. "Bizet does not know what he is doing when he writes *a tempo animato* in the score? I do not know what I do when I conduct *animato*? All these fine gentlemen in the orchestra, they do not know what *animato* means? Only her highness Geraldine Farrar knows the correct tempo?"

"The orchestra does what you tell them to do," I snapped. "And if Bizet were here he would *weep* when he heard what you're doing to his music!"

"Ah, yes, the *orchestra* does what I tell them to do! An example certain sopranos would be well-advised to follow!" He picked up his baton. "We try again."

"*Coraggio*," Caruso whispered to me from the wings.

I muttered under my breath and went back to my place on the stage. We were rehearsing Act II and it was Carmen's *Gypsy Song* that was the bone of contention between Toscanini and me. The aria starts off fast and then gets faster. But it wasn't the music that was causing trouble; it was the words. The *Gypsy Song* has some real tongue-twisters in it; if I could just go *la-la-la* I could sing it as fast as the Maestro wanted. But lines like *Les Bohémiens à tour de bras de leurs instruments faisaient rage* simply cannot be sung at the tempo Toscanini was setting. I'd explained this to him a dozen times, but all he ever did was shrug and say something like "Ah yes, French—it is not a reasonable language."

We tried again. I got through it somehow, but neither Toscanini nor I was satisfied with the result. But that epitome of Italian ego in the orchestra pit decided we couldn't spend any more time on *Gypsy Song* and should go on to the next part. Gatti-Casazza was in the auditorium watching, listening; but he never interfered in rehearsal, never. That's probably why he and Toscanini had made such a good team for so long.

Almost immediately it was time for the toreador to do his turn. Act II takes place in an inn, but we were rehearsing without sets. Onstage were a number of singers playing army officers and gypsies; offstage left a men's chorus waited to follow the baritone on when he made his entrance. But Philippe Duchon was standing upstage center; and when the orchestra played his cue, he simply walked straight downstage and started to sing. Two or three of the men's chorus hurried on from the left and looked at Toscanini uncertainly.

The Maestro rapped his baton; the orchestra trailed off. "Monsieur Duchon, you see our stage set only once and you forget. Escamillo enters from the left—you see the chorus waiting offstage to the left?"

"I see, and I do not forget," Duchon replied stiffly. "I am accustomed to making my entrance from upstage center. I do not like coming in from a *corner*."

"But Monsieur," Toscanini said patiently, "the set has no door there. It is impossible to enter from upstage center. You come in from the left."

"No, I come in from upstage center," the baritone answered just as patiently. "You will have a door put in the set."

Everyone on stage stared at him. I've had my own say about the Metropolitan's stage sets on occasion, but to demand that a set be rebuilt two-thirds of the way through the season—well, I'd never heard the like before.

"It cannot be done," Toscanini said waspishly.

"It *must* be done," Duchon thundered. "You will have a door put in the set, and you will do so before the next performance!"

You could almost see the steam coming out of Toscanini's ears; *nobody* spoke to him like that, absolutely nobody. He let loose a stream of Italian invective that would have withered a lesser man than Duchon.

Then Duchon did an unforgivable thing: He went over

Toscanini's head. "Mr. Gatti?" he called to the general manager, who'd been sitting quietly through all the uproar. "You will see that a door is installed in the back flat of the set, please?" That was doubly insulting to the conductor, for Toscanini saw himself as the man who truly ran the Metropolitan Opera while Gatti-Casazza just tended to money matters and mundane things like that.

Then all three of them were jabbering at once, and before long Gatti and Toscanini were shouting at each other—which made no sense, because as far as I could tell they were in agreement: no new door. Caruso wandered out on to the stage from the wings and announced, "I have a suggestion."

"*No!*" everybody roared.

He shrugged and went back to the wings.

While Toscanini and Gatti were still arguing, Duchon came over to where I was sitting at a table downstage right. "The *Gypsy Song,* it is not easy to sing. But if you took fewer breaths you could manage it better. After rehearsal I will give you a breathing exercise you can practice." He gave me a quick smile and walked away.

I was so astounded I couldn't say a word at first. Emmy Destinn was right; the man wanted to run everything. I jumped to my feet and shrieked, "There's nothing wrong with my breath control!"

Toscanini broke off his argument with Gatti to stare at me, puzzled. "I do not say anything is wrong with your breath control."

"Not you. *Him!*" I pointed accusingly at the offending baritone.

"So!" Toscanini fumed at Duchon. "Now you are directing my singers for me as well?"

"I merely make a helpful suggestion," Duchon replied calmly.

"No suggestions permitted!" a tenor voice sang out from offstage.

Duchon lifted his upper lip in a soundless sneer as he turned to walk away—and fell over a chair. A dozen hands reached out to help him up, but he waved them off. "Who put that chair there?" he shouted. "It was not there a

minute ago!'' He got back to his feet. "I asked a question
and I expect an answer. Who put that chair there?"

"There are chairs all over the stage," I snapped. "Watch
where you're going."

"*That* chair was not in *that* place before," Duchon said
icily. "Someone just now put it there. To trip me."

"Oh, Monsieur!" Gatti sighed. "No one wants to trip
you. You mistake."

"Did you hope I'd fall and crack my head open?"
Duchon demanded of the stage at large. "Is that what you
had in mind?"

"*Ridicolo,*" Toscanini muttered.

"You would not find it ridiculous if it happened to you,
Maestro! And Mr. Gatti-Casazza—you will have a new
door put into the set! I insist!"

"Monsieur Duchon," Gatti said worriedly, "the bud-
get, it has no money for building new sets, you understand?"

"Then you must find the money somewhere," Duchon
replied implacably.

Toscanini got a wicked gleam in his eye. "Monsieur,"
he said in the sweetest manner imaginable, "if you persuade Mr. Gatti to spend the money for a new door, I have
no objection."

Oh, that was naughty. Gatti was a notorious penny-
pincher; he would lose an arm rather than spend money on
a singer's whim, even when that singer was Philippe
Duchon. Toscanini had just made it Gatti's battle instead
of his own. Duchon didn't know it, but he didn't have a
chance of winning this one.

Gatti stared at Toscanini with murderous dislike, and the
conductor returned the look glare for glare. There really
was bad feeling growing between the two men, and ultimately that could cause more trouble than anything Duchon
might do. "Can we get on with the rehearsal?" I asked.

"Not until we settle the matter of the door." Duchon
dismissed me with a wave of his hand.

He dismissed *me*. With a wave of his hand! "Maestro,"
I said angrily, "who is in charge here?"

Before Toscanini could answer, Gatti said, "Gerry,

please, do not be angry. I am sure Monsieur Duchon is simply trying to achieve the best production possible—''

''Why are you siding with him?'' I demanded. ''Don't you understand it's *your* job he's after?''

And then I realized what I'd said. Gatti turned white, Toscanini snickered, and Duchon shot me a look that told me our previously friendly entente was now at an undeniable end. There was no way to unsay what I'd said, so I just sat back down at my table and waited. Gatti recovered quickly enough and informed our imperious baritone that there would be no door installed in the set for him, and that he would have to make do with a stage-left entrance.

''In that case,'' Duchon said, ''I do not rehearse.'' He turned to go.

''Monsieur!'' Gatti cried. ''You sign a contract!''

''And I intend to honor it,'' Duchon nodded. ''I will sing every performance I am contracted for. But I do not rehearse.'' And with that, he walked off the stage and out of the opera house.

An absolutely *dead* silence fell. Everyone avoided looking at everyone else. Then Caruso said from his place in the wings, ''I think he means it.''

Nothing like stating the obvious to relieve the tension a little. Toscanini became all business, deciding what we would rehearse next, issuing orders, snapping at people, being Toscanini. Gatti resumed his seat in the auditorium, but he looked a little shaken and kept pulling at his beard in distress. I wished I had kept my mouth shut. Duchon had indeed lost the management of his own opera house because of the war and undoubtedly was looking for a replacement, but I shouldn't have said anything about it. Not here, not under these circumstances.

Caruso finally got to come out of the wings. Once on stage, he started acting the clown, trying to lighten the mood. While I was doing my dance with the castanets, he made all sorts of improper remarks that normally would have had me in stitches. And when he knelt at my feet to sing the *Flower Song* he kept tickling my ankle. But the Caruso magic just wasn't working; when rehearsal finally ended, everyone left in a sour mood.

I was stopped on my way out by a shabby figure that materialized out of the shadows backstage. "The Duchon wrong," he said earnestly. "You not listen."

"Don't you worry about that, Uncle Hummy, I have no intention of listening. You were here the whole time?"

He nodded vigorously. "Here since last night."

That stopped me. "You spent the *night* in the opera house?"

A look of alarm grew on his face. "Tell Mr. Gatti?"

"No, I'm not going to tell anybody. But I don't think that's such a good idea, Uncle Hummy. Maybe you'd better not do it again." He looked so distressed I added, "Well, maybe you'd better not *tell* anybody, I mean."

He understood; his thin lips stretched back in a big grin. He bobbed his head and mumbled something I didn't understand and shuffled off to whatever niche he'd staked out for himself.

When I got home I telephoned Emmy Destinn. "You're right," I said. "He's a monster."

She knew right off whom I meant. "What did he do?"

So I told her everything that had happened at rehearsal—Duchon's demand that a door be installed upstage center, his insulting suggestion about my breath control, his walking out of rehearsal. I even told her my own imprudent remark about Duchon's wanting Gatti-Casazza's job.

"You know, I was wondering about that," Emmy said. "Duchon is so overbearing—he just has to run things. He is not a man to take the loss of his own opera house lying down."

"You think I'm right, then?"

"Probably." She giggled. "You may have sabotaged him a little, though, bringing it out into the open like that. He truly did just walk out of rehearsal?"

"He truly did."

"Sure of himself, isn't he? One performance in this country, and already he is dictating terms."

"Well, he thinks he has Gatti over a barrel. As long as Pasquale Amato is out, Duchon can pretty much do as he pleases."

"He must not know about Jimmy Freeman, then."

"Ah, but he does!" I told her about our encounter with Jimmy in Delmonico's.

"You've had a busy day," Emmy remarked.

When I'd hung up, I sat and thought about Philippe Duchon. At the time we left the restaurant, we'd been friendly if not actual friends. But that was over now, little as it was. Now we were all going to have to go into our next performance with a baritone who refused to rehearse and with all the ill-will such presumptuousness generated. The man's behavior was unpardonable. Duchon seemed to have forgotten that *Carmen* was the *woman's* opera; he should have taken his cue from *me*.

I called Scotti and told him I was going to need some unusually sympathetic company that evening.

◻ **5** ◻ "At least Tiffany's does not change," Caruso said, looking around with an appreciative sigh. "Everything else in the world changes, but not Tiffany's."

"It's only been here ten years, Rico," I remarked. Caruso had come along to help me pick out a silver jewel box I wanted to give my mother for her birthday. It was the kind of shopping expedition Jimmy Freeman usually accompanied me on, but I hadn't seen the angry young baritone for more than a week.

"Look at Fifth Avenue!" Caruso went on plaintively. "It turns into the street of commerce! And the lobster palaces, they close down. Rector's, Shanley's—gone, gone!"

Restaurants were important to the tenor. "I miss Rector's too," I admitted. "It was a good place to be seen."

"Lobster Newburg and White Seal champagne," he sighed. "Venison chops. Lynnhaven oysters. The Café de l'Opéra, it is gone too. And this year they make Hammerstein's Victoria into motion picture house!" He made a gesture of disgust. "Motion pictures—pah!"

"You're getting old, Rico," I laughed. "I remember a time when you were delighted by everything new. It didn't matter what it was, just so long as it was new! Besides, aren't you being a little hard on the motion pictures?"

"But they have no sound!" he cried. "How can you have opera without singing?"

He was thinking of my acceptance of Mr. de Mille's invitation to go to California in the summer and make a film version of *Carmen*. "Don't think of it as opera," I said. "Think of it as something different."

Just then the Tiffany's assistant who was helping us and *his* assistant came back with four silver jewel boxes, which they placed ceremoniously on the velvet-covered table where Caruso and I were sitting. The tenor immediately went into a paroxysm of ecstasy; he loved *objets d'art* and couldn't keep his hands off the jewel boxes.

"Look at this one, Gerry, it has secret drawer that you open from the back! And here is one with cherubs on the lid, and fancy posies on the side . . . and this one! This one, it plays a little tune!''

They *were* nice. My mother would like any one of them—but then she always liked everything I gave her, bless her. Eventually I made my selection. Caruso bought the other three.

We asked that the boxes be delivered and left. Caruso's motor car and chauffeur were waiting out front for us; we climbed in hurriedly to get out of the cold. "The Hotel Astor," Caruso told the chauffeur, and to me: "We pay Pasquale a little visit, yes?"

I hadn't been to see Amato since the day after the *Madame Sans-Gêne* première. I am as terrified of infection as any other singer, and even that first visit to Amato's sickroom had been motivated more by remorse than by anything else, since I was the one who'd given the baritone his cold. I wanted to go see him . . . but I didn't want to go see him.

Caruso knew what I was thinking. "Do not worry, *cara* Gerry. I and Scotti, we figure out way to talk to Pasquale safely. You see."

Well, I saw, all right. Scotti was already there, demonstrating the procedure. What they'd figured out was an arrangement whereby the visitors would sit in one room and shout through the open bedroom door to Amato. Amato, resting his voice, would scribble an answer on a notepad, and a valet would then run into the other room carrying the message. It wasn't the latest thing in rapid communication, but it worked.

Even the ever-cantankerous Dr. Curtis approved. He was putting on his coat to leave, but paused long enough to say, "Amato needs cheering up. He could use some company."

"And what am I?" Scotti asked indignantly. "A piece of furniture?"

Dr. Curtis ignored him and said to me, low, "Gerry, if Amato asks you about Duchon, tell him you were all a little disappointed in him, or some such. He's feeling just well enough to start worrying about a new rival taking over his roles."

I glanced at Scotti. "Did you tell Toto?"

He shook his head. "Amato knows Scotti and Caruso both will lie to him and tell him anything they think might cheer him up. But for some reason he trusts you. Tell him what he wants to hear."

"*For some reason!*" I exclaimed. "Well, I like that!"

"Don't be so touchy, Gerry, you know what I mean. Just don't stay too long." And with that, the good doctor hurried away.

The valet came running in and handed me a piece of paper. It had one word written on it: *Duchon?*

I could see only the foot of Amato's bed from where I was sitting. "Frankly, we're a little disappointed in our French import," I called out, taking my cue from Dr. Curtis. "He sings well enough, but he's not the shining star we'd all been led to expect."

The valet rushed into the bedroom and returned with another piece of paper: *Trouble?*

"Yes, I think you could say there's trouble," I shouted. Caruso half-laughed, half-groaned. I said, "Duchon is as big a bully as Toscanini."

Scotti's face lit up. "Is it true?"

"Didn't Rico tell you? He's refused to rehearse."

"Oh, that. Yes, Rico tells me. I think there is something more."

"Good heavens, Toto, isn't that enough? But come to think of it, there is something more. He's holding me to a promise I made, to sing a joint concert with him."

Caruso looked surprised. "You go through with it?"

I sighed. "I did say I'd do it."

Scotti asked, "Do you sign anything?"

"No, but it's a benefit concert, Toto. For Alsatian war relief. If it were just a regular concert, I wouldn't do it. But I feel obligated to help." I hadn't told anyone about Duchon's tragic encounter with the Germans when he was a boy; that was his private story and for him to tell, not me.

Amato's valet was back with a new piece of paper: *Talk louder.*

I raised my voice and said, "Duchon invited me to

lunch at Delmonico's last week. He apologized for insulting me when we'd first met and was nice as could be. Then we went to rehearsal and he insulted me again! Why did he bother trying to make friends if he was going to insult me all over again?''

"Because he wants something from you," Scotti said dryly.

"No, no," Caruso protested. "Duchon is not so, ah, calculating. He is but moody. Good mood one minute, not so good the next." He asked the valet to bring him some paper from Amato's notepad.

Note from Amato: *How did he insult you?*

"The first time, he called me a German-lover," I shouted. 'The second time, he implied I didn't have good breath control.''

Scotti looked amused. "Which is worse?"

"The second one," I snapped, "and stop smirking. *You* don't have to sing with him.''

"Che fortuna!" Scotti rolled his eyes heavenward.

"Do you know he complains of sore throat?" Caruso said, sketching away. He was drawing caricatures of Scotti and me. I knew what mine would look like: all mouth and teeth.

"Who is complaining of a sore throat?" I asked. "Duchon?"

"For two days now," the tenor nodded. "I send him my throat spray.''

Oh, wonderful. That was all we needed. Another baritone flat on his back.

Scotti laughed. "Your young protégé may get his chance after all, Gerry.''

"No, no, it is not that bad," Caruso said hastily. "Duchon still sings. But we must all be very careful," he added ominously. "So much sickness around!"

In the next room Amato coughed pitifully, once.

"Poor Pasquale!" Caruso sang out on cue. "Is there anything we can do for you?"

The note the valet brought in was for me. *Move in with me, Gerry, and nurse me back to health and vigor.*

"He's feeling better," I told the others.

Caruso had finished his sketches and held them up for our inspection. "Very nice," Scotti said expressionlessly.

"Do I really have that many teeth?" I murmured. But what Caruso had done to me was nothing compared to what he'd done to Scotti. In his sketch he'd made Scotti's long nose droop down below his chin. Caruso sent the caricatures in to Amato.

We talked on for a while, the three of us, and then it was time to leave. It occurred to me I'd been sitting there chatting away and hadn't even *seen* Amato, so I went to the door of his bedroom and looked in. He was asleep, Caruso's caricatures of Scotti and me lying on the covers. Amato was a handsome man, when he wasn't wearing that black wig and drooping mustache he preferred for most of his stage roles. He was still washed-out and weak looking, but he looked better than the last time I'd seen him. Our ailing baritone was definitely on the mend. So, it was only a matter of enduring Duchon just a little longer.

Caruso was singing the following night and wanted to spend the rest of the day practicing, so Scotti took me home. In the lobby of the apartment building we found Jimmy Freeman's vocal coach waiting. The doorman told us he'd been there over an hour.

Osgood Springer came straight to the point. "James wishes to talk to you, Miss Farrar. But he's not sure you're still speaking to him."

"Well, of course I'm still speaking to him," I said lightly. "Whyever not?"

"He's afraid that scene he made in Delmonico's might have offended you. May I tell him you'll see him?"

"What scene in Delmonico's?" Scotti wanted to know.

I waved a hand at him vaguely and asked Springer where Jimmy was.

"Across the street."

I went to the lobby door and looked out. On the other side of West Seventy-fourth a forlorn-looking figure stood shivering in a doorway, a petitioner awaiting permission to enter the palace. "For heaven's sake, Mr. Springer, tell him to come in. He must be freezing."

Springer glanced quickly at Scotti. "He would like to talk to you alone."

I turned to my escort. "Do you mind, Toto?"

"Yes," he answered shortly. "I mind. You are with *me*."

That surprised me. Scotti had more or less taken it for granted that there would always be young men flocking around me, just as I had taken it for granted there'd always be young women flocking around *him*. But by acting jealous, he was making Jimmy Freeman into a serious rival.

"Miss Farrar," Springer said urgently, "James won't work, he won't even practice his scales. He won't do anything until he talks to you."

"He can talk to her another time." Scotti wasn't giving an inch.

"Please, Miss Farrar. I beg you." Springer's face had darkened, making the scar on his jaw more livid than ever. It struck me he must hate what he was doing—acting as go-between for a sulking young man who up to now had done exactly as he was told. A demeaning position for Springer.

I suggested a compromise. "Go on up, Toto," I said, "the maid will let you in. I'll join you in a few minutes. Mr. Springer, tell Jimmy I'll talk to him down here."

Springer looked at the doorman, who was doing his best to appear as if he weren't listening. "That will have to do, I suppose. I'll get him."

He left, and Scotti headed toward the elevator. "Five minutes!" he commanded.

I made a noncommittal noise and waited for Jimmy. When he came in, he looked downright hangdog. *Stand up straight*, I wanted to shout; but Jimmy had enough problems without my fussing at him.

It took him several efforts, but he finally managed to blurt out, "I'm sorry!"

I went over to the doorman and asked him to go out and get me a newspaper. He looked disappointed, but he went. Then I told Jimmy to sit down, on one of those uncomfortable love seats decorators of apartment buildings seem to favor for lobbies, and I sat beside him. "Now, Jimmy, what's this all about? Surely you're not still upset over that little incident in Delmonico's? There's no need to be. Look at me—I'm not upset at all!"

He looked as if he wanted to cry. "I made such a fool of myself!"

"Well, yes," I agreed. "But only a little bit. It's certainly not worth all this *anguish*."

"I called you my girl! Right out loud in public! All those people heard me call you my girl. Oh, I'm so ashamed!"

Keep it light. "Do you mean you're ashamed of *me*?" I laughed.

"Oh no, Miss Farrar, you know how I feel about you! I meant I was ashamed of being so presumptuous. As if *you* would ever consent to be *my* girl," he said bitterly. "I'm not blind, you know. I know about the others, Scotti and that Dutch actor and—"

"Never mind that," I interrupted hastily. "Now listen to me, Jimmy. I was not offended by what you said. I don't want you to do it again, but that one time was all right. Do you hear me? It was all right."

He grasped my hand. "Oh, Miss Farrar!" was all he could think of to say.

"From now on we can dispense with 'Miss Farrar,' I think. Call me Gerry."

"Gerry!"

Suddenly I found myself caught in a strong embrace while Jimmy's fervent kisses landed in all sorts of odd places, like on my nose. He smelled good, fresh and clean and with a touch of the winter air still on his cheek. He smelled so *young*.

But—strongly disciplined creature that I am—I pushed him away. "Enough of that, Jimmy. Next time wait for *me* to do the grabbing."

"I'll wait, I'll wait!" His face was beaming, his eyes were glistening; he'd gone from the Slough of Despond to the top of Mount Olympus in thirty seconds flat.

"Mr. Springer tells me you aren't working," I said

sternly. "You aren't even practicing your scales. I don't *ever* want to hear that again. Do you understand?"

"I understand," he said happily. "I can work now."

"You can work no matter what," I lectured him. "*Nothing* must be allowed to get in the way of your singing, not ever again. Will you promise me this will never happen again? That you'll always work, regardless of what happens?"

"I promise, oh yes, I promise!" Right then he would have promised to rob the Knickerbocker Trust if I'd asked him to.

The doorman came back with my newspaper; he must have run both ways. "Go find Mr. Springer," I told Jimmy. "You have a lot of lost time to make up for. You must work every day. Start now."

"I will, I promise you. Oh, thank you, Miss . . . Gerry. Thank you for being so understanding."

Being understanding is only one of my virtues. I sent young Jimmy Freeman on his way and hurried upstairs to soothe Antonio Scotti's ruffled feathers.

On the whole, I rather like days like that one.

The following night Duchon sang *The Huguenots*.

I sat in the artists' box at the Met, and Scotti sat there with me—after changing his mind half a dozen times. The baritone lead in *The Huguenots* was a role that he and Pasquale Amato took turns singing, and that night Duchon was filling in for Amato. So this was the first time Scotti had a chance to hear the Frenchman in one of *his* roles. He wanted to hear him, but he didn't like being seen checking up on his new rival. So there he sat in the box, grumbling and unhappy.

Caruso was in the cast, and so was Emmy Destinn; they helped, but only a little. *Les Huguenots* is a long opera, and Meyerbeer's music only intermittently exciting. I found my attention beginning to wander.

Emmy looked terrible. She was wearing a costume that made her appear twice as wide as she already was. Emmy simply had no sense of style whatsoever. Her costume was pink and reminded me of one she wore when we sang together in *Tannhäuser* at the Royal Opera in Berlin, with me as Elisabeth and Emmy as, heaven help us, Venus. She'd come on stage swathed in voluminous folds of a particularly horrendous shade of pink satin, absolutely the worst color and fabric for any woman even slightly on the plump side. In addition to that, Emmy had been further burdened by a wreath of violent red roses. Then, to top it all off, she'd worn a red wig coiled in the fat-doughnuts style of Greek statues in a museum. And this was the goddess of love? Her *Huguenots* wig was blonde and her pink costume was brocade instead of satin, so she looked a little better than in Berlin. But not much.

A nudge from Scotti brought me back from my reverie. "They may come to blows," he whispered.

I focused my attention on the stage, and what I saw was a championship bout of upstaging in progress. The whole point of upstaging another singer is to draw that singer around to face you, so that his or her voice is lost upstage. It's a nasty trick, and it takes lots of practice to get it right, believe me.

Duchon upstaged Emmy. She turned her back to him, which is all you can do when somebody upstages you. He crossed down to her and sang to the back of her head, which made her look awkward. She crossed to the other side of the stage, just to break up the tableau. He moved center stage and sang directly to the audience. She upstaged him. He moved up to join her and stood in a way that blocked her face from the audience. She didn't move.

"He's standing on her dress," I whispered to Scotti.

Eventually Emmy was able to pull loose and the maneuvering continued. The scene ended with both of them singing a long sustained note—which Emmy held for just a second longer after the conductor had indicated the cut-off, making Duchon sound as if he'd run out of breath. So Emmy Destinn had the last word. The audience cheerfully applauded the winner.

But the next time Duchon appeared, he positioned himself at center stage and never budged from the spot. Absolutely *refused* to move. That threw everybody else's stage movement off and the scene was a shambles. *The Huguenots* needs seven strong principal singers to make it work, but our visiting Frenchman was acting as if the entire opera revolved around *him*. I didn't think Philippe Duchon was winning a lot of friends at the Metropolitan.

At the act break we slipped out of the box and hurried backstage. What we found was absolute chaos—everyone yelling, and no one yelling louder than Emmy Destinn. (When Emmy yells, watch out for your eardrums.) Duchon wasn't anywhere in sight. In the center of it all was Gatti-Casazza, desperately trying to calm everyone down. Poor Gatti; it was one of the few times I've ever felt sorry for him.

"He is impossible!" Emmy was shouting. "He is ruining the performance!"

"Shh!" Gatti cautioned. "They hear you out front!"

"I do not *care* if they hear me out front! How do you expect me to sing with that monster undercutting everything I do?"

Even Caruso was angry. "This time he goes too far. Mr. Gatti, you do something, yes?" He caught sight of Scotti and me. "Toto, Gerry—am I not right? He does not care what he does to the rest of us. He does not care about the opera. Am I not right?"

"*Assolutamente*," Scotti said without hesitation. "No question of it."

"Everyone out front can see what's going on," I added.

"There, you see!" Emmy yelled at Gatti. "We are being made to look like fools, all because of that . . . that . . ." she sputtered ineffectually, unable to think of a word nasty enough. "You must replace him. Now!"

Gatti pulled anxiously at his beard. "I think it is not so bad as you believe. Besides, he has only one more scene, yes? It does not look good, to replace him now."

"Then why do you have Jimmy stand by if you do not use him?" Caruso demanded.

Jimmy? Jimmy Freeman?

"Or Scotti," Emmy interjected. "Scotti is here—he can finish."

"Only one more scene," Gatti pleaded.

I looked around for Jimmy while the argument went on.

I didn't see him, but I did spot Osgood Springer listening intently to everything that was being said. I made my way over to the vocal coach and asked, "Did I understand correctly, Mr. Springer? Jimmy is on stand-by?"

He nodded dourly. "Duchon was complaining of a sore throat. I told Mr. Gatti James was not ready for this role, but he wanted someone at hand anyway."

That was just like Gatti, building up Jimmy's hopes a second time for nothing. "Where's Jimmy now?"

"Getting into costume. Just in case."

Just then an uproar broke out from the direction of the stairs leading to the dressing rooms. Duchon came thundering down the steps, hauling poor old Uncle Hummy along by the neck of his shabby overcoat. "Mr. Gatti!" Duchon bellowed. "Is this the kind of opera house you run in America? Where *tramps* can come in off the street and give instructions to the singers?"

"Uncle Hummy!" Caruso rushed over and grabbed the old man's shoulder. "Let him go, Duchon!"

"How did he get in here?" Gatti cried in exasperation, and went off to bawl out the doorkeeper. (Or to escape.)

"Let him go!" Caruso repeated. A brief tug-of-war took place between the two singers that ended only when Uncle Hummy's well-worn overcoat ripped all the way down the back. The old man began to cry.

"Do not cry, Uncle Hummy," Caruso said hastily. "I buy you new coat."

"Uncle," Duchon repeated unbelievingly, "Hummy. This man is your uncle?"

"No, no, I mean yes, I mean he is everybody's uncle. You do not treat him this way!"

"Well, *everybody's* uncle," Duchon said sarcastically, "invited himself into my dressing room and told me I was spoiling the performance. At least I think that's what he said—he does not speak well, this one."

Scotti decided to get into the act, speaking to Duchon for the first time ever. "Uncle Hummy is a sort of fixture at the Metropolitan, Monsieur. He is here longer than any of us, yes? He means no harm."

Duchon examined the most famous baritone in the world

from head to toe and then said, insolently: "I do not believe I know you, sir."

Every mouth in the place dropped open. Scotti waited a moment and then said in a quiet manner, "There seem to be many things you do not know, Duchon."

Good for him! But the one I was really impressed by was Uncle Hummy. He'd actually gone into Duchon's dressing room to try to talk the baritone into mending his ways. In the nine seasons I'd been at the Met I'd never once seen him do anything like that before. Uncle Hummy had always worked at being inconspicuous, at staying out of the way; his presence would not have been tolerated otherwise. Speaking to Duchon was a big risk for him, and it was a thing even Gatti had not found the courage to do.

Duchon was saying something when his voice suddenly tightened up on him. He put his hand to his throat in alarm.

"The spray!" Caruso commanded.

Duchon looked around vaguely. "I think it's in my dressing room."

"I get! I get!" said Uncle Hummy, and hurried off up the stairs, the two halves of his ruined overcoat flapping behind him.

"You see," I said to Duchon with a smile, "he can be useful if you let him."

"Mm." A noncommittal sound.

Gatti was back. "Places, please! Places!" he cried frantically, now that everyone else had calmed down. "The curtain is late!"

"I am not ready," Emmy announced firmly.

"Then *get* ready!" Gatti screamed.

"Ssh!" Emmy frowned. "They hear you out front."

Uncle Hummy came back with one of the atomizer bottles Caruso had given Duchon. The baritone sprayed his throat, tried a few notes, and sounded fine.

Scotti and I decided to watch the rest of the performance from backstage. We were joined by a forlorn-looking Jimmy Freeman, dressed in a costume he would not be wearing on stage that night. Even Scotti felt sorry for him and tried to cheer him up. We all agreed that Giulio Gatti-Casazza was just about the lowest form of life on earth and fully deserved to be consigned to Dante's version of hell. But we could not agree on whether he belonged in the fourth circle with the misers or the eighth circle with the hypocrites and evil counselors.

"I really thought I'd have a chance to sing tonight," Jimmy lamented. "The way Mr. Gatti talked, Duchon was practically on his deathbed. Mr. Springer worked with me all day getting ready for tonight."

"You chance comes soon," Scotti said encouragingly. "It seems not so, but it comes."

I added, "Everyone goes through this, Jimmy—don't be discouraged. You have to work your way up." Or so conventional wisdom said. As for myself, I'd started out singing leads and never looked back.

Jimmy shook his head. "I don't know. I'm beginning to think the only time I'll get a chance is when some other baritone drops dead." He shot a sudden horrified glance at Scotti. "Oh . . . ah, I didn't mean, uh . . ."

"Put your conscience at ease," Scotti said wryly. "I do not, ah, drop dead, not I."

The Huguenots resumed. In his final scene, Duchon pulled the same stunt he'd used earlier; he staked out center stage for himself and wouldn't yield to anybody. But they got through it somehow; Duchon made his final exit—and gave me a start. The minute he was off the stage, one leg flew out from under him and the other buckled. If it hadn't been for a quick-thinking stagehand who caught him, he'd have fallen straight back and taken a nasty crack on the head.

"*Water* on the stage floor? Right where I make my exit?" Duchon looked around. "Nowhere else—just where I make my exit!"

The stagehand mumbled something.

"Why is there *water* on the stage floor?" Duchon was making no attempt to keep his voice down. "Why only there, where I come off the stage?"

Mumble mumble from the stagehand.

"How did it get there? You must have seen who put it there!"

Mumble.

"Why did you not clean it up? Did someone pay you to spill water where I was sure to slip in it?"

Mumblemumblemumblemumblemumble!

Duchon took a deep breath and next spoke in more moderate tones, but what he said wasn't moderate at all. "I shall insist to Gatti-Casazza that you be dismissed immediately." He turned and walked away.

"Of all the ungrateful . . . !" I exclaimed, outraged. "That man saved him from injuring himself, and he's going to get him fired!"

"No, he does not get him fired," Scotti said tightly. "I speak to Gatti and tell him what transpires. I tell him his Monsieur Duchon is accident-horizontal."

"Accident-prone," I said. "He actually thought that water was spilled there deliberately—to *make* him fall!"

"He does have a high opinion of his own importance, doesn't he?" Jimmy murmured.

The Duchon-less scenes that followed went smoothly enough, but the curtain-call applause was not the most enthusiastic I'd ever heard. The opera was too long and there'd been that delay between acts and the audience had just had enough. That happens, sometimes. Caruso came off the stage scowling, unusual for him. Emmy steamed up to her dressing room without a word. Duchon started up the stairs but then caught sight of the three of us in the wings and came over.

There I was standing between two baritones, either of whom could replace Duchon on a moment's notice. He ignored both of them and lifted my hand to his lips. "Ah, *la belle* Geraldine! If only you had been singing tonight instead of that Bohemian sow! The entire production would have been elevated."

Well, of all the *ungracious* things to say! Duchon had evidently decided he wanted me on his side again and *this* was his way of winning me over? He'd figured all he had to do was insult my rival and I would be all smiles and simpering acquiescence. Emmy Destinn wasn't the only one he'd insulted; I was not so easily manipulated as that! He was undoubtedly right in asserting I'd have been better in the role than she, but I wouldn't be caught dead in *The Huguenots*—and said so. "Emmy probably made you look as good as any soprano could," I added sweetly.

A tic appeared beneath Duchon's eye. Scotti was laughing while Jimmy Freeman just looked uncomfortable. Duchon forced down his annoyance and said, "You and I, we will still make beautiful music, *ma charmante*."

I thought the *ma charmante* a bit familiar but simply said, "I hope so, Philippe." But I said it in a way that let him know I had my doubts. He bowed stiffly and left.

Scotti laughed again and gave me a light kiss (partly to show off in front of Jimmy, I suspected). "He wants to make beautiful music with you, Gerry! Perhaps you need bodyguard? I volunteer!"

I accepted with a laugh, but turned down his invitation to stop in at the Hotel Knickerbocker for a bite to eat. It was late and I wanted to get to sleep; I'm a morning lark, not a night owl. Scotti hesitated only a moment before asking Jimmy Freeman if he'd like to join him. Surprised, Jimmy stammered out his acceptance. So the two baritones in my life delivered me to my apartment and then went off together for a late supper, and perhaps for a man-to-man talk.

Poor Jimmy.

❑ **6** ❑ The next morning I telephoned Gatti-Casazza. "You owe Jimmy Freeman a major role. Right now. And two new roles next season."

He moaned. "So, Gerry, you are now Jimmy Freeman's manager? Already this morning Osgood Springer is here, demanding the moon for his star pupil. I tell you same thing I tell him. The schedule is set for the rest of the season, yes? For next year, I will try to find him a role."

"You'll 'try'? Is that all? Just 'try'? Well, that's not good enough. As long as you're going to keep calling him in to stand by for Duchon—"

"One time!" he protested.

"—then he deserves a firm commitment from you for next season at least. Jimmy is a professional, Mr. Gatti. You're treating him like a schoolboy."

"I do not like all this pressure!" he said testily. "It is not yet eleven o'clock and already I have Springer and then a complaint committee from the orchestra and now you. It is too much! I tell you I will *try* to find Freeman a role next season."

I considered. "Gatti, tell me the truth. Will you truly try, or are you just putting me off?"

His sigh echoed along the telephone wire like a dying wind. "I tell you the truth, Gerry. Upon my word, I will try."

I'd have to be content with that, then. "What's the orchestra committee complaining about now?"

"Toscanini, as usual. He is calling them names again."

"What's he been calling them?"

He didn't want to tell me, but I insisted. "*Castrade,*" he said, "words like that. I tell them they should hear what he calls me."

That seemed like a good opening. "There's trouble between you and Toscanini, isn't there? Anyone can see it. What's the matter?"

"Money is the matter!" he growled. "The board of directors has ordered a policy of retrenchment, yes? And Toscanini, he refuses to accept! He *refuses*!"

"He wants more salary?"

"More salary, more other things—things that all cost money. More rehearsal time, for one. Better sets and costumes. And he wants me to stop hiring what he calls the 'second-rate' singers. He wants me to spend a fortune, that is what he wants! Where does the money come from?"

The same old excuses, I thought in irritation. "None of those things sound so dreadful to me."

"Not dreadful, no. But impossible! You and Toscanini and Caruso, all of you, you think I have endless supply of money to spend! I know you call me penny-pincher and other names behind my back—do not deny it! But the directors decide these matters, not I. Come into my office, Gerry, I show you the books."

"No, thank you, you've shown me the books before." Personally, I was convinced that Gatti kept two sets of books, one for the directors and the other to show to singers. "You know what I think of your policy of retrenchment, Mr. Gatti. It's nothing more than an underhanded attempt to take advantage of the singers, now that a lot of your competition has disappeared." The Manhattan Opera House had closed; opera had been suspended in Boston and Chicago—temporarily, one hoped. And if Antonio Scotti was right, there'd soon be an influx of singers from Europe, all of them looking for a new home at the Metropolitan. The more I thought about it, the angrier I got. "Don't use that excuse with me, Gatti, and don't use it with Toscanini. You never gave up anything you didn't have to!"

He screamed something at me, and I screamed something back at him, and it went on like that until I hung up the telephone so hard I broke the little hook off the side. Sometimes Gatti made me *furious*! The Metropolitan was in a good position, from the board of directors' point of view. It was already more than fully staffed for its own needs, and the number of available singers was bound to increase if the war dragged on much longer. In a year Gatti might have *fifteen* baritones standing by the next time Pasquale Amato got sick. That meant he didn't have to listen to any of the singers' demands; he could pretty much do what he wanted.

My contract wasn't due for renewal yet, but I thought a little preliminary work wouldn't hurt. I decided to ask my manager to start negotiating my new contract now, before things got worse. Before I left home I told my maid Bella that we needed a new telephone and to notify whomever one notifies about such matters.

Morris Gest kept offices on the third floor of a new building on West Forty-fifth Street, a big jump up from his ticket-scalping days. Morris's private office had three windows that started at the floor and extended about three-fourths of the way up the wall. I sat in the client's chair, framed by the middle window and fully visible to anyone down on the street who cared to look up. Quite a few did; one man I didn't know blew me a kiss. I waved.

"So, darling Gerry, what can I do for you?" Morris asked.

"You can challenge Gatti-Casazza to a duel!" I explained what I thought was going to happen during the next few years, during the period of "retrenchment" that was to be the excuse for all sorts of inevitably shabby treatment we were bound to receive. "Gatti's sitting pretty right now. I think we'd better work out a new contract now, before things get worse."

He gave me a big grin and started pawing through the papers in his desk. He came up with a handwritten copy of a letter he'd sent to Gatti a week ago, spelling out new terms he wanted for my next contract. "You see, darling, you have nothing to worry about. Morris Gest always has his ear to the ground." The terms of the contract were exorbitant; Morris liked to leave himself plenty of room to maneuver.

I congratulated him on his perspicacity. "You think I'm right, then? Things are going to get worse?"

"Well, let's just say they're not going to get any better for a while. But we don't have anything to worry about. Mr. Gatti's not going to risk losing you, you sell too many tickets." He scowled. "Look, as long as you're here, there's something else." He pawed through his desk drawer again and pulled out another sheet of paper. "That concert you're doing with Philippe Duchon—this here's what he wants you to sing.''

I took the paper automatically. ''Excuse me?''

Morris visibly braced himself. ''Now don't get mad, darling, but he says—and I'm quoting directly—he says, 'Tell Miss Farrar she is to sing these numbers.' Something about complementing his own choices.''

I was on my feet, shaking. ''*He* is telling *me* what *I* am to sing? Do I understand you correctly? *He* is telling *me*?''

''Told him you wouldn't like it,'' Morris said glumly.

''How dare he!'' I exploded. ''Who does he think he is, telling *me* what to sing! Has he forgotten *I* am helping *him*? He doesn't consult me, he doesn't talk it over, he just decides . . . what arrogance! How *dare* he treat me like this!'' I furiously tore up the list without reading it and flung the pieces at Morris, who flinched. ''You can tell that, that *baritone* he can sing them himself—because *I* won't be anywhere near the concert hall! The idea!''

''Now, Gerry—''

''Don't you *now Gerry* me! And what were you doing, Morris Gest, the whole time Duchon was deciding what *I* was going to sing? Which one of us are you representing, Duchon or me?''

He looked uncomfortable. ''Well, as a matter of fact, both of you.''

''*What?!*''

He looked *very* uncomfortable. ''I'm setting up a tour for him. Benefit performances. All over the country.''

''You signed Duchon?''

''He's reading the contract now. I already got seven dates set, firm. Possibility of twenty more. We can make some of 'em joint concerts—Duchon's suggestion, darling,'' he added hastily. ''He really wants you to sing with him. So he's a little high-handed, so what? The tour will be good for you, Gerry—it's patriotic, it shows you aren't really on the Germans' side. You want to help all those poor, er, Alsatians, don't you? You haven't toured for a while anyway.''

''What are you getting out of all this, Morris?''

''Only expenses, darling,'' he said innocently, ''only

expenses. Plus Philippe Duchon under contract, of course. But that's for the future. On this tour, I won't be making a cent.''

I believed that the way I believed Enrico Caruso would develop a sudden aversion to Italian food. ''He expects me to tour with him? Of all the gall! I suppose he's already decided what I'm to wear as well?''

Morris brightened; you could just see him thinking, *safe ground!* ''Not a bit of it, darling. He didn't even mention clothing. Come on, Gerry. We can all sit down and work out the program. He just doesn't know how we do things over here, that's all. Be nice, darling. We don't want to scare him off.''

So that's the way the wind was blowing. I smiled coolly. ''That's right, he hasn't signed the contract yet— you did say he was reading it, didn't you? So you don't mind putting *me* on the spot just to land *him*! Morris, you're fired!''

''Not again,'' he sighed. ''Look, even the Old Man thinks it's a good idea, you touring with Duchon. If you don't believe me, ask him.''

That was a sort of dirty trick. Morris knew I liked his father-in-law and respected his opinion. But I wasn't ready to give in. ''What does he know about concert tours?''

''He knows *publicity,* darling, and he says joint appearances would pack 'em in. Besides, think of all the other sopranos who'd give their eye teeth to be invited to tour with Duchon.''

''*What* other sopranos?'' I asked scornfully.

He started to name some names but then thought better of it. He argued a little longer, until I cut him off.

''I tell you what,'' I said. ''When Philippe Duchon appears at my door carrying two dozen orchids and apologizes *on his knees*—''

''Then you'll do it?''

''Then I'll think about it.''

We left it at that. As a matter of fact, I had no intention of going on tour with Philippe Duchon. I couldn't stand the man and the thought of actually traveling with him set my teeth on edge. But I might do one joint concert here in New York, the one I'd originally agreed to.

If he asked me nicely enough.

Scotti and I were scheduled to sing a *Tosca* the next Wednesday, and fortunately a tenor other than Caruso was doing the third leading role. I say fortunately because it was my turn to be the target of one of Caruso's little tricks. He "got" either Scotti or me every time the three of us sang together, and the last time it had been Scotti. What Caruso had done had been a masterpiece of artlessness. He'd simply gone on stage and handed Scotti an egg. Poor Toto—he didn't know what to do with it. He didn't want to put it down someplace where Caruso could pick it up again and do something really messy with it. He couldn't put it in his pocket because he knew Caruso would find some reason to slap him on the hip or bump up against him before the curtain closed. So he'd had to sing out the rest of the act with this *egg* in his hand.

Tosca was one of my best roles—Tosca and Butterfly, with their hauntingly beautiful music that I never tired of singing. Puccini's *Tosca* was special to me, an opera about an opera star. Scotti had been singing the villainous Scarpia for a long time and he'd helped me learn the opera some years back, during one long idyllic summer we'd spent together in Como. In performance I'd fallen into the habit of apologizing right before I killed him in the second act. Scotti said that when he sang *Tosca* with other sopranos he was sometimes late picking up his cue to fall to the floor, unconsciously waiting for that whispered *Sorry, Toto* right as he was being stabbed.

My acting in *Tosca* had been highly praised. And why not? I'd been coached in the role by Sarah Bernhardt— lovely, generous woman. But even more importantly, the composer liked my Tosca. He'd told me I was exactly what he'd visualized *and heard* while he was writing the opera. From Puccini, that was high praise indeed—especially when you considered the fact that the man and I were barely speaking to each other.

I'd seriously offended the composer four or five years

ago, when I refused to learn his *Manon Lescaut*. But the circumstances were such that I *couldn't* accept his offer. Since the originally scheduled soprano had fallen ill a week before the performance, I would have had to learn the role in only six days—and I'd have had to learn it while on board ship crossing the ocean. Some roles can be learned that fast, but *Manon Lescaut* was simply too subtle, too complex to be mastered in so short a time. So I'd had to tell Puccini no.

But he got even—oh, did he get even! He made a point of telling everyone that I'd turned down *Manon Lescaut* because he had chosen Emmy Destinn to create the title role of *La Fanciulla del West* instead of me! That hurt. That really hurt. Of course I'd wanted the role; every soprano at the Met had wanted it. *Fanciulla* was Puccini's opera about America's Wild West and it had had its world première at the Metropolitan, in 1910. Caruso and Amato had sung the male leads, and those two choices were understandable. But why Puccini had selected an overweight middle-European to sing the role of a young girl in a California mining camp—oh, it was beyond me! Surely an *American* girl would have made better sense? But no, Puccini had wanted Emmy, and Emmy it had been. Losing the role to Emmy was bad enough, but when Puccini made me out to be a bad sport about it—well, what can I say? Has anyone ever been more injured, more wronged?

"Gerry?" said Emmy, inviting herself into my dressing room. Now she was dropping in backstage *before* performances! "Do you know that Duchon is out front?"

"Duchon? Whatever for? Scarpia isn't one of his roles."

"Not yet."

Oh-oh. "Are you saying what I think you're saying?"

She nodded. "He's thinking of learning a Puccini role, I've been told. And he likes *Tosca*."

Oh dear. "Does Scotti know?"

"He's the one who told me."

So that made two of Scotti's roles Duchon was after, Rigoletto and now Scarpia. "What's he doing learning a new role at his age?" I grumbled. "He should be thinking of retiring."

"That's what Scotti said." She looked around my dressing room. "You know, this would be quite nice if it were a little larger." She left before I could answer.

But I didn't need to answer. It galled Emmy that I had my own private dressing room; it galled everybody. Too bad. The other principal singers had to take turns using the star dressing room. But nobody used *my* dressing room except me. It had been an old storage room that I'd had decorated in bright and cheerful colors; then I'd had a lock installed, the only key to which stayed with *me*. I didn't share my dressing room with anybody.

I put Philippe Duchon and his lusting after Scotti's roles out of my mind; there were more important things to think about. Tosca's entrance, to begin with. Toscanini was not conducting tonight; that meant I'd have more leeway in what I did on stage. The other conductors at the Met weren't nearly so unreasonable about following *my* tempo as Toscanini was.

Jimmy Freeman was singing the small role of the Sacristan, and I was pleased to see he was looking more chipper than the last few times I'd seen him. I soon found out why; while we were waiting for the opera to start, he told me that Gatti-Casazza had said he could have Amato's role in the next performance of *Madame Sans-Gêne* if he could learn it in time.

"I start studying tomorrow," he grinned. "I wanted to start today, but Mr. Springer wouldn't let me. He said today should be spent thinking only of *Tosca*."

"Oh, Jimmy, I'm so glad!" And I was. Gatti had *sort* of kept his word about finding a role for Jimmy. *Madame Sans-Gêne* would not be in the repertoire next year, but I didn't want to remind Jimmy of that. At least Gatti was giving him a chance; if he sang well in *Sans-Gêne*, other roles would follow.

"It might be for only one performance," Jimmy said realistically. "Amato is recovering from his bronchitis. But it's one of the leads, and I'll be singing opposite *you*!" He took my hand. "Gerry, I can't tell you how much this means to me. I—"

Just then the harsh chords that signaled the opening of

Act I sounded from the orchestra. Jimmy had to enter almost immediately, so we both forgot about everything except Puccini's tragic opera.

The first act went swimmingly—a little faster than we usually sang it, but everyone's energy was running high, so why not use it? We slowed down for Act II, deliberately, allowing the menace in the music to swell to its full sinister level. My big aria drew a standing ovation, which I was in no hurry to end. From the back of the auditorium came the wonderful chant "Ger*ee*, Ger*ee*"; Mildredand-phoebe and their friends were out in force. Immediately came the scene in which Tosca murders her oppressor. I thrust the knife against Scotti's chest in an overhead sweep, whispered *Sorry, Toto,* and stepped back out of the way as he collapsed to the stage floor.

Right before the third and final act began, I heard Gatti-Casazza explaining to the firing squad what they were to do. Oh-oh—three things wrong with that. First, it was not Gatti's job to explain stage actions to the supers, it was the production manager's job. Second, the time to explain those actions was in rehearsal, not two minutes before the curtains were due to open during a performance. Third, they shouldn't have to be given instructions at all, not this late in the season. A closer look at the six-man firing squad told me they were strangers; I knew all of our regular supers, by sight if not by name, and I didn't know any of these six.

"It is very simple," Gatti was saying. "You follow Spoletta on and line up beside him in a row, yes? When he raises his arm, you lift your rifles to the firing position. When he drops his arm, you fire. That is all there is to it."

"Who's Spoletta?" one of them asked.

"He is the police officer who leads you on. He will be here shortly—you do not go on right away."

"What's the story?" another asked. "What's happening in the opera?"

"There is no time for that now," Gatti said hurriedly, and sent one of the stagehands to look for the man who was singing Spoletta.

"What's all this?" I asked Gatti. "Who are they?"

"Students from Columbia University," he muttered, plucking nervously at his beard. "*Cielo m'ajuti!* How do these things happen? Somehow the call for supers is over-looked for tonight and everyone is blaming everyone else! I do not find out until the performance is already started!"

"So you recruited six college boys to do the job," I said in amazement. "Why not just get the regular supers?"

"There is no time to round them all up! I tell my assistant to go to one place where he can expect to find six reasonably intelligent men together."

"But they don't even know the story of the opera!"

"They do not need to. It will work out, Gerry. They are on stage only a few minutes."

I wondered whether he was reassuring me or himself. The orchestra had started playing the quiet prelude to Act III when one of the new firing squad thought of something. "How do we get off the stage?" he asked Gatti.

"Just follow the principal off," he said, meaning Spoletta. It was so standard a stage direction for supers that Gatti had forgotten these newcomers wouldn't know it.

The third act of *Tosca* is exciting, both dramatically and musically; its sole drawback is that the tenor has the only aria. The curtain opens to show the parapet of a prison, where Tosca's lover (the tenor) is awaiting execution. Tosca arrives with the news that she'd managed to strike a bargain with the villainous Scarpia (recently deceased). Scarpia had offered to arrange a mock execution if Tosca would yield herself to him; the rifles would be loaded with blank cartridges. She'd agreed. But as soon as the lustful villain had made the necessary arrangements, Tosca had plunged a knife into his heart.

So Tosca's lover goes through with the charade; everyone connected with the mock execution acts out his part. But when the firing squad is gone, Tosca's lover fails to get up from the ground. Scarpia has had the last word—the bullets were real. A couple of men rush in; Scarpia's body has been discovered. In despair, Tosca hurls herself from the parapet to her death below.

Oh, how I love that part of it! Tosca's cries of excitement as the firing squad leaves turning quickly to cries of horror as she discovers her lover is not just feigning death, he really is dead. Then her mad dash to the parapet—where she leaps to her death not with the name of her lover on her lips, but the name of the man who has posthumously defeated her: *O Scarpia, avanti a Dio! We'll meet before God.*

Everything went well at first. The tenor sang his aria, I made my entrance, we sang our love duet. Just as we finished, Spoletta marched in from stage right with his college-boy firing squad. I moved over to stage left, leaving the tenor to face his doom upstage center.

Right away I knew something was wrong. The six young men of the firing squad looked uneasy and kept exchanging questioning glances. A couple of them tried to get the attention of Spoletta, but the man singing the role was right in the middle of his big moment on stage and wasn't paying any attention to the supers. I found out later our last-minute substitutes had come on the stage expecting to find one person there to shoot, only to be confronted with *two*—who weren't even standing together! Pretty much left to their own devices, they reasoned out that the opera was a tragedy and its title was *Tosca* . . . so, when Spoletta gave the signal, they all pointed their rifles stage left, at *me*—and fired away!

Upstage center, the tenor fell down dead.

The audience roared. All during the tense moments that followed, the audience was laughing its collective head off. I looked at the conductor; he was desperately calling for more volume from the orchestra, trying to drown out the laughter. There was nothing to do but go on with it.

But that fool firing squad was still on the stage, disconcerted by the laughter. Spoletta had exited, but instead of following him off the college boys were still standing around looking lost and blocking me from the audience. My big dramatic scene, discovering my lover was dead—ruined, totally ruined! But the end was in sight, thank God! I ran to the parapet, shrieked *Avanti a Dio!* as loudly as I could, and jumped down to the mattress on the floor behind the set.

Only to look up and see all six members of the firing squad jumping down after me.

That's right. The firing squad jumped too. Well, Gatti-Casazza had *said* follow the principal off. So they'd followed me over the parapet.

I did a little unrehearsed screaming—have you ever had six college boys land on top of *you* when you were least expecting it? The resulting bedlam backstage was more than matched by the noisy hilarity out front. Had ever a performance come to so humiliating an end! I was furious! "You imbeciles!" I screamed. "You were supposed to leave with Spoletta! You've spoiled the opera!"

They looked first shocked and then crestfallen. "I, I'm sorry," one of them stammered, shamefaced. "We didn't know."

Well, of course they didn't know; their instructions had been hurried and vague. "Ah, it's not your fault," I grumbled. "*You* aren't the ones I should be yelling at." I extricated myself from the tangle of arms and legs I was caught in and stood up. "*Gatti!*" I screamed.

He was right there, behind me, too thunderstruck even to move. We were surrounded by screaming people—singers, backstage crew, maids and valets—all of them anxious to tell the firing squad what they now already knew. The firing squad decided to yell at Gatti for sending them out on the stage so poorly prepared; I helped them. The noise level kept rising and rising.

Finally Gatti grabbed me and screamed into my ear, "The curtain call! You will miss the curtain call!"

"Are you crazy?" I screamed back. "Go out in front of that hysterical audience after a fiasco like this? Never!"

"But they will think . . ."

"And they'll be right! I'm no fool! I'm *not* taking a curtain call tonight!" I pulled away from him and tried to work my way through the crowd. The tenor, as far as I could tell, had managed to disappear; smart man.

Scotti came up to me laughing so hard the tears were running down his face. "Let me examine you! What, no bullet holes? Remarkable! But still, the first *Tosca* in history in which the *soprano* is executed—although I can think of a few productions that would improve with such an alteration.''

''Do you mean me?'' I shrieked.

''Of course not, *cara* Gerry! I mean all those *other* Toscas, the ones who only wish they could sing like you! But what an ending! A firing squad that heroically leaps to its own death! In remorse over shooting so charming a lady, no doubt.''

''It's not funny, Toto!''

''The curtain call!'' Gatti shouted desperately. ''The curtain call . . . somebody . . . Scotti?''

Scotti gestured apologetically. Traditionally the baritone does not take a curtain call at the end of *Tosca*, since his part ends in Act II; Scotti had already changed into his street clothes. With my refusing to go out and the tenor turned suddenly invisible, not one of the opera's three lead singers was available for the curtain call.

So who did take the curtain call? Why, the firing squad, of course. The audience rose to its feet and cheered.

Emmy Destinn came backstage, wearing an expression that said I-saw-it-but-I-don't-believe-it. The last thing in the world I wanted to hear was some undisguised crowing from Emmy Destinn, so I pushed my way over to her and screamed, ''Emmy, if you say one word—*one word!*—I shall pull your hair right out of your head! Every strand of it!''

She pressed her lips together and tried to look sympathetic.

Jimmy Freeman, also changed into street clothes, was wearing a face that could have been a model for a tragic mask. ''What a terrible thing!'' he cried. ''Oh, Gerry, I'm so sorry!''

At last, a friendly shoulder to cry on. The trouble was, I didn't feel like crying. *Killing*, maybe, but not crying.

''And wouldn't you know,'' Jimmy went on, ''old Duchon is over there talking to the chairman of the board. Capitalizing on the mistake.''

''Over where?''

''There.'' He gestured with his head. I made my way over to where Philippe Duchon was standing with Otto Kahn, chairman of the Metropolitan board of directors.

"In an efficiently run house," Duchon was saying, "such amateurishness would not be tolerated. *All* details must be seen to, including adequate coaching of the supernumeraries."

The Frenchman was doing his best to undermine Gatti-Casazza; I wondered how far he'd go to usurp Gatti's place. If it ever came down to a choice between Gatti and Duchon, there wasn't the slightest doubt as to which was preferable. "Oh, hello, Mr. Kahn," I said gaily to the chairman. "How did you like our little comedy?"

He shook his head. "Unfortunate. But these things are bound to happen once in a while, I suppose."

So he hadn't been taken in by Duchon's self-promoting spiel. Good. "Yes, it was unfortunate—but it *was* funny, you have to admit." I laughed lightly. *Ha ha, oh yes, very funny, ha ha.* "Come now, Mr. Kahn, you did laugh, didn't you?"

The corner of his mouth twitched. "I must confess I did indulge in a chuckle or two."

Better and better. "That was a stroke of genius on Gatti's part, wasn't it? Sending the firing squad out to take the curtain call, I mean. There's no way to pretend what happened did *not* happen—so, we might as well make the most of it!"

"Yes, that was a clever move," Mr. Kahn agreed. "Send the audience home in a good mood—it never hurts. But, dear Miss Farrar, you did not get to take your own well-earned curtain call."

I waved a hand dismissively. "I'll take twice as many next time." I gave him my most brilliant smile, and he smiled back automatically.

Through all this Duchon had stood like a statue, working hard at keeping his face impassive. I chatted with Mr. Kahn another minute or two and then went looking for Scotti. I found him with Emmy Destinn, both of them doubled over with laughter. The minute they saw me they straightened up and put on sober expressions.

"Oh, stop that," I said crossly, "I know you both think it's a big joke. Toto, I want to get out of here. Now."

"Certainly, *bellissima*," he purred. "As soon as you change, we—"

"I'm not going to change. I want to get out of here *right now*." Very unprofessional, leaving the opera house in full costume and make-up; I'd never done it before. But tonight was an unusual night.

Outside the stage door Mildredandphoebe were waiting with a million questions, but I hurried by without answering; I'd never done *that* before either. It was snowing—wet and clingy snow, the worst kind of stuff to fall out of the sky on you on a bad night.

In the back seat of the limousine Scotti did his best to reassure me. "Gerry, that firing squad—it does not make *you* look bad. You are wonderful. You always are, but tonight even more wonderful than usual. I am wonderful too! Do not be sad, Gerry. *I* am not sad!"

I sighed. "But we had such a good one going, Toto."

"Yes, we have a good one tonight. And next time will be good too. Smile, *gioia mia*. Tell me what I can do to make you feel better."

I told him.

◻ **7** ◻ A few days later I was in the music room, deep in the daily drudgery of scales, when my maid Bella came in and told me a Mr. "Dew-shone" was there to see me. I told her to show him in to the music room.

Then Duchon was standing stiffly just inside the door, as if unsure of his welcome—as well he might be! He carried a long florist's box. "Even singing scales," he said softly, "you make beautiful music, Gerry."

"What a charming way to start a conversation," I said. "Do come in, Philippe, don't stand there in the doorway. What do you have there?"

He ceremoniously handed me the florist's box. "Two dozen orchids, I believe you said," he smiled wryly.

I'd also said *on his knees*, but I pretended to forget that part of it. "You've been talking to Morris, then."

"Mr. Gest explained I may have been precipitate in my suggestions. It seems I am always apologizing to you, Gerry. It is not my intention to keep offending you—I don't know what happens."

What happens is your personality keeps getting in the way, I thought. I turned my attention to the florist's box. The lid said Wadley & Smythe, Fifth Avenue—he'd not stinted on the expense. The orchids were lovely, that delicate rose variety with yellow throats; I wished I'd said three dozen. I told Bella to bring some shallow bowls filled with water.

Plunge right in. "Did you really think I'd let you pick out my program numbers for me?" I asked Duchon.

A Gallic shrug. "I was mistaken to presume. Your Mr. Gest says you now refuse to sing in concert with me at all. Gerry, I beg you—please reconsider. Your presence would mean so much to the Alsatian war relief. France needs you, Gerry."

Oh, my. "You should have thought of that when you were making out my program for me."

"*Ma chère*, do not let my personal clumsiness dissuade you. We need money, much money. The only way I can help is by giving benefit concerts. And possibly by persuading you—'' He broke off abruptly, his eyes staring at something across the room.

I followed his glance. He was looking at a framed photograph I kept on the piano, a picture of the Crown Prince. Handsome Willi, son of Kaiser Wilhelm—my friend, Duchon's enemy.

He picked up smoothly where he'd left off. ''And possibly by persuading you to sing with me. You could help so much, if you would.''

Bella came in with the shallow bowls, making two trips. I busied myself floating the orchids on the water while Duchon walked about the room. ''What a charming place you have, Gerry! Both comfortable and elegant. And so much room!'' He swung out both arms expansively—and ''accidentally'' knocked Willi's picture off the piano to the floor, where the glass splintered into a dozen pieces.

I made no fuss, simply told Bella to clean it up. When she'd left the room, I interrupted Duchon's apologies and told him to sit down.

I sat in a chair facing him. ''Philippe, you come here to ask me to do a special favor for you. And then you do something like that, breaking Willi's picture, that you know will offend me. Is this your subtle way of telling me you don't really want me to sing with you?''

He looked horrified. ''No, no—never think that! I *do* want you to sing with me! More than anything!''

''Then why do you *do* things like that? Ever since we met, you've been complimenting me in one breath and insulting me in the next. You're no stumbling schoolboy,'' I said, thinking of Jimmy Freeman. ''You must know what you're doing. So what is it you hope to accomplish by acting in this outlandish way?''

He didn't say anything. But his face grew pinched, his eyes squeezed together, and to my dismay I realized the man was crying. I fidgeted a bit, not really knowing what to do; finally I handed him a glass of wine, which he took one sip of and then handed back.

When he could talk again, he said, ''You are mistaken when you say I must know what I'm doing. I do not. I come to this strange land so full of noise and color and money, and I . . . I do not always know what is best to do. I am not a young man, Gerry. So many changes—so many *violent* changes, and so quickly. I lose my opera house, I am in danger of losing my country, and now I think I may be losing my, eh, eh.''

Voice. He was afraid of losing his voice.

Oh, that explained so many things! The alternating moods, the arrogance, the quickness to attribute accidents to the malevolence of others. The eagerness to find an opera company he could manage. It even explained his wanting to learn a new role at this late stage of his career. Singing Scarpia in *Tosca* would be a way of denying any loss of vocal power—a way of denying death, in fact.

But I thought he was mistaken about losing his voice, and said so. "Your voice is strong and true, Philippe, and it has a resonance and timbre that neophyte singers would give ten years of their lives for. What makes you think you're losing it?''

"A tightness, a closing up without warning. Several times in rehearsal, and even when I practice those same scales you were doing so effortlessly a few minutes ago— suddenly the voice is just not there. Nothing comes out. It hasn't happened in performance yet, but it's only a matter of time.''

"Have you consulted a physician?''

"Yes, Gatti-Casazza recommended a Dr., ah . . . ?''

"Curtis?''

"Dr. Curtis, yes. He says there is nothing to worry about. I must admit Caruso's throat spray does help, if only for brief periods of time. Do you know what's in it?''

"It's basically Dobell's Solution with several other things added,'' I said, "salt water and the like. Caruso's always changing the formula. Philippe, this tightening up in your throat—do you think it might have an emotional cause instead of a physical one? You've obviously had a lot to distress you lately.''

He smiled sadly. "That is what Dr. Curtis suggested. He says it is all in my mind and not in my throat. Perhaps what is needed is not a throat spray but a spray for the head.''

As jokes go, it was a pretty feeble one; but it told me Duchon was making an effort, trying to regain control over a life that had suddenly gone haywire on him. On impulse, I leaned over and patted his hand. "I'll sing your fund-raising concert with you, Philippe. We can talk about a tour later. And don't worry about losing your voice—you'll outlast us all."

A while later he left, each of us reassured a little about the other. I felt more comfortable with him now than at any time since we'd first met. When a singer is under such stress that his voice is affected, obviously his behavior is going to be erratic. If it were happening to me, I'd be running around and screaming and breaking things. Or maybe even jumping off the Brooklyn Bridge.

The evening had started off badly. I'd insulted one of society's *grandes dames* in a strong, clear voice that carried all the way across the room—and I'd done so because *she* had insulted *me*. The most annoying thing about the entire interchange was that the stupid cow wasn't even aware she *had* insulted me.

We were at a dinner party at the Vanderbilt mansion on Fifth Avenue. I was wearing a white taffeta evening frock trimmed with lace and rosebuds, and I was the only woman there whose arms were not bare. The upper part of my left arm still sported a bruise, the result of my unforeseen collision with a foot belonging to somebody in that disastrous *Tosca* firing squad. Toscanini was my escort for the evening, and the only other person there from the Met was Caruso. I'd barely gotten my wraps off when this cow started pestering me to sing. I said no politely several times, even pointing out once that I'd come to be entertained, not to do the entertaining myself.

This is something all singers have to put up with. We accept invitations to a social occasion and there's always somebody who expects us to perform in a professional capacity. Caruso sometimes accepts a fee to sing at such events. But I never do, because that puts you on some ambiguous level between honored guest and hired help.

When I'm a guest, I want to be treated as a guest and nothing else.

"Dear little songbird," the cow mooed, "do sing that nice little aria from *Madame Butterfly* for us. I so seldom get to hear it."

That nice little aria. That's actually what she called *Un Bel Dì*, one of the greatest pieces of music for soprano voice ever written—*that nice little aria.* "I am sorry," I announced, projecting my voice so all could hear, "but if you would arrive in your box before the middle of the second act, and stop chattering, you *would* hear it—in the opera house, where it belongs."

Caruso looked shocked. Toscanini smothered a laugh. The cow's friends frowned at me, while her enemies smiled in approval. But at last she understood and importuned me no further. In fact, she hasn't spoken to me since.

All this before we sat down to dinner.

Toscanini didn't really want to be there. He wasn't good at parties—he had no small talk. Gatti-Casazza was the same way; whenever I invited him and Toscanini both to a party, they created two little islands of gloom in the midst of all the gaiety. Those two were alike in so many ways; if one of them had been a woman, they would have been married.

Married, but now thinking of divorce. Somewhere between the quail in aspic and the *bombe Moscovite* Toscanini confided that he probably wouldn't be at the Metropolitan next season. He said it so casually that at first I didn't pay too much attention; he'd threatened to quit before. But he insisted that this time he meant it.

"It is this 'retrenchment,' " he complained. "Everywhere I look, Gatti cuts the corners. Anything to save a few dollars, yes? How does he expect me to produce the first-class productions with so little money, so little rehearsal time? He expects me to work the miracles? *Questo non si può fare!* I am not magician!"

For once I found myself seeing Gatti's side of it. "The retrenchment wasn't his idea, you know. The board decides these things. Gatti is simply carrying out his instructions."

"Then he should resign with me. We leave La Scala together, now we must leave the Metropolitan together."

It was that statement, I think, that made me realize Toscanini wasn't just making empty threats. The idea of the Metropolitan Opera without Toscanini and Gatti at the helm—why, it was unthinkable! A chill ran through me.

Toscanini noticed. "Gerry?"

I shook my head. "I just realized what it meant. What would the Metropolitan do without you?"

"It would deteriorate," he said matter-of-factly. Then he put on what I'd come to recognize as his romantic face. "The one thing that makes me hesitate," he whispered, "is the thought of leaving you, *cara mia*."

Just then one of the other dinner guests said something to me and the conversation took a different direction. Across the table and three or four chairs down, Caruso was seated between two lovely women with whom he was flirting with gusto. They were both laughing and having a good time; Caruso's only problem was deciding which one to concentrate on.

Caruso had tried to flirt with me when we first met. But I could never take him seriously; such a *funny*-looking man, and so unintentionally comical when he put on the airs of a languishing lover. I remember the first time I ever saw him—at Monte Carlo, at the first rehearsal for the *Bohème* we were to sing. He'd come in wearing a suit of shrieking green checks and bright yellow gloves, brandishing that ubiquitous gold-headed cane of his. But he was so pleasant and affable to everyone, so kind, that I couldn't help but like him.

That was back in the early stages of both our careers. I had never heard Caruso sing; and all during rehearsals he sang half-voice, saving himself for the performance. On opening night when I first heard the magnificent sound that came pouring out of the throat of that funny-looking Neapolitan, I was literally struck dumb with amazement. I stood like a statue on the stage until the conductor rapped sharply with his baton to bring me back to my senses. I'll never know another pleasure quite like that one—singing with Enrico Caruso for the very first time. At the end of

Act III Caruso had lifted me bodily in full view of the audience and carried me all the way to my dressing room. Oh, what a moment that was! The Monte Carlo audience went wild. (Caruso has never even *tried* to heft up any other soprano he's sung with!)

Talk at the table turned to the war, and I let my mind wander, remembering. Toscanini murmured, "Where are you, *cara mia*? Of what do you think?"

"Monte Carlo," I answered.

That place, it seemed to me, epitomized all that was both good and bad about the Europe that was now being torn to pieces. Frankly, I missed the glitter of Monte Carlo, the cultivated frivolity, the carefree abandon with which money was spent. Not only at the gaming tables (where I gambled just enough to learn not to gamble!), but in the little everyday gestures. Whether it was a Russian overtipping or an American calling out *All join in!* at the bar, it made for a kind of good-humored camaraderie and display for its own sake. Surfeited grand dukes, wearied kings incognito, phlegmatic John Bulls, American millionaires new to the international playground, sophisticated Parisian elegants—they all contributed to the pageantry that springs from the irrepressible urge for human expression.

Yet a lot of it was mere bravado. Monte Carlo has always paraded a snobbish indifference to less fortunate mortals; the well-being of the common man was not a popular topic of conversation. American millionaires found it hard to break into the inner circles, and European nobility found that marriage to American heiresses was not enough to arrest the decay of old families. Those centuries-old coats of arms were too tarnished; they could never again be burnished to their original brightness, not even with American money. Something was dying in Europe; and I think that underneath all the frenetic gaiety, Monte Carlo knew it.

Dinner ended, and the guests began drifting to other rooms in search of entertainment. I announced it was time for me to leave. My hostess made no attempt to dissuade me; she understood, as did everyone else there, that I do not keep late hours. As my escort, Toscanini then had an excuse to leave himself—for which he breathed a barely disguised sigh of relief. Caruso had settled on the younger of his two dinner companions (don't they always?), but he abandoned her long enough to say goodbye.

"Go straight home to bed, Gerry," he ordered, eyes twinkling. "Although I do not understand why you insist you need your beauty sleep." A nice compliment.

"Don't be too charming tonight, Rico," I answered in the same vein. "Your lady may not let you go at all."

He tried to look dismayed and failed. "How terrible! I will be careful."

Toscanini and I were turning to go when a bass voice boomed out from across the room. "Miss Farrar! Do wait a moment—please!"

The bass voice had said *please*, but it was clearly a command. The owner of the voice was an oversized woman in her sixties wearing enough jewels to weigh down an elephant. She was one of those obtrusive people who thrust their faces into yours when they talked, and I'd always had trouble being polite to her. She never took hints; she was worse than the cow who'd wanted me to sing.

"Dear Miss Farrar, I have a favor I want to ask of you." (*No*, I thought automatically.) "I have been racking my brains trying to think what to wear to the war relief costume ball. But when I saw you here tonight, I had the answer! Do allow me to wear one of your Butterfly costumes, my dear—it will be just the thing!"

I gritted my teeth. "Sorry, I never lend my costumes."

"Ah, but you can make an exception this one time, can't you?"

"I'm sorry, no. There's still time for you to get an Oriental costume made up, isn't there?"

"But that's not the same as wearing one from the Metropolitan Opera!" she boomed. "If I show up in one of Geraldine Farrar's costumes, I'll win the prize!"

For what? I wondered. I had lent some of my costumes to a few of these society matrons when I was new at the Met. They'd come back with the seams stretched and some of the ornaments missing; the costumes hadn't even been cleaned before they were returned. I told the woman no again, but she didn't want to hear me. She was about my height but outweighed me by a good sixty pounds, and she was closing in.

"Now, Miss Farrar, I'm just not going to take no for an answer! Do lend me one of those exquisite costumes—I'll let you choose which one! I will take good care of it and make sure everyone knows it belongs to you. And a wig. I'll need a wig."

I stepped back from that overendowed dowager and looked her up and down. "Dear lady, until you can lift your façade and restrain your posterior, you would need not one but several of my Butterfly costumes. You would do better to choose something from Emmy Destinn's wardrobe."

"Gerry!" Caruso looked horrified. The others within hearing distance tittered. Toscanini had his back turned, so I couldn't tell what he was thinking.

"Well, I *never*!" My buxom adversary flounced off, and believe you me, nobody flounced better than she did. I was heartily glad to be rid of her.

"Gerry, why you insult Emmy?" Caruso said in a low voice. He looked hurt.

"Oh, I don't know," I muttered. "I can't stand women like that one. Look how fat she is—she'd ruin my costumes!"

"And that is why you insult Emmy? Because she is not slim and beautiful? You have no tolerance, Gerry, no understanding."

"Don't scold me, Rico, I'm in no mood for it." I tapped Toscanini on the shoulder. "Come."

Toscanini's face was a mask until we got into the limousine and were snuggled comfortably under the fur lap rug. Then he laughed. And laughed and laughed and laughed. "Ah, Gerry! All these things I think to myself but cannot say to the ladies—you say them! *In fede mia!* You have heart of the lion!"

"Mmm," I murmured. "But Rico's mad at me."

He took my hand. "Eh, you must remember, Caruso

and Emmy—they are friends for many years, many. Caruso feels protective, you understand?''

I snorted, and didn't even care that it was such an indelicate sound. ''Emmy Destinn needs a protector the way you need conducting lessons.''

''Nevertheless, Caruso *thinks* he is protecting her, and that makes the difference, no?''

''I suppose.''

We rode in silence for a while, holding hands like a couple of schoolchildren. I wasn't concerned about Emmy and Caruso; it was my companion I was worrying about. There was a time when I'd actually thought about leaving the Metropolitan Opera—because of Toscanini. During his first year in New York we hadn't seen eye to eye on *anything*; the Maestro was so rigid, so demanding! But Toscanini had made the first gesture of reconciliation, and since then I'd sung in the best-conducted performances of my life. ''You aren't really going to leave the Metropolitan, are you?'' I asked.

''Is possible,'' he shrugged. Then his voice took on a note of excitement. ''Why do you not come with me, Gerry? You have never sung in *Italia*. Let my countrymen hear you, let them see you!'' He laughed. ''They make me national hero! I return home, and I bring America's brightest star with me, yes?'' He laughed again. ''It could be glorious, *cara mia*.''

That's all I needed—to start all over again in a new country, in the middle of a war. I put my head on his shoulder and said: ''I don't want you to go, you know. I want you to stay right where you are and go on doing what you're doing now. I want you to keep on screaming at me in rehearsal and whispering compliments in my ear whenever we're alone. I don't want anything to change.''

''Ah, but the change, it starts already,'' he reflected sadly. ''But I understand you. There are things you want to keep in your heart, to cherish forever, yes? Even moments, special moments. Like this one.''

What a nice thing to say. ''Tell me something. How is it possible for a person to be so nasty in rehearsal and so sweet the rest of the time?''

"Strange," Toscanini said. "I am just wondering the same thing."

The place where Fifth Avenue and Broadway meet is the windiest corner in town and no place to be in midwinter. But around the corner on East Twenty-third Street is the Bon Ton Tea Shoppe, where I was meeting Morris Gest. I like the Bon Ton; they serve a good tea and they know how to treat celebrities. When the staff had assured itself that Miss Farrar's chair was comfortable and Miss Farrar's order had been taken and there was nothing else that Miss Farrar desired, I turned to Morris. "Well?"

He reached in his pocket and pulled out a small porcelain jar. "They've made a good offer," he said, "but I think I can get them to go higher."

The label on the jar said *Creme Nerol*. I took off the lid and sniffed; it smelled good. "Very well, I'll try it tonight." The makers of Creme Nerol had asked me to endorse their new skin and beauty product, but I wanted to test it first.

"They plan on running your picture in the advertisement. That should be good for a few more sales. By the way, the Old Man will be joining us here—I hope you don't mind."

"Not at all, I'm glad he's coming." And I was; I hadn't seen Morris's father-in-law for a while. Just then our tea arrived. I stirred and sipped and nibbled a little of the cream cake we were served—just a taste.

Morris took a big swallow of tea and made a face, obviously wishing it were something stronger. "Your contract will be ready in a day or two."

"For Creme Nerol? I haven't said yes yet, Morris."

"Naw, the contract for your joint concert with that double-crossing, underhanded, tight-fisted, no-good Frog you're determined to sing with."

Oh my. "Philippe Duchon? Why, what's he done?"

"He's ratted out on me, that's what he's done." Morris's face was angry; a big vein stood out in his forehead. "He let me go ahead and arrange his tour for him, and then he up and tells me he's decided not to sign a personal management contract after all, mercy beau-koo. Ain't that a nice howdy-do?''

It was a rotten trick. "Is he signing with someone else?''

"Not so far as I know. I could cancel his tour, but there's no point. He's got the schedule I made out for him—all he has to do is pick up a telephone and reconfirm. That slimy son of a bitch!''

"Morris!''

"Sorry, Gerry. But I could chew nails! He's got you to sing for him for free and he got me to arrange his tour for him for free . . . I could throttle that damned Frog! Who does he think he is?''

"Calm down, Morris, this can't be good for you. Here, have some more tea.'' I filled his cup, understanding full well why he was so bothered; it wasn't often that someone pulled a fast one on Morris Gest. "You might as well forget about it. There's nothing you can do.''

"The hell there isn't,'' he muttered. "I can sue the oily-tongued bastard.''

"But you had no contract!''

"We had a *verbal* contract. And if I can prove we had one, it'll stand up in court. That's why I asked the Old Man to meet us here—he knows the ins and outs of a courtroom, he's been sued more than anybody else I know. And Gerry, you'd help my case if you refused to sing with Duchon.''

On again, off again. "How would that help?''

"Oh, you could testify that you knew he'd welched on his agreement with me and that made you leery of him, since his word wasn't worth much, something like that. We can work it out.''

I didn't like Morris's asking me to take sides in his quarrel with Philippe Duchon; my relationship with the baritone was precarious enough as it was. But Morris was in the right, and he was an old friend. If it ever came down to it, I'd have to side with Morris.

"Here comes the Old Man,'' he said.

I looked up to see a distinguished-looking older man in priest's raiment approaching, his thick silver hair carefully waved and his face calm. He ignored his son-in-law and took my hand. "My dear Geraldine," he said in that soft, mellifluous voice of his, "when are you going to abandon the opera house in favor of the theatre? We need you, you know."

I gave him my best smile. "Get thee behind me, Satan. Your offer becomes more tempting every time I hear it."

"Ah, that is music to my ears!" He sat down at the table, finally acknowledging his son-in-law's presence. "I told Morris I couldn't leave rehearsal to meet him, but then he mentioned you'd be here. How could I resist?"

So I was the bait. "I'm glad you didn't resist. What are you rehearsing now, David?"

"We're reviving *A Celebrated Case.* I'll try it out in Boston next month before bringing it to New York. Why don't you let me find a play for you?"

David Belasco had been after me for several years to act in one of his productions. Playwright, director, producer—Belasco was the single most important and influential figure in New York theatre, and I was frankly flattered by his attention. He even had his own theatre building, on West Forty-fourth Street; but he always had half a dozen other productions playing in town. He'd worked his way up from nothing to become high priest of the theatre world—which, I suppose, is why he always wore ecclesiastical garb. Also, it helped hide his growing pot belly.

Belasco and Morris talked a while about Morris's intended litigation, and Belasco too seemed to think I would make a good witness for the plaintiff. He gave his son-in-law the names of a couple of attorneys. Morris was always on the lookout for a new lawyer; he distrusted the profession and was convinced that all its practitioners were out to fleece him.

Meanwhile, I'd been thinking. When there was a lull in the lawyer-talk, I said, "David, I could use your help."

"Name it, dear lady," he smiled.

"I'm concerned about the final duet in *Carmen*—the acting, not the singing. The way Caruso and I do it, well, there's something wrong with it."

Belasco frowned. "I saw your *Carmen* in December,

but I'm afraid I don't remember the acting in the final duet at all.''

"That's what's wrong with it—there's nothing to remember! Caruso and I stand there like two blocks of wood and wave our arms at each other. I've tried doing a few things on my own, but they haven't worked very well. David, I would appreciate some suggestions.''

"When do you next sing *Carmen*?''

"Friday night. Can you come see what we're doing? Or not doing, rather.''

"I'll be there. And don't worry, Gerry, I'll work out something for you and your partner.''

"If he cooperates,'' I sighed.

Belasco smiled. "I've dealt with Mr. Caruso before, remember.''

That's right; he had. Belasco had directed the stage action for the première of *La Fanciulla del West*, Puccini's cowboy opera that had starred Caruso and Pasquale Amato. And Emmy Destinn—instead of me.

Instead of me.

I had to see my dressmaker and left soon after that, feeling much relieved. If anyone could solve the staging problems of *Carmen*'s final duet, it was David Belasco. It occurred to me that on Friday night Belasco would also be seeing the man his son-in-law was planning to sue; Duchon would again be substituting for Amato.

Unless he lost his voice before then. I almost wished it would happen. And then I was almost ashamed of myself for thinking such a thing. Almost.

□ **8** □ "It's still too fast, Mr. Springer," I said. He grimaced and forced himself to play more slowly. I'd invited him and Jimmy Freeman to my apartment to rehearse those parts of *Madame Sans-Gêne* Jimmy would be singing. Jimmy was doing fine; the only problem was keeping Osgood Springer's piano accompaniment to the pace the orchestra would be following. But I could understand his desire to speed things up once in a while; the music was rather bland in places.

But Jimmy thought it was wonderful. It was his first major role, after all, and—let's face it—he was doubly excited because he would be singing with me. I didn't mind. When we finished, I announced I could see no major problems, Mr. Springer declared he was satisfied, and Jimmy proclaimed himself in seventh heaven, no less. We would do all right.

Bella and one of the other maids brought us refreshments. As I was pouring Mr. Springer's coffee, he mentioned that he and Jimmy would be seeing me on Friday night, at *Carmen*. It seemed Jimmy would be standing by for Duchon again.

"I don't object, not really," Jimmy said happily. "I'll gladly stand by every night as long as I have *Madame Sans-Gêne* to look forward to."

So with the promise of that one performance, Gatti-Casazza had gained himself a willing slave. "Duchon is still complaining of throat problems, then?" I asked.

"Mr. Gatti didn't actually say so," Osgood Springer replied, "but that was the impression I got. Do those two dislike each other?"

"Who?" I said, startled. "Gatti and Toscanini?"

"Toscanini? No, I meant Gatti and Duchon. Our general manager seems uneasy every time he speaks of the Frenchman."

Worried about his job. "I don't think there's any actual dislike between them," I said, "but Duchon is not easy to work with. He makes so many demands."

"*You* work with him," Jimmy said loyally.

"Only through the exercise of superior self-control," I

smiled modestly. "The man isn't easy to get along with. I'd much rather sing with you.

Jimmy almost dropped his cup. "You would? You really would?"

"I really would."

Jimmy put down his cup and got up and did an impromptu little dance. "Hear that, Mr. Springer? She'd rather sing with me than Duchon!"

His voice coach laughed, enjoying the moment almost as much as Jimmy. "Things will be returning to normal soon. I hear Pasquale Amato is up and about now. He'll be back soon, and then Philippe Duchon can go back to where he came from."

Oh my. Did they really think that? "Mr. Springer, Jimmy—I don't want to tell you this. But Duchon isn't going back to France. Not right away, at least."

A silence heavy enough to feel came into the room. Then Jimmy said, "What do you mean, he isn't going back? All he's doing is filling in for Amato."

"No, that's not all he's doing," I said. "He's going on tour, for one thing—my manager arranged it for him. And Duchon and Gatti have been talking about next season's schedule, I know."

The silence returned. Abruptly Mr. Springer stood up and walked over to stare out the window.

I felt compelled to explain. "Philippe Duchon is an ardent patriot, you know that. But there's nothing he can do in France. Here he can raise money—that's why he came in the first place, to solicit funds for Alsatian war relief. I think you'd both better get used to the idea that he's going to be around for a while." I didn't have the heart to tell them I'd agreed to sing a joint concert with Duchon; they'd find out about that soon enough.

"I thought he'd be leaving," Jimmy said, stunned.

"So what happens to James?" Mr. Springer asked, still staring out the window.

"Oh, I'm sure Gatti will give him another leading role next season," I said in as optimistic a voice as I could summon. "Maybe even two roles."

Mr. Springer whirled from the window. "With *three*

lead baritones on the roster? Scotti, Amato, and Duchon? There's no room left for James!''

''You can never have too many good baritones!'' I was *determined* to be optimistic.

Mr. Springer made a sound something like *pshaw* and turned back to the window. ''I thought he'd be leaving,'' Jimmy repeated dully.

I shouldn't have told them, I thought miserably. But I couldn't let them go on living in a fool's paradise; the later they found out the truth, the more it would hurt. Confound Gatti-Casazza anyway! He should have explained things to them.

Mr. Springer roused himself and made an effort to help cheer Jimmy up. But Jimmy wouldn't be cheered. ''Damn that Frenchman!'' he cried. ''I should have punched him in the nose, that day in Delmonico's! I should have punched him in the *throat*!''

''Jimmy!'' I protested. ''You don't mean that.''

''I do mean that!'' he shouted in full youthful bravado. ''Everything was going fine until *he* came.''

''Control yourself, James—this is not like you,'' his coach said. ''Miss Farrar, I apologize for this outburst. Perhaps we'd better leave.''

I hated for them to go on such a sour note, but a brisk walk in the nippy February air might do Jimmy some good. I saw them out and leaned against the closed door for a moment. At least one good piece of news had come out of that unpleasant scene: Osgood Springer had said Pasquale Amato was up and about. I decided to go see him.

It was my chauffeur's day off, so that meant I'd have to drive myself. Operating a motor car is not one of the things I look forward to when I wake up in the morning; but I refuse to ride those noisy trolleys or call one of the taximetre cabs, because I do not relish the thought of entrusting my life to the driving skills of a stranger. So I steered my way down icy Broadway—doing it, but not liking it.

I was relieved when I got to the Astor and happy to find Amato was indeed out of his sickbed. He was wearing several thicknesses of red flannel wrapped around his throat, but he was talking instead of scribbling notes on little pieces of paper. "Gerry!" he cried happily. "Look at me! Like Hercules, eh?" He thumped a fist against his chest. "Now I am ready to move mountains, to swim oceans, to sing! Am I not picture of health?"

"Pasquale, you are as healthy and handsome as ever," I laughed. "And I can't begin to tell you how glad I am you're well again! When are you coming back?"

His face fell a little. "Dr. Curtis is cautious man. He says another week. I miss two more performances—*Carmen* tomorrow night and *Madame Sans-Gêne*." He brightened. "But I am back for *Aïda*!"

Emmy Destinn's opera, but I didn't care. Amato was looking so good I just had to give him a little hug. "You don't know how much we've all missed you. You just don't *know*."

He winked at me. "You are not happy with your Monsieur Duchon?"

"He's not *my* Monsieur Duchon," I shuddered, "thank goodness. Do you know, Pasquale, the entire atmosphere at the Met has changed since he's been here?" I realized that was true only as I said it. But it *was* true—Amato had always been an oasis of stability and calm in the middle of the chaos that was normal in an opera house, but Duchon had generated nothing but dissension from the day he arrived. From calling me a German-lover to double-crossing Morris Gest, there'd been just one troublesome thing after another. But there'd been nice things too, luncheon at Delmonico's, a box of orchids. Ah, what was the use? I gave up trying to understand the man. "I'm glad you're better," I told Amato again.

"*Grazie*. I am so much better," he announced, "that I come to hear your Carmen tomorrow night."

"You're coming to hear Duchon's Escamillo, you mean," I said. "But Pasquale, do you think you should be going out so soon? That's not summer weather out there. Does Dr. Curtis approve?"

"Dr. Curtis accompanies me! I am in the cold air only

un momento—when I get into limousine and when I get out. We take precautions, *cara* Gerry. Do not worry."

"Well, if Dr. Curtis will be with you, I suppose it's all right."

"Dr. Curtis and my *nurse*," Amato laughed. "Emmy Destinn casts herself in role of angel of mercy. She says she will carry the medicine and assist Dr. Curtis."

"What does Dr. Curtis say to that?"

Amato raised his shoulders, spread his hands. "He is resigned."

Amato wanted to be brought up to date on the latest gossip; I chattered on for half an hour, hearing myself mention Philippe Duchon's name a little more often than I really cared to. I'd just about run out of things to say when Amato pulled a watch from his pocket and reluctantly announced it was time for his nap.

"I am instructed to sleep two hours every afternoon," he said with a sigh. "Dr. Curtis says that if I do not, my knees start to bend the wrong way and green feathers grow on my back."

"Good heavens! Well, we can't have that." I stood up to leave. "Besides, two hours in bed every afternoon sounds like a good idea."

He gallantly invited me to join him, but I declined.

Scotti lounged elegantly in the chair beside my dressing table while Bella arranged my hair; I never wear a wig for *Carmen*. "You seem in high spirits tonight, Gerry," Scotti said.

I smiled at my reflection in the mirror. "Amato is almost completely recovered. This is the last *Carmen* I'll have to sing with Duchon."

"Ah. Also your last chance to upstage him."

"Why, Toto, the idea! I don't *have* to upstage him." My hair didn't look quite right; I told Bella to brush it out and start over. "He's coming tonight, you know. Amato."

"*È vero?* That is good news, yes? He must indeed be better, to brave this weather." He sighed. "New York winters are not easy for us Neapolitans."

"Poor Toto."

Just then a timid knock came at the door. Bella let in Uncle Hummy, who was wearing an expensive-looking new gray tweed overcoat.

"Uncle Hummy!" Scotti cried. "How dashing you are! Turn around—let us see."

The old man beamed, showing off his new coat. "Meeztair Caruso buy me."

It's incredible what a difference the change of *one* garment can make (as I am always telling Emmy Destinn). Uncle Hummy didn't exactly look like a new man, but oh my, what an improvement! Having that expensive coat on his back had given him a sense of pride; he was standing up straight and grinning from ear to ear. No one would mistake him for a tramp now.

Uncle Hummy held out a folded piece of paper to me. "Note you, Miz Zherry." He bobbed his head once or twice, grinned a toothy grin, and left.

The note said:

> *My dear Gerry,*
> *I would be most grateful if you would not remain seated at your table during the Toreador Song. You are the only one on stage who is not standing at the time, and I fear you draw attention away from the aria. I thank you in advance for indulging me in this whim.*
>
> > *Votre ami,*
> > *Philippe Duchon*

Silently I handed the note to Scotti.

He read it and shook his head. "He does enjoy telling others what to do, does he not? And now he uses Uncle Hummy to run the errands. What are you going to do?"

"What do you think I'm going to do? I'm going to *glue* myself to that chair! He wants me to fade into that mob of people who stand around and *cheer* him. Ha! That'll be the day!"

"Foolish man," Scotti murmured.

"Toto, why on earth did you never learn Escamillo? It's a simple enough role."

"Eh, that is why."

"You could still learn it," I persisted. "You already know the *Toreador Song*—everybody does. And you could learn the rest of the role in twenty minutes."

"Fifteen."

"Then why haven't you ever done it!" I cried, exasperated. "Why must I be subjected to this, this pillar of vanity telling me what to do?"

"Now, now," Scotti said in his most soothing voice. "Only one more performance with Duchon, remember? Amato is back for the next one."

I let him *now now* me into a state of something resembling calm. If Amato had made a similar request, I wouldn't have thought a thing about it. But coming from Duchon, after all the other things that had happened—well, it was just too much. All this fuss over the *Toreador Song*.

"*To-ré-a-dor, en ga-a-a-r-de,*" sang a friendly, familiar voice from outside the door. In came Pasquale Amato, radiating good cheer and well-being. "Gerry! And Toto! I come to wish you well tonight, *cara* Gerry! And perhaps to frighten Monsieur Duchon a trifle, no? I am back!"

"Not yet, you're not," Dr. Curtis growled, following him in. "And I told you not to do any singing yet."

Amato gave an exaggerated sigh and rolled his eyes. "Where is my nurse?"

"She's coming," Dr. Curtis said.

"She is here," Emmy Destinn announced, marching in like the soldiers' chorus in *Faust*. For once she was wearing a flattering gown—wine-colored velvet with a minimum of flounces and ruffles. But the effect was spoiled by what she was carrying over her left shoulder. It looked for all the world like one of those saddlebags you put on horses.

"Charming accessory, Emmy," I said dryly.

"Pasquale's medicine," she explained. "You never know what might be needed."

"I told you not to bring so much," Dr. Curtis grumbled. "We'd never even need most of those things."

"You never know," Emmy repeated.

My small dressing room had become crowded; I shooed

the maid out. "So, Pasquale," I asked, "have you seen
Duchon yet?"

"No, Duchon has not seen me yet," he answered blithely,
putting things in their proper perspective. "I save that little
treat until last minute."

"Childish," Dr. Curtis muttered.

I handed Duchon's note to Emmy. "Here's something
you might find interesting."

She draped the saddlebag over the back of a chair and
read the note. She made a tsk-tsking sound and said, "You
are going to remain seated, aren't you?"

"Need you ask?"

"At least he's polite. He signs it *votre ami* instead of
ton ami."

Scotti was peering down Amato's throat. "It looks well
to me, Pasquale."

Dr. Curtis shifted his weight. "So glad you agree, Dr.
Scotti. It's almost time for the curtain. We'd better take
our seats."

"First we seek out Duchon," Amato said, "and then
we take our seats. Come."

They were going out when Scotti called, "Oh, Emmy—do
you not forget something?" He pointed to the medicine
bag draped over the chair.

"Oh—thank you, Toto." She saddled up and left.

I started warming up while I finished putting on my
make-up. After a while Scotti began humming along with
me, just for fun, until I told him he was distracting me.
That was about the five hundredth time I'd told him. As
usual, he said he'd forgotten and wouldn't do it again. We
both knew he would.

I made one final check of my appearance in the mirror;
then we went down to the stage level. I asked Scotti where
he'd be watching from.

"The first act—from out front. Thereafter, we will see.
Cielo! What bothers Rico so?"

Caruso was running around backstage with a look of
absolute desperation on his face, and he had half the
backstage crew running around too. Caruso always panics

right before a performance, but this wasn't his normal stage fright. "Rico, what's wrong?" I called.

"My throat spray!" he cried. "It is disappeared! Vanish-ed! I cannot sing four acts of Bizet without my throat spray! Impossible!"

"Then why not send your valet back to the Knicker-bocker for more?"

He stared at me blankly for a moment, then whirled on his heel and dashed away yelling, "Mario! Mario!" Caruso's apartment at the Hotel Knickerbocker was only three short blocks away; the valet could get there and back in no time.

I barely felt Scotti's good-luck hug as he slipped away to take his seat out front; I'd already started the process of shutting out everything except Bizet's music. Carmen doesn't make her entrance immediately, but I like to be there from the very beginning. We got the word; it was time. Applause from out front told me Toscanini was making his way through the orchestra pit to the podium. The applause increased slightly—he was taking a bow. Then the orchestra crashed into *Carmen*'s noisy prelude, and it would be only a few minutes until the curtain opened. Gooseflesh time.

La voilà! I don't believe I thought of that irritant Duchon once during the entire first act. I sang the *Habanera* and was rewarded with a nod of approval from Toscanini as well as with thunderous applause from the audience. I got into a fight with another woman, I was arrested, I had my wrists bound, and I was turned over to Don José/Caruso to be guarded. But when a little later he was supposed to set me free, Caruso "forgot" to loosen the ropes. So I had to finish singing the *Seguidilla* with my hands tied behind my back. Caruso thought that was very funny.

But he wasn't laughing during the act break. I made a quick costume change, picked up my castanets, and came down to find our tenor looking like a storm about to break. He'd found out what had happened to his throat spray. Uncle Hummy had taken it.

"I mistake! I mistake!" the old man cried pitifully. "I think it other!"

Caruso threw up his hands. "What does that mean, you think it other?"

"*Other*," Uncle Hummy insisted. "Duchon."

Just then Duchon himself came strolling up. "I do apologize if I've caused you any inconvenience, Caruso. I told your uncle here to see if he could find my throat spray, and evidently he picked yours up by mistake."

"Mistake," Uncle Hummy agreed.

Caruso could never stay mad long. "Eh, well, it does not matter. I have more now."

Uncle Hummy tugged at his sleeve. "Sorry. Sorry."

Caruso busied himself with reassuring the old man that all was well, but Duchon had already forgotten the incident. He headed straight for me with fire in his eye. "Gerry, I want you to have a word with your protégé. He keeps watching me. As if *willing* me to suffer a totally unexpected heart failure or something equally incapacitating. No finesse, that one."

"Jimmy? Surely you exaggerate."

"See for yourself." He gestured angrily behind him.

I looked over to where Jimmy Freeman stood once again in his thankless role of waiter-in-the-wings. Jimmy was in costume, listening to useless last-minute advice from his ever-present mentor, Osgood Springer. Listening to Mr. Springer, but never taking his eyes off Duchon. It was eerie, the way he kept staring at him.

But I was in no mood to do Philippe Duchon's dirty work for him, not after that bossy note he'd sent me, politely worded though it was. "So he's watching you," I shrugged. "You let the strangest things bother you, Philippe." I gave a little rattle with my castanets for emphasis.

His eyes hardened. But before he could say anything, Gatti-Casazza came lumbering up. "Ah, Monsieur Duchon! Everything goes well? No problems?"

"If you mean do I still have my voice, yes, I do," Duchon said harshly. "I will tell *you* if I need a replacement—you do not need to keep inquiring. You might as well send that boy home." He flapped a hand in Jimmy's direction.

"Eh, well, now that he is here . . ."

"Mr. Gatti, I do not want that boy around boring holes into me with his eyes! I *insist* you get rid of him."

"But he is here only because you—"

"I know why he is here and I am telling you there is no longer any need for him to be here! *Send him away!*" Duchon was shouting.

Caruso rushed over to us. "Send who away? Why? Something is happening, yes? What is wrong? Who—"

"*Tacete,* Rico," I whispered.

Gatti was looking worried. "Monsieur Duchon, it is almost time for the second act—"

"I should have smashed that insect when he presumed to attack me," Duchon snarled, "that day in Delmonico's." He stared at me. "And I would have, too—if you had not kept encouraging him!"

"I!" I said, astounded. "I did no such thing!"

Caruso's eyes were wide. "Someone attacks you in Delmonico's? Who?"

Duchon ignored him. "Oh, you are denying it now? You did not, ah, egg him on?"

"I most certainly did not!" I underscored my denial with a roll on the castanets. "You are rewriting what happened to suit yourself!"

"*What* happens?" Caruso cried plaintively. "Who attacks you?"

"I did, Mr. Caruso," came Jimmy Freeman's voice from behind me. "But only with words. I should have used my fists."

Duchon laughed. "You? You are good only for making scenes in restaurants. To impress a woman old enough to be your mother."

Jimmy lunged at him, almost knocking me over. Gatti and Caruso both got between Jimmy and Duchon and prevented a fight. The two Italians were both talking loudly in their language, Duchon was answering in French, and Jimmy contributed some downhome American cussing. I decided to join the party.

"*Bâtard!*" I screamed at Duchon. "Old enough to be his mother? I would have had to give birth at age ten!"

Mr. Springer was there, trying to pull Jimmy away. We were surrounded by stagehands and the other singers, all of whom seemed to find this intermission feature far more interesting than the opera. "And I had nothing to do with what happened in Delmonico's!" I went on. "Did I encourage you in any way, Jimmy?" He shook his head. "There—you see!"

"Oh, how innocent you are," Duchon sneered. "You know perfectly well you enjoyed seeing that boy make a fool of himself!"

I threw the castanets at him.

I didn't stop to think; I just threw them. If I had stopped to think, I undoubtedly would have thrown them harder. As it was, it was quite hard enough, thank you. I was using the hardwood castanets that night, not the ivory ones; and the edge of one of the clappers had a little rough spot on it—not much, just a little place. But evidently that rough spot caught Duchon just at the hairline, and . . . well, you know how scalp wounds bleed.

Duchon stood there with the blood running down his face, bellowing like a bull.

Caruso stood there staring at Duchon, horrified.

Gatti-Casazza stood there staring at *me*, horrified.

Jimmy Freeman stood there staring at me, openly admiring.

I stood there listening to my conscience and waiting for remorse to set in. It didn't happen.

Then everybody was screaming and waving their arms and accomplishing nothing. Gatti sent someone out front to fetch Dr. Curtis. He came, followed by Emmy Destinn with her saddlebag of medical supplies, followed by Pasquale Amato, who wouldn't dream of missing out on the fun. Osgood Springer recovered my castanets and handed them to me with a wry smile.

Dr. Curtis got the bleeding stopped and was applying a miniscule bandage. Gatti hovered over Duchon anxiously. "Can you sing?"

"Of course I can sing," Duchon snapped. "I do not sing with my *scalp*."

"Somehow," a soft voice said out of nowhere, "I do

not think this is a good time to visit." It was David Belasco, who I'd completely forgotten was coming to-night. He stood there in the midst of the pandemonium, a serene figure in his priestly garb, with a bemused expression on his face. "Even opening nights aren't as hectic as this. Are you all right, Gerry?"

I said I was. Morris Gest stood beside his father-in-law, gawking at Duchon. "Did *you* do that?" he asked me.

"I did," I replied. "And I should have done it long ago."

"That must be an interesting story," Belasco murmured. "You must tell it to me sometime."

"I'm sorry you had to see this, David," I said. "I'm not sorry it happened—but I'm sorry you had to see it."

Morris grinned at me. "You really did that?"

"I came back to tell you how impressed I was by your performance in the first act," Belasco said, "but I can see this is not the time. Perhaps after the opera? A late supper?"

Before I could answer, Amato came over and made a show of feeling the muscle in my upper right arm. "I am glad we are friends, *cara mia*," he whispered.

And then—just what we all needed—Toscanini stormed out onto the stage and demanded to know what was holding up the performance. When someone told him what had happened, he started screaming at me—but suddenly broke off in mid-scream. In fact, he looked as if he was trying not to laugh. "With the castanets?" he asked.

"With the castanets," I nodded.

"Highly unprofessional behavior," he snickered and moved away without another word. I was glad he left; I was starting to feel crowded. David Belasco and Morris Gest had tactfully interposed their bodies between me and the mob of people backstage, but it was beginning to seem that almost everyone in the world that I knew was there.

Everyone except Scotti. Where was Scotti?

Places, please!—at last! Carmen is on stage when the curtain opens on Act II, so I moved down to my place. The last thing I heard before the curtain opened was a baritone voice rumbling, "And she didn't even apologize!"

And she wasn't going to, either. The second act began,

and I didn't waste any time getting into it. I was still angry and keyed up and *fed* up and my nerves were on edge and I couldn't stand still and this and that and the other—and I whipped through the *Gypsy Song* at a speed that had Toscanini's eyebrows climbing his forehead. For once *he* had to labor to keep up.

Gypsy girls danced, gypsy men banged away at their tambourines, I sang a few lines with one of the officers, and then it was time for Escamillo's entrance. I'd made up my mind to keep my back turned to Duchon during his entire aria, so I sat down at the table and stared determinedly offstage—at Caruso, who was standing there insouciantly wearing a chamber pot on his head.

I kept my mouth covered with my hand until I was sure the laugh was under control, and then gazed blankly out at the audience. On the other side of the stage, the chorus was singing *Vivat! vivat le Torero!* But when Duchon's cue came—nothing. Something ran through the other singers on the stage—a gasp, a quick intake of breath—and I swiveled in my chair to see what was the matter.

There stood Duchon, his eyes big as saucers and his face *horribly* contorted, one hand grasping his throat. The other arm he held straight out in front of him, one finger pointing at *me*. He staggered to center stage; one of the chorus men tried to help him, but Duchon shrugged him off.

No sound came out of his mouth, but his lips kept forming the word *You!*—over and over again. I wanted to stand up, but my legs were paralyzed. Duchon staggered across the stage toward me, still mouthing *You, you!*—and then collapsed across my lap. The chair gave way under the sudden extra weight, spilling both of us to the floor.

His huge body lay over me, twitching, twitching—until somebody thought to yell, "Curtain! Close the curtain!"

Twitching.

□ **9** □ It was the throat spray, of course. Someone had put something in the spray that turned Philippe Duchon's throat into a raging furnace.

Dr. Curtis had rummaged through Emmy's saddlebag and provided what immediate relief he could before hustling Duchon off to a hospital. The rest of us watched them go in a state of shock. What a vicious, *ugly* thing to do—there was no imaginable way it could have been an accident. Attacking a singer's throat . . . unthinkable, simply unthinkable!

But somebody had thought of it. Somebody right there.

Duchon had been all right when we started the second act; I'd heard him say *And she didn't even apologize* right before the curtains opened. That meant that sometime during the *Gypsy Song* or right before he made his entrance he'd used the spray—and set his throat on fire. That was bad enough, but also it was clear Duchon thought *I* was the one who had tampered with the spray. The way he came straight at me across the stage, the accusing finger, his mouthing *You!* at me—no doubt about it, Duchon was blaming me.

Gatti-Casazza had acted with an alacrity that surprised everyone. He'd recovered from his shock first and announced in a voice that brooked no disagreement that the performance would continue. He told an ashen-faced Jimmy Freeman to get ready. He decided that picking up where we'd left off would simply emphasize Duchon's scary collapse and so we would start the second act over, meaning I'd have to sing the *Gypsy Song* again. Toscanini gave him no argument; he was quite willing to let Gatti shoulder this one alone.

"The spray bottle?" Caruso asked weakly.

"Dr. Curtis took it with him to have the contents analyzed," Gatti said. "Do not use your own spray, Enrico—it too may have been tampered with, no? And take that ridiculous object off your head!" He came over to me and placed his hands on my shoulders. "You are not hurt, Gerry? Duchon is a heavy man, I know."

It seemed to me he should have inquired about that

121

before he started announcing what we were going to do, but nobody was thinking straight yet. I was feeling a little dizzy and I couldn't seem to stop trembling, but I wasn't *hurt*. I told him I could go on, feeling only slightly like a martyr.

"Try this," said Emmy Destinn, holding an open ammonia bottle under my nose. I made a noise and pushed the bad smell away, but it did help. The dizziness left. And then Scotti was there, back from wherever he'd disappeared to, wrapping both arms around me and *willing* my trembling to stop.

Gatti went out in front of the curtain and made the necessary announcement. He downplayed Duchon's collapse, saying only that he was indisposed. Then he enthusiastically informed the audience that they were in for a special treat, that they were going to witness the début performance in a major role of that rising young baritone, Mr. James Freeman. He was trying to generate some curiosity about Duchon's replacement, but from behind the curtain I couldn't tell whether he was succeeding or not.

We started again. This time I sang the *Gypsy Song* at a much slower tempo and Toscanini, God bless him, followed me. Not that it mattered much; everyone was only half-listening anyway, including me. I was worried about Jimmy. In fact, I was willing to wager that everyone on the stage was thinking of that untried baritone who was about to step into Philippe Duchon's shoes.

And step he did! These weren't the most auspicious of circumstances for a young singer's début, but Jimmy didn't even hesitate; he sang his aria like the professional he was. He looked good and he sounded good; I was proud of him. It was a pity he had to sing his first major role in a performance that had such a cloud over it, but the audience greeted his performance warmly and Jimmy enjoyed his first taste of real success.

That gave us all a lift. Toscanini picked up the tempo and we went through the rest of the act with something like our previous *élan*. (I'd have to tell Jimmy he'd saved the performance.) I did my vamping dance with the castanets, and Caruso did nothing at all to distract me. No more pranks tonight.

I came off the stage feeling flushed and excited, the way a good performance always leaves me; nothing like the healing power of music. I was surprised to find David Belasco and Morris Gest waiting in the wings. "Didn't you watch from out front?"

"We did," Belasco said dryly, "until we were ordered to come back here."

"Ordered? By whom?"

"By that man." Belasco gestured majestically toward a tall, lanky stranger with a derby perched on the back of his head. "That is none other than Lieutenant Michael O'Halloran of the New York Detective Bureau. We have met before."

"*I* never met him before," Morris said. "And I'd just as soon skip it this time. But since we were backstage during the time somebody diddled with that throat spray, he says we gotta hang around."

"But who called the police?" I asked.

"Mr. Gatti. That's a surprise, isn't it? The lieutenant brought some of his buddies with him. Look there," Morris pointed, "and there. And over there."

I looked at the three other policemen, asking questions of anyone they could buttonhole. I felt a chill run down my back and said, "I must go—I have to change." I ran up the stairs to my dressing room.

Gatti had called the police! I approved, wholeheartedly; I had no desire to go on working with someone capable of such a vicious act as the one we witnessed tonight, whoever he might be. But I was surprised at the speed with which Gatti had acted, and even that he'd called the police at all. I'd have thought his first reaction would have been to keep things quiet, to avoid scandal. Impressive, the way ne'd stepped in and taken charge.

What had been in the spray? Was the damage permanent, would Duchon be able to sing again? I was especially anxious for the villain to be found since Duchon had accused me, and he'd done so in front of a packed house! Three thousand people had watched him accuse me. How could he think I'd do such a thing? Just because I'd thrown those silly castanets at him, that didn't mean—oh, it was absurd.

The last two acts of *Carmen* went well enough. The brief tussle between Jimmy and Caruso in the third act was not convincing—they'd never rehearsed it together, after all. But that was a minor matter; the important thing was that Jimmy Freeman had clearly established his right to a place on the stage of the Metropolitan Opera. After the performance was over I gave him a big kiss and told him he was wonderful. Everyone was happy for Jimmy, but the shadow of what had happened to Duchon still hung over all the congratulations. Not a début to be remembered with undiluted joy.

The police lieutenant, O'Halloran, had been busy during the last two acts. Scotti told me O'Halloran and his men had been questioning stagehands and maids and valets and chorus singers as to their whereabouts up to the time Duchon made his entrance in Act II. According to the baritone's valet, Duchon had sprayed his throat once upon arriving at the opera house but had not asked for the bottle again until immediately before his entrance.

"This means," Scotti mused somberly, "that the spray is safe when he brings it here, no? Someone backstage is responsible." He was sitting in his usual chair by my dressing table while I creamed the make-up off my face. "Everyone who is backstage before the first act, during the first act, and during the first-act intermission—any one of them can do it."

"Which is just about everybody," I pointed out. "Even Dr. Curtis could have done it."

He cocked an eyebrow at me. "You suspect Dr. Curtis?"

"Certainly not! I just named him as the most *un*likely person I could think of. But even he was back here, Toto."

Someone knocked and quickly opened the dressing room door; it was one of the policemen I'd seen downstairs. "Miss Farrar? Lieutenant O'Halloran would like you to come down to the stage as soon as you've changed."

Oh, wonderful. "Couldn't this wait until tomorrow? I'm exhausted."

"No, ma'am, I'm afraid it can't." He looked at Scotti. "You are . . . ?"

"Antonio Scotti," Toto announced regally.

"Ah, Mr. Scotti, yes. The lieutenant wants you to come down too, please. Now if you'll tell me where I can find Mr. Caruso, I'll be on my way."

"On the men's side," I said, and sent the maid with him to show him the way. "I hope it doesn't take long—I really do want to get out of here."

"I also. Are you almost ready?"

"Heavens, no. And I am *not* going to hurry."

But I did. I wanted to get the interview over with so I could go home and crawl into bed and not get up for seventeen days.

It turned out to be a sort of mass interview. The fourth-act set had been struck and chairs placed in a semicircle on the stage. We made quite an assembly: me, Scotti, Caruso, Emmy Destinn, Pasquale Amato, Jimmy Freeman, Osgood Springer, David Belasco, Morris Gest, Gatti-Casazza, and Toscanini. Everyone looked as resentful of being there as I felt.

Lieutenant O'Halloran was standing with his back to the auditorium, facing our semicircle. The other three policemen moved around behind us here and there, making everyone nervous. The lieutenant cleared his throat. "I know you are all wondering about Philippe Duchon's condition. One of my men just got back from the hospital, and the news isn't good. Dr. Curtis says the vocal cords are destroyed—Duchon won't be singing any more. In fact, he won't even be able to talk. The damage is irreversible."

We sat in stunned silence for a long time; I couldn't even hear myself breathing. I had wondered whether Duchon would be able to sing again, but not really; I mean, I kept thinking he would recover or Dr. Curtis could operate or *something*. I'd been denying the possibility that the voice might be gone forever. But the lieutenant had just scotched that.

Finally Scotti stirred. "So easily," he murmured.

I knew what he was thinking. Every singer on the stage was thinking the same thing. *If a lifetime of singing can be ended that easily—then how safe am I?*

Lieutenant O'Halloran went on: "The substance added to the throat spray was ordinary ammonia, in sufficient quantity and of sufficient strength to burn the lining of his throat and trickle down to the vocal cords. Since the ammonia was in a bottle with an atomizer spray screwed on tightly, it evidently didn't give off enough odor to warn Duchon."

Ammonia. Emmy Destinn had held a bottle of ammonia under my nose when I felt faint.

"I've asked you folks to stay," Lieutenant O'Halloran said, "because most of you have some sort of grudge against Philippe Duchon. You—"

"*I* have no grudge against Duchon!" Caruso cried.

"I said *most* of you, Mr. Caruso. Maybe even all of you—now wait a minute, wait a minute!"

Several people had started to protest at once, but it was David Belasco who won the floor. "Lieutenant, I have never even met Philippe Duchon!" he objected. "Why would I possibly want to harm him?"

"You're here because you're a witness who was backstage during the crucial time, Mr. Belasco. You are all witnesses, to some degree or other. As to motive, all I've had time to find out is that there was a lot of bad feeling between Moan-sewer Duchon and just about everybody else here. I don't know all the details yet, and I sure don't know which are the important ones. But you were all backstage sometime during the period the ammonia was added to the spray bottle. Now I want you all to think back. When was the last time you saw the bottle?"

Caruso shrugged. "How can we tell? They both look alike."

"Both? What both?"

"*My* spray bottle and Duchon's. Uncle Hummy took mine by mistake and gave it to Duchon. I had to send Mario back to the Knickerbocker for more."

O'Halloran stared at him. "Uncle . . . Hummy, did you say? Who's he?"

Caruso explained, and told about the confusion of the two bottles. The lieutenant thought that over and said, "Mr. Caruso, do you realize what that means? That means the bottle with the ammonia in it may have been meant for *you*."

"*No*," we all said emphatically.

The lieutenant looked surprised. "Why are you so sure?"

Emmy Destinn spoke up. "Because Caruso does not make enemies, Lieutenant. Not that kind, at any rate. Oh, we have all wanted to strangle him at one time or another—"

"Emmy!"

"—but not seriously and not for long. Duchon, on the other hand, made an enemy every time he opened his mouth. That ammonia was meant for him, no question."

"She is right, Lieutenant," Gatti-Casazza said as a murmur of agreement ran across the stage. "No one wishes Caruso harm. Duchon was the, ah, intended victim."

"Mm, maybe. So where's this Uncle Hummy now?" It turned out no one had seen him since the opening of the second act, and the lieutenant was suddenly very interested in the old man. "What's his real name?" No one knew. "Well, then, where does he live?" No one knew that either. "Then how about a description?" he asked in exasperation. Gatti provided a description, and O'Halloran sent one of his men to start the search.

"Surely you do not suspect Uncle Hummy," Scotti protested. "He is a harmless old man!"

"Maybe he is and maybe he isn't, but he did handle Moan-sewer Duchon's spray bottle. Where's your own spray bottle, Mr. Caruso?"

"In the dressing room."

Lieutenant O'Halloran sent another of his men up to fetch it. "We have three bottles, right?" he asked. "Mr. Caruso's original bottle, Mr. Duchon's original bottle," (he'd given up on *Moan-sewer*) "and Mr. Caruso's second bottle, the replacement for the one Uncle Hummy supposedly picked up by mistake. Dr. Curtis gave us the bottle

with the ammonia in it, and if Mr. Caruso's bottle is in his
dressing room—there should be one more bottle around
here somewhere. Anybody know where it is?''

Nobody did, of course, so the lieutenant put his third
man to work looking for it. The second man came back
with Caruso's bottle. Bottles, bottles, bottles! What would
finding the third bottle tell him? I wished he would get on
with it.

He did. He walked over to where I was sitting, planted
himself squarely in front of me, and said, ''Miss Farrar, I
have to tell you—right now you are my prime suspect.''
The first words he ever spoke to me.

''That's ridiculous!'' Jimmy Freeman shouted.

''*Stupido*,'' Pasquale Amato muttered.

I agreed with both of them. I was also pleased to see
that everyone else on the stage was looking disgusted.

Lieutenant O'Halloran counted off on his fingers. ''Number one, Mr. Duchon accused you of being a German
sympathizer.'' Well, well—the lieutenant *had* been busy.
''Number two, you threw your castanets at him hard enough
to draw blood.''

''She throws a chair at me once,'' Caruso sighed.

''And a vase of flowers at me,'' Toscanini smiled.

''And an open bottle of wine at me,'' Amato added,
''alas.''

''I am lucky,'' Scotti said. ''At me she throws nothing
harder than a pillow.''

I gave O'Halloran my tenth-best smile. ''I throw things,
Lieutenant.'' The first words I ever spoke to *him*.

''*Number three*,'' he plowed on, determined to make his
point, ''Duchon himself accused you of doctoring his throat
spray. The way I get it, he staggered out on the stage and
pointed his finger at you. He was going for you when he
collapsed. Or did I get it wrong?''

A dead silence descended over the stage; there was no
way of arguing that point away. Finally I said, ''No, you
didn't get it wrong, Lieutenant. But Duchon did. I didn't
put ammonia in the spray bottle. Good heavens, I'm a
singer myself! I couldn't do a thing like that. Besides, I
don't carry ammonia around with me!''

"I do," Emmy spoke up. "At least, I did tonight. There's a bottle in the medicine bag."

Lieutenant O'Halloran pounced on that. "Is there any missing? Was the bottle full when you got here?"

Emmy wasn't sure. "You'll have to ask Dr. Curtis—it is his medicine bag."

"Was this bag out of your possession anytime during the evening?"

"Oh, I put it down three or four times. While I was waiting for Pasquale."

"Pasquale?"

"Me, Lieutenant," Amato said. "Emmy carries the medicine, to help Dr. Curtis. I am not in the opera house for a few weeks because I have been ill. So I go visit and say hello, I am back—you understand?"

"So the bag was left unattended several times during the evening. Meaning anyone could have taken the ammonia bottle." He looked directly at me. "Anyone."

"Oh, cut it out, Lieutenant," Morris Gest snarled unexpectedly. "You're barking up the wrong tree. Gerry wouldn't seriously harm anyone—it's not her way."

O'Halloran raised one eyebrow. "A lady who throws things?"

Toscanini chimed in, "But that is precisely *why* she does no serious harm! She lets the anger out often, in little spurts. This does give her the unfortunate reputation of being stubborn, selfish, unreasonable—"

"Thank you very much," I snapped.

"—but she does not let the anger, eh, *pile up*—you see? She does not hold it in and let it grow and become dangerous. *Per dio*, Lieutenant—Gerry is the *last* person you should suspect!"

T'amo, you funny man.

"Mm, that's as may be," the lieutenant was saying, "but we'll save that for later. Right now, I want to go over everything that happened here up to the time Duchon pointed his finger at Miss Farrar. I want you to think back over what you saw, and be sure to check each other on details. Mr. Caruso, you start."

That sounded like a simple enough procedure, but it

turned out that nobody remembered anything the same way. It was incredible, the number of different versions of the same incident that came out! Even simple little things, like where Emmy had put down the medicine bag in my dressing room, I distinctly remembered seeing her drape it over the back of a chair, Scotti said she put it on the dressing table, Emmy claimed she put it on the floor because she remembered having to stoop over to pick it up, and Amato didn't remember her putting it down at all!

Everything that had happened came out that same garbled way. Osgood Springer said my castanets had hit Duchon at the corner of the mouth (it was the hairline), David Belasco said he'd seen Scotti backstage at a time Scotti insisted he was still out front, Toscanini said Dr. Curtis was attending to Duchon on the right side of the stage when in fact it was the left, Jimmy Freeman said he didn't get into costume until the first act was well under way (I could have sworn I'd seen him dressed earlier than that), Caruso thought he saw Gatti go into Duchon's dressing room but Gatti said he hadn't been upstairs all evening, Emmy was convinced that Uncle Hummy's new tweed coat was brown instead of gray, Amato said he'd bumped into Morris Gest backstage before the first act but Morris said it was *after*, and on and on and on. Lieutenant O'Halloran was beginning to get a glazed look in his eye.

David Belasco finally spoke up and put an end to it. "If I may make a suggestion, Lieutenant," he said with that surprisingly soft-voiced authority that got him attention whenever he wanted it, "these people have had a long and stressful evening. They're tired and upset. A good night's sleep can sometimes work wonders toward clearing the memory. Perhaps we can continue this tomorrow?"

I was glad to see Lieutenant O'Halloran was a man who could take suggestion. "Not a bad idea, Mr. Belasco— we're not getting very far this way. Go on home, folks, and thanks for your help. Somebody'll be around to talk to you tomorrow."

A cheering thought. Morris Gest headed straight for me. "Are you all right, Gerry?"

"Dead on my feet, but otherwise unscarred. I'm all right, Morris—don't worry."

He gave my arm a little squeeze and went back to collect Belasco. Toscanini gave me an encouraging wink and Scotti came over to help me with my coat.

Caruso went up to O'Halloran. "Lieutenant, you worry about these conflicting stories, no? Do not distress yourself. *I* will help you get the truth! I assist you in your questioning and—"

"You'll do nothing of the sort, Mr. Caruso. You will keep your nose out of it this time. You will do no 'investigating' on your own. None at all. Understand?"

"But I help you before!" Caruso protested. "You tell me I am a help! You stand right here on this stage and you say—"

"Mr. Caruso, listen to me. Listen carefully. Don't meddle. Don't ask questions, don't eavesdrop, don't read other people's mail. Don't do any of those things you did the last time we met. Whatever occurs to you—don't do it. If I catch you playing detective even *once*, I'm going to throw you in the pokey for obstructing justice."

Caruso's mouth dropped open and his eyes grew huge. "You do not do such a thing!"

O'Halloran leered. "Just give me the excuse. I mean it, Mr. Caruso. Keep out of it *completely*. I'll tolerate no interference from you this time."

"But . . . but . . . but . . ." Caruso sputtered.

"No buts. No nothing. *Keep out of it!* Do you understand?"

Emmy and Amato exchanged a knowing look, and without speaking a word marched over to Caruso. They each took an arm and gently steered the sputtering tenor off the stage.

That "last time" they'd been talking about had been just a little over four years ago, when a small-time impresario had been killed shortly before the world première of *La Fanciulla del West*. Caruso had taken it upon himself to find the killer, of all things. I wasn't involved in it, but Emmy Destinn told me Caruso had poked and pried and made such a pest of himself they were all ready to drop

him into the East River. But his bumbling around *had*
helped turn up the killer, and I guess he was thinking of
doing the same thing again—until Lieutenant O'Halloran
wrote paid to *that* little plan.

"Ready?" Scotti said. "One good thing about all this—no
fans waiting at the stage door at this hour, yes? They are
all home in bed like good sensible people."

But he was wrong. Mildredandphoebe were outside,
huddling together against the cold. "What happened?"
Mildred said instead of hello. "The doorkeeper wouldn't
let us in—he said something about a police investigation."

"Police," Phoebe nodded.

I was so tired I was ready to drop, but they'd been
waiting there in the cold all this time and I couldn't just
brush them off. I told them as briefly as I could what had
happened.

"That's terrible!" Mildred exclaimed. ("Terrible!"
Phoebe echoed.) "And they have no idea who did it?"

"Oh, they have an idea," I said dryly, "but they're
wrong. Look, I'll talk to you about this some other time.
Right now, I am dreadfully tired."

"Perhaps in a few days?" Scotti suggested.

"Of course," Mildred agreed quickly. "Take care of
yourself, Miss Farrar." Phoebe nodded vehemently; they
really are nice girls.

It wasn't until I got home that I remembered David
Belasco had said something to me about a late supper—but
that was before Duchon had made his dramatic entrance in
Act II. Belasco must have forgotten about it, as I had.
Fortunately.

"*Riposi bene,*" Scotti whispered, and kissed me good-
night.

□ **10** □ I didn't sleep well, but I rose at my usual hour and got in my daily practice—scales, *lieder,* a few arias. Scotti called and tried to persuade me to come to the Knickerbocker for lunch, but I didn't want to go out. I knew I was going to have to talk to Lieutenant O'Halloran sometime during the day, and I didn't feel like being sociable with that impending interview hanging over my head.

One thing I did was write a congratulatory note to Jimmy Freeman. Poor Jimmy. He'd done a remarkable thing last night, taking over for Duchon that way—under circumstances that would have shaken even a seasoned singer. But he'd done it, and he'd done it well. Last night was a big step forward for Jimmy, and we should all have been fussing over him afterward instead of sitting in a semicircle arguing about who saw what when.

Sometime during the morning I called the hospital and inquired about Philippe Duchon's condition: no change. Also, no visitors. I tried to imagine what Duchon must be going through, not only the physical pain but also the devastating knowledge that his life as a singer was over. Not even during those moments when I outright hated him had I ever wished so horrible a fate for him. I called Wadley & Smythe and ordered two dozen orchids to be sent to the hospital. Maybe he'd remember.

It was late afternoon before Lieutenant O'Halloran arrived. The maid had to ask him twice for his derby hat; he was obviously used to wearing it indoors. "Well, Lieutenant," I said once he'd settled on a sofa, "have you come to arrest me?"

He gave a lopsided grin. "Now, Miss Farrar, I just want to ask you some questions."

"Oh, is that all? And here I was thinking that last night you virtually accused me of putting ammonia in Duchon's throat spray. Did I dream that?"

He sighed. "Miss Farrar, one thing I've found out today is that you and Duchon fought like cats and dogs—and that alone makes me think you're not the one who tampered with the spray. Someone bent on destroying a man would be more circumspect. But I'm not allowed to go on hunches. I have to deal with evidence, and I have to account to my superior for what I do—you understand?''

I didn't believe that at all; I thought he was trying to put me off my guard. I sat down in the chair farthest away from the sofa and said, ''Very well, Lieutenant, ask your questions.''

He gave me a mildly reproachful look and left the sofa for a chair nearer mine. ''First of all, tell me what you and Duchon fought about.''

''Everything. Philippe Duchon is arrogant and overbearing, and impossible to work with.'' The lieutenant wanted details, so I told him about Duchon's refusing to rehearse *Carmen,* his presuming to pick out the numbers I was to sing in our joint concert—now canceled, I suddenly realized—and a number of similar things. ''But Lieutenant, that's only half the story. We disagreed a lot, yes, but we always made the effort to work together. Duchon is as adept at apologizing as he is at causing trouble. He'd bring me flowers, take me to lunch, write me little notes—''

''Like this one?'' He pulled out a notebook and found the single sheet of paper he'd slipped between the pages.

It was the note Duchon had written last night, instructing me not to stay seated during his aria. ''How did you get this?'' I asked.

''Never mind how I got it. Is that what you were fighting about last night?''

''That started it, yes.''

''Miss Farrar—why did you throw your castanets at him?''

Oh, I didn't like this! We were getting into a personal area that was really none of the police's business. What had tipped the scale for me last night was that one final insult, when Duchon accused me of enjoying seeing Jimmy Freeman make a fool of himself in Delmonico's. The story made me look bad, it made Jimmy look bad, but—worst of all—it did *not* make Duchon look bad.

So I told that nosy police detective that I didn't remember. ''You must understand, Lieutenant, Duchon was a constant irritant—he was always doing something to make me angry. It could have been anything.''

"The way I hear it, he said you enjoyed watching James Freeman make a fool of himself.''

Oh, for . . . I felt like throwing something at him. If he already knew the answer, then why did he bother asking me? To see what I would say, obviously. "That could be right,'' I smiled coolly.

"Miss Farrar,'' O'Halloran said in a way that let me see how patient he was being, "I know about the rivalry between your protégé and Philippe Duchon. I know about the scene in Delmonico's. What I don't know is your version of it. So why don't you tell me?''

Jimmy must have already told him about Delmonico's, or perhaps one of the people *I* had told about it. "What did you do, Lieutenant, talk to everybody else before you came here? Were you saving me for last?'' He just smiled, so I went on and told him about Jimmy's ineffectual verbal attack on Duchon in Delmonico's. In fact, I ended up telling him just about everything he wanted to know; he knew it all anyway.

When I'd finished, I asked him a question. "How is all this going to help you find the killer?''

"The *killer*?''

"Killer, yes. Killing Duchon's voice is the same as killing the man. For all practical intents and purposes, Duchon's life is over. He can't sing. He'll never manage an opera company without being able to talk. He can't even coach. So what's left for him? You don't spend your life creating music and then switch over to permanent silence without batting an eye. That's *death*, Lieutenant.''

"Mm, I suppose it is, in a way.''

"So why aren't you trying to find out who put the ammonia in the throat spray? Why do you keep asking about irrelevant matters like that little scene in Delmonico's?''

"We might not find an eyewitness to the act, so now I'm looking for motives. Who had a reason to want Duchon out of the picture, that sort of thing.''

"But surely you don't mean—" I caught myself in time and clamped my lips together.

It didn't make any difference. "Go on and say it, Miss Farrar. Surely I don't mean James Freeman? Ask yourself one question: Who gains the most from Duchon's removal from the scene?"

"That's absurd, Lieutenant. Jimmy Freeman is a sweet boy who wouldn't harm a fly."

He didn't think that worth commenting on. "Freeman was scheduled to sing Pasquale Amato's roles while Amato was ill, until Duchon showed up and took his job away from him. Freeman was demoted to standing by for his rival, and Duchon was planning to sing at the Met next year—making Freeman's chances for getting ahead even slimmer. And there was bad feeling between the two, on the verge of erupting into something nasty, looks like. Last night Duchon wanted Gatti-Casazza to get rid of Freeman, didn't he? Freeman has a motive, all right."

"Oh, Lieutenant, *everybody* has a motive if you want to be picky about it. I'm telling you, *nobody* liked the man. Why single out Jimmy Freeman?"

He grunted. "Unfortunately, you've got a point. Everyone does have some kind of motive—including you, don't forget. Gatti-Casazza was worried that Duchon was after his job, for instance."

"He needn't have been. The board of directors would never have fired Gatti to hire Duchon."

"But could he be sure of that? And if Gatti went, what would happen to Toscanini—who was already at loggerheads with Duchon?"

"Maestro Toscanini has a place at the Metropolitan for as long as he wants. He'll leave only when *he* chooses to go." Not for another hundred years, I hoped.

"Then there's your manager. Duchon cheated him, and from what I can find out, nobody cheats Morris Gest and gets away with it."

I was silent. That was true.

"Duchon and Emmy Destinn have been enemies for years, dating back to their singing together at . . ." He flipped through his notebook until he found what he wanted.

"At Covent Garden. Her reasons for disliking him seem to be about the same as yours. She told me their working relationship had settled down into a good, dull, solid hatred."

"Ha! Good for her."

"The other two baritones, Amato and Scotti—they were both in danger of losing their roles to Duchon." He sighed. "Ten years ago I wouldn't have believed something like that could be an adequate motive for attacking a man. But that was before I'd worked with opera people. Now I know better, if you'll excuse my saying so. So I'd have to say both Scotti and Amato had motives too. In fact, about the only ones who don't have motives are David Belasco and Enrico Caruso. Belasco didn't even know Duchon. Caruso got along with Duchon better than anyone else managed to, but he still got mad enough one night to ask Gatti-Casazza to replace him. That was during a performance of . . ." He started flipping through his notebook again.

"The Huguenots," I said.

He couldn't find the page. "That sounds right. But even so, Caruso could never stay mad long enough to carry out an act of retaliation."

I smiled, halfway meaning it. "You sound as if you know Rico well."

"Well enough," he said dryly. "I know he fancies himself a detective. If you're his friend, Miss Farrar, you'll convince him I meant what I said last night. I'll lock him up if I catch him snooping this time."

"But you wouldn't really."

"Yes, I would," he said simply—and I believed him, Lord help us. "Now, Miss Farrar," the lieutenant went on, "I want to go over your movements last night one more time. Don't rush; try to remember everything you saw and name everybody who saw you. Take your time, get it straight."

How tedious. I told him basically the same thing I'd told him the night before, but with more detail. He'd interrupt now and then to get something clarified, and he asked a few questions when I'd finished—such as did I actually see Uncle Hummy pick up Caruso's throat spray or did I only hear about it afterwards? I'd only heard about it. "By the way," I said, "have you found Uncle Hummy?"

"Not yet," he admitted. "Everyone at the Metropolitan knows who he is but nobody knows where he lives."

"Well, I shouldn't worry, if I were you. Uncle Hummy can't stay away from opera very long. He'll show up soon. And Lieutenant, you're wrong about Jimmy Freeman. He didn't put the ammonia in the spray. I'm as sure of his innocence as I am of my own."

He scratched his cheek with a long bony finger. "But I'm not sure of either, you see. No matter how many other motives I'm able to dig up, we still can't get away from the fact that it was *you* Duchon accused."

"That's *ridiculous*!" I stormed. "He was just guessing! If he *knew* I'd tampered with the spray, would he have gone ahead and used it?"

"But he must have had some reason for suspecting you—"

"He was angry with me! I'd just thrown my castanets at him!"

"True, but there might be something more. I'm going to ask him about it as soon as he's able to write out his answers. Dr. Curtis says a couple more days. Well, I think that's all for now. I'll be going. My coat and hat?"

I called the maid, and just like that he was gone. No thank you for your help or I'm sorry I took up so much of your time, no attempt to reassure me or promise to keep me informed. I didn't think I liked this Lieutenant O'Halloran very much. But whether I liked him or not, I was going to cooperate in every way he asked me to. A person capable of destroying a singer's voice was capable of anything. What if that person ever got mad at *me*?

But who was it? I couldn't imagine any of the people I knew doing a thing like that. Guns, poison, knives, nooses, heavy clubs for banging people over the head—I could imagine certain people I knew using those; heavens, I'd thought of using them myself on occasion. But *going for the voice*—that was simply unimaginable. Yet someone had done it. I sat down at my writing table and took out a piece of paper and wrote the word *Suspects* at the top.

Lieutenant O'Halloran seemed inclined to eliminate Belasco and Caruso, and I could see no reason to disagree with him. So who was the first suspect? Well, there was no way around it: I wrote down my own name. Next came Jimmy Freeman, as preposterous as that might be. A thought occurred to me: If Jimmy Freeman belonged on a list of suspects, shouldn't Mr. Springer's name be there as well? He had a big investment in Jimmy. I didn't think Toscanini had any real motive, but as long as O'Halloran considered him a suspect, he should be included. I ended up listing just about everybody: *Geraldine Farrar, Jimmy Freeman, Osgood Springer, Arturo Toscanini, Giulio Gatti-Casazza, Morris Gest, Emmy Destinn, Pasquale Amato, Antonio Scotti, Dr. Holbrook Curtis.*

Once I had my list, I didn't have the foggiest notion what to do with it. I couldn't believe any one of those people was guilty. It must have been a chorus singer. Or a stagehand. Perhaps a member of the orchestra? Or someone from the audience had sneaked backstage without being seen and . . . oh, how absurd! I went back to studying the list, thinking vaguely about the process of elimination. But when you came right down to it, there was only one name there I could eliminate with absolute certainty—my own.

I was still mulling it over when the doorbell rang and Enrico Caruso erupted into the room before the maid had a chance to announce him. "Gerry! You are alone? *Bene*, we talk!" He was carrying a small rectangular box tied with bright yellow ribbon that he put down on my writing table while he shrugged out of his overcoat.

"What's this?" I said, picking up the box.

"A birthday gift for you. Brr, I am cold! Do you have coffee?"

"It's not my birthday, Rico."

"I know, I know! But I think if Lieutenant O'Halloran is here, I need reason for coming to see you. I must have coffee!" He charged off to the kitchen to ask the maid to make some.

I opened the box. It contained a slip of paper that read: *I.O.U. one birthday gift, E. Caruso.*

He came back from the kitchen. "Is he come yet?"

"O'Halloran? He left just a little while ago."

"Do you know what he does? He sends one of his men to me this morning, to show me big, heavy manacles." Caruso made a face. "*Manacles!* The man, he tells me they are what I wear when he leads me through the streets to the jailhouse if the lieutenant finds out I am 'snooping' again. Snooping, that is what they call it!"

I had to laugh. "You don't suppose the lieutenant is trying to intimidate you, do you?"

"He succeeds," Caruso nodded, wide-eyed. "He means it, Gerry—he puts me in the, ah, pokey if I investigate." Then a sly look came over his face that immediately put me on my guard. "But he does not say *you* cannot investigate!"

"I! What do I know about investigating?"

"It is not difficult, Gerry. I do it before, I know how. I help."

"But Lieutenant O'Halloran—"

"Yes, yes, you see?" he cried excitedly. "*I* cannot investigate—so I stay in the background, I look innocent and unconcerned. The lieutenant keeps one eye on *me*, he never notices that you conduct investigation of your own. Is good plan, no?"

It was a *crazy* plan. But Caruso's enthusiasm had a contagious quality to it. Farrar and Caruso, Consulting Detectives! I laughed out loud at the thought of it—but I didn't say no. "Rico, what would I *do*? I can't ask questions the way the police do."

"You can, you can! And people we know talk to you more freely than they do to Lieutenant O'Halloran. You listen. You read things. You watch."

"I snoop, in other words."

Caruso let loose a whole arpeggio of sighs. "Why does everyone like that word so much?" he complained. "Eh, well, you snoop. Then we talk over what you find out and decide what you do next."

My maid Bella came in with the coffee, poured us each a cup, and left us alone again. What Caruso proposed was patently ludicrous. The very idea, Geraldine Farrar doing

the police's work for them! It would make a good plot for
a farce. But what if I could find something Lieutenant
O'Halloran could not? Surely it wouldn't *hurt* for me to
ask a question or two?

I thought about it for a while and then gave in. As long
as Lieutenant O'Halloran seriously considered me a suspect, I'd better do something to protect myself.

"But understand this, Rico," I said. "I'm not going to
do anything *outré* like hide under Jimmy Freeman's bed to
see if he talks in his sleep. *I'll* have the final word on what I
do and don't do. Will you agree to that?"

"*Certo,* yes," he answered quickly. Too quickly.

"I'm not just talking, Rico. *I* make the decisions."

"I agree, I agree! That is the way it should be!"

Well, we'd see. "So what do we do first?"

"First, we make a list of all possible suspects. Detectives always make lists."

"D'you mean like this one?" I handed him the list I'd
already made out.

Caruso whooped and caught me in a bear hug that
almost cracked my ribs. "I *know* you make good detective! You already start without me!" When he read my
name at the top of the list he rather ostentatiously insisted
on adding his own to the bottom.

By unspoken agreement we ignored the first and last
names and argued over the rest of them. "I don't think any
of these people did it," I said.

"Nor I," Caruso agreed. "So perhaps we prove they
did not do it? Then Lieutenant O'Halloran looks elsewhere."

I groaned; it sounded like an impossible job. "I just
now thought of something—there should be one other
name on that list. Uncle Hummy."

"*Ridicolo.*"

"I agree. But isn't it equally ridiculous to suspect any of
those other people?"

"What is his motive?"

"I have no idea. Duchon was using him to run errands,
so they must have made some sort of peace. But Uncle
Hummy was there at the right time, Rico."

He scribbled the old man's name on the list. "Eh, well,

we talk to him the next time he comes to the opera house.''

''*We* talk to him?''

Caruso slapped his forehead. ''*Per dio!* I must remember—stay out of things, watch quietly, say nothing. It will be hard, very hard!''

I could believe that. ''So how do we go about eliminating names from this list?''

''Choose one name, start with him. Or her, if you choose Emmy.''

''Him.'' There was one name I wanted to eliminate right away. I picked up the telephone and gave the operator Scotti's number. ''Toto? I want to ask you one question.''

''Anything, *cara mia.*''

''Did you put the ammonia in Duchon's throat spray?''

''*What?* What do you think I am?''

''Yes or no, Toto.''

''No!''

''That's good enough for me. *Ciao.*'' I hung up.

Caruso threw his arms up in the air. ''Is that what you call investigating? *Impossibile!*''

''He said he didn't do it, and I believe him. I've thought of something I could investigate, though.'' I told him about the note Duchon had written telling me not to stay seated while he was singing the *Toreador Song.* ''Lieutenant O'Halloran has that note now. Not that there's any reason he shouldn't have it. But when I asked him where he got it, he wouldn't tell me. Don't you find that peculiar?''

Caruso jumped on it like a starving dog on a bone; it was a starting point. ''Very peculiar, very peculiar indeed! When do you last see the note, Gerry? Think back.''

''I've been trying to remember, and I think it was when I gave it to Emmy to read. I don't believe she gave it back.''

''Emmy?'' Caruso drew his brows together. ''Why does she keep the note, and then why does she pass it on to the police?''

''And why is it even important?'' I didn't think it was important at all; but like my partner, I was eager to find a starting point. ''I'll talk to Emmy, see what I can learn.''

"*Bene, bene.* Now. Last night—all those conflicting stories? Perhaps we, eh, unconflict a few?"

"Which ones?"

He thought a moment. "Amato and Morris Gest do not agree about the time they bumped into each other backstage. Amato says before the first ace, Morris says after. How do we find out who is right?"

"That's easy. I can ask David Belasco if Morris was with him the whole time before the opera started."

"Yes! *Magnifico!*" Caruso gave a little bounce of joy, causing me a moment's concern for the chair. "You talk to Mr. Belasco, yes."

"Also, I'd like to try to pin down exactly when Jimmy Freeman got into costume," I said. "The way he told it last night, it sounded as if he didn't dress until we were well into the first act. But I'm pretty sure I saw him in costume before the opera even started."

"You must be wrong, Gerry. Jimmy, he has no need to get into costume before . . . oh." It sank in on him. "*O cielo!* Unless he knows ahead of time he sings that night?"

We were both quiet while we mulled over the significance of *that*. Then I said, "It can't be true."

Caruso looked at the list again. "What else?"

"I thought we were going to select one name and concentrate on that one at first."

He waved a hand dismissively. "Eh, a good detective must be flexible. Can you think of anything else?"

"Don't we have enough to start?"

The telephone rang. It was Scotti, demanding an explanation. Caruso decided that would be a good time to pick up his hat and coat and tiptoe out, leaving me to smooth the troubled waters as best I could.

Detectives always make lists, Caruso had said, so after a light evening meal I made another one. Only three items: Duchon's note, Jimmy's costume, Morris's whereabouts before the opera started.

Asking Emmy Destinn about Duchon's note would have to wait; Emmy was scheduled to sing that evening and I didn't want to bother her during a performance. David

Belasco would probably be at his theatre or checking on one of his other productions in town, so the question of Morris Gest's whereabouts would have to wait too.

That left Jimmy Freeman and the costume I *thought* I saw him wearing before he said he put it on. If only I could be sure! But I couldn't, which meant I'd have to find corroboration—one way or the other—from someone else. Gatti-Casazza would be tied up at the opera house all evening. I preferred not to call Scotti again, because I wasn't *quite* ready to confess I'd undertaken the role of detective. I'd explained away my earlier telephone call as a bit of foolishness I was indulging in and wasn't exactly flattered by the ease with which he accepted that explanation.

The logical person for me to ask about the time Jimmy got into costume was Mr. Springer. But he'd be sure to tell Jimmy I'd asked; besides, I was certain he'd back up his star pupil in any story Jimmy chose to tell. No, they were just too close; I needed someone disinterested. I considered asking some of the other singers in the cast of *Carmen*, or the chorus members, or the stagehands—some of them must have seen Jimmy early in the evening. But backstage gossip being what it is, it would soon be all over town that Geraldine Farrar suspected Jimmy Freeman of doing dastardly deeds, etc. No, best keep it to the circle of people O'Halloran had called together after the performance.

So who else was backstage before the opera started? Pasquale Amato, for one. I looked up his number and called, but his valet said he was asleep. Next I tried Dr. Curtis and this time was in luck. I told him what I wanted to know—whether he had seen Jimmy Freeman backstage before the performance started.

"Yes, I saw him," Dr. Curtis rasped, "him and his nanny both. Springer was busy coaching away—does he ever stop? I remember thinking what a pathetic little scene it was, since there was no chance Freeman would get to sing. Huh."

"Dr. Curtis, this is important. When you saw Jimmy, was he in costume yet?"

"Why do you want to know that?"

"I think I remember him in costume before the first act, but he says no, he didn't get dressed until later."

"So? What difference does—" He broke off suddenly as he understood what I was getting at. "You mean he wouldn't have gotten into costume early unless he'd known . . . oh, I must say, Gerry—that's pretty far-fetched. You don't seriously think Jimmy Freeman is our culprit, do you?"

"No, I don't I don't think so at all. But it's been bothering me and I'd like to prove myself wrong. *Was* he in costume when you saw him?" There was a long silence. "Dr. Curtis?"

"I'm sorry, Gerry, I just don't remember. Why don't you ask Amato? He was there. Or Emmy—she was there too."

"Emmy is singing tonight and Amato is asleep. I'll ask them tomorrow."

"Let me know what you find out."

I said I would and hung up. Suddenly I was exhausted. One telephone call and I was all detected out; it occurred to me that perhaps I'd bitten off more than I could chew. But then I glanced at the clock and was surprised to see it was already past my usual bedtime—where had the hours flown to? I was tired, that was all.

I was just getting into bed when the telephone rang. It was Caruso, wanting a "report."

"For heaven's sake, Rico, I just got started!" I protested. "I don't have anything to tell you yet."

"You have had *hours*," he insisted. "Surely you do something!"

I explained that the only person available had been Dr. Curtis and summarized our conversation for him. Then I explained what I planned to do next.

It didn't satisfy him. "You could have gone to the opera house—there you talk to Emmy, to Mr. Gatti, to *thousands* of people! You can still go! It is not late, you—"

I hung up on him. Impossible man! But he did have the sense not to call back, thank heaven for small favors.

❑ **11** ❑ Monday I got an early start. Caruso telephoned just as I was leaving, but one of the maids took the call and I was able to slip away without talking to him.

My first stop was the Hotel Astor. I'd decided to start with Pasquale Amato because he was an old friend and could be counted on to cooperate. I found him seated at a small table writing a letter; when I told him what I was doing, he put his head down on his arms and his whole body began to shake. For the life of me I couldn't tell whether he was laughing or crying.

He was doing both. "Oh, Gerry, Gerry! You let our friend Rico talk you into this, yes?"

"Not completely," I said, slightly miffed at his reaction. "He just . . . encouraged me, so to speak."

"He is afraid to play detective himself—he fears the police lieutenant and his threats of imprisonment, no? So he makes *you* do the, ah, foot work?"

"Leg work. And he's not *making* me do anything, Pasquale. All I want is to ask you a question. Now are you going to answer, or are you just going to sit there and moan and wail and laugh and cry?"

"Oh, ask your question, by all means, do ask your question," he moaned and wailed and laughed and cried.

I asked him if he'd seen Jimmy Freeman before the curtains opened on the first act of *Carmen*. He had. "Was he in costume?"

Amato squinted his eyes as he peered back into the recent past. "Yes, he was. He was ready to go . . . aha, long *before* Duchon's accident. Too long. I see."

My heart sank. I was so hoping he'd tell me my imagination was running away with me and I only thought I'd seen Jimmy in costume that early. But if Amato had seen him too, then that seemed to settle it.

Amato understood my concern. "Gerry, it means nothing. I often get into costume early myself—we all do, yes?"

"But not when we think we won't be singing that night.

146

Besides, why does Jimmy say he was not in costume before Act I when you and I both saw he was?''

''He says that? Ah. That makes a difference, yes? But perhaps he is merely embarrassed at appearing so eager. Is this not possible?''

''Possible, but not very probable.'' I thought about it a minute. ''Jimmy lied, and I can think of only one reason why he'd lie. To hide the fact that he knew ahead of time that something dreadful was going to happen to Duchon. But I can't believe it. He has to have some other reason for lying.''

''Or perhaps we are both mistaken, Gerry. Backstage before a performance—chaos, always! Perhaps we confuse the time we see him. Ask Emmy, she was there with me. And Dr. Curtis—Dr. Curtis was there! Ask him.''

''I've already asked him. He doesn't remember.''

''So, what do you do now? Confront Jimmy?''

''I think I'll talk to Emmy first,'' I hedged. ''I don't want to accuse Jimmy.''

''But eventually you accuse someone, do you not? That is your goal, no? *Cara* Gerry, is there no way I can dissuade you? Caruso was lucky, the time he 'investigated' but he knows nothing of detective work. Do not let him influence you. Leave it to the police.''

''The police suspect *me*, Pasquale—how can I leave it to them? I've got to find out everything I can.''

''But Gerry, how do you hope to find out what happened when the police—''

''Pasquale, don't argue with me, please. I've made up my mind.''

He threw up his hands. ''*Cielo!* Why do I bother! You are even more stubborn than Rico! Go, then! Ask your questions! Make trouble!''

It was the only time I'd ever seen him angry with me. I hated to leave him in that mood, but I had a lot of things to do that day. I left the Hotel Astor and crossed Times Square; on the corner of Forty-second Street and Broadway I hesitated. Across the street was the Hotel Knickerbocker, and I would dearly have loved to go in and talk to Scotti. But Caruso lived in the apartment directly above Scotti's, and I didn't want to risk running into *him* just yet. Besides, I was due at the Metropolitan in forty-five minutes and I wanted to allow time to see Gatti-Casazza first.

So I hurried down Broadway to the opera house, and I found Gatti upstairs in his office. He was arguing with someone on the telephone when I went in, so I sat in a chair and stared at him until he hung up.

"Is it important, Gerry?" he asked waspishly. "I have many things to attend to."

"It's very important," I assured him. "Did you see Jimmy Freeman backstage any time before Friday's performance of *Carmen* started?"

He blinked. "*That* is important?"

"Extremely. Did you see him?"

"I did."

"Was he in costume?"

Gatti went through the same eye-squinting process as Amato. "No, I do not think he was."

I almost jumped out of the chair with excitement. "When did you first see him that night?"

"Eh, it cannot have been too early. Early in the evening, most of you were upstairs getting ready. I did not go up to the dressing-room level that night."

"So it must have been right before the curtain opened?"

"I do not remember. It could have been any time after he came down from the dressing rooms. I did not go upstairs at all."

That was twice he'd made a point of saying he'd not been near the dressing rooms that night. Because of something Caruso had said when Lieutenant O'Halloran was questioning us? What was it . . . ah. Yes. Caruso had said he thought he'd seen Gatti going into Duchon's dressing room. *I* had not seen Gatti upstairs that night. Nevertheless, Gatti was making a point of denying something I hadn't even asked him about.

I did ask him if he'd seen Morris Gest backstage before the opera began, or if he'd seen Scotti between Acts I and II. He hadn't. He muttered something about not having time to gossip so I left.

Downstairs in the main auditorium, the others were there and waiting for me with expressions of martyred patience on their faces even though I wasn't late. Toscanini had called a rehearsal of *Madame Sans-Gêne*. It wasn't to be a full rehearsal; we were going to sing only those scenes in which Jimmy Freeman would appear. Osgood Springer was seated beside the piano accompanist, ready to turn the pages of the score once we started.

Jimmy was in the wings, eager to make his first entrance. "The Maestro called this rehearsal just for *me!*" he exulted. "I hope I don't make a fool of myself."

"Rather hope that you do," I cautioned. "Rehearsal is the place to make your mistakes." I did a few warm-up exercises and told Toscanini I was ready.

It was a rather uninspired rehearsal, as rehearsals always are when a newcomer is being taught what everybody else already knows. Jimmy plugged away at it, doing everything Toscanini told him to do and not even minding the few times the Maestro yelled at him. He was being treated like a star! Osgood Springer looked as though he wanted to speak up and make suggestions once or twice but he clamped his mouth shut and said nothing. Everyone knew how little Toscanini welcomed suggestions.

When we'd finished, Springer made a beeline toward me. "What do *you* think?" he asked in a low voice.

"I think he sounds good," I answered truthfully.

"I don't know," he said worriedly. "Something is missing. I can't put my finger on it."

"What's missing is an audience. Don't worry, Mr. Springer, Jimmy will do just fine." And he would, once he had a full house to sing to and a full orchestra to accompany him.

Just then Toscanini came up and made a big show of kissing my hand. Springer raised one eyebrow and faded discreetly away. "Ah, *cara mia!*" Toscanini purred. "You are in good voice today!"

"Am I? But you didn't yell at me once," I teased. "My feelings were hurt."

"I promise to yell next time. But for now—you join me for lunch, yes?"

"I wish I could, but I must go see Emmy Destinn."

"Last night she sings, remember."

"I know, but it's almost one o'clock. It'll be all right." Emmy always slept until noon the day after a performance.

Lunch would have been a good opportunity to ask Toscanini some questions, but for the life of me I couldn't think of a single one to ask. He hadn't been backstage at all until I'd already beaned Duchon with my castanets right before Act II. And then he'd come back only to see what the delay was and left immediately, after only a minute or two—not long enough to see anything or do anything.

I'd told my chauffeur to meet me at the Thirty-ninth Street entrance. Emmy Destinn next.

"I don't know why I let you talk me into this," Emmy grumbled. "I have my own dressmaker."

I said something about a change being nice once in a while and steered her away from the lavender silk she was looking at. My own dressmaker had taken one look at Emmy and knew she had her work cut out for her. Together we'd managed to talk Emmy out of the design she'd initially favored—puff sleeves, gathers on the hips—and settled on something a little more flattering to her ample figure. Now all we needed was the material.

"Don't you have any bright colors?" Emmy complained.

"These are troubled times, Madame," the dressmaker murmured discreetly. "Muted colors are perferred. Or blacks and whites. Now here is a lovely pearl gray that would suit Madame perfectly."

"It does not suit Madame at all. What about that dusty rose over there?"

We finally convinced her that a green so dark it was almost black would best complement her complexion and hair color. Once that was settled, the dressmaker started the discouraging business of taking Emmy's measurements; for that she called an assistant.

While Emmy was being measured, I casually brought up the subject of Duchon's note. I asked her if she remembered it.

"The one asking you not to sit down during the *Toreador Song*? Yes, I remember it. Why?"

"Do you remember what you did with it when you finished reading it?"

She shrugged, a gesture that involved her whole body. "I thought I gave it back to you."

"If Madame could stand still . . . ?" the dressmaker's assistant whispered.

"Oh, sorry. Is the note missing, Gerry? Why is it important?"

"It's not exactly missing. A certain police lieutenant has it."

"O'Halloran? Well, I didn't give it to him, if that's what you are hinting at."

"If Madame could hold out her arm . . . ?"

"In Prague I never have to go through this," Emmy grumbled. "I tell my dressmaker what I want and she just makes it. I don't even have to bother with fittings."

I believed that. Finally the measuring was finished and we left. It was, for February, a nice day. The wind was taking a rest, the sun was valiantly trying to shine, it was dry underfoot. "Let's walk," I said on impulse.

"Walk?" Emmy looked at me as if I'd just suggested we burn down the Metropolitan Opera House.

"I could do with a little exercise. Come on." We strolled up Fifth Avenue, my limousine trailing us. The street traffic was solid with hansom cabs, carriages, bicycles, and most of all motor cars—which were more and more taking the place of horses. In addition to my limousine there were sedans, touring cars, open-top busses packed with people now that the weather had cleared a little; and I saw one electric brougham. I wondered if the latter was easier to drive than a gasoline-powered motor car; with no big engine in front of him, the driver could look almost straight down at the street.

We passed B. Altman's, where a gaggle of girls flocked around us asking for autographs. A few asked Emmy too.

"Where do they come from?" she asked when we eventually got away. "Your gerryflappers. They are *everywhere*."

I told her I didn't remember ever seeing those particular girls before. We walked on toward the Knabe Piano Building. "How old do you think they are?" I said. "Those girls that stopped us?"

"Mm." Not particularly interested.

"Do you think they're as old as Jimmy Freeman?"

"No."

"Speaking of Jimmy, did you happen to see him in costume before the first act of *Carmen* Friday night?"

She stopped stock still and put both fists on her hips. "Gerry. How did we get from gerryflappers to Jimmy Freeman's costume?"

"Oh, I don't know," I answered in what I hoped was a disarming manner. "Just a natural leap, I suppose."

"Well, if you can make that kind of leap, so can I. Thinking of Jimmy Freeman reminds me that my feet hurt."

I didn't see any connection, but then I wasn't meant to. I signaled my chauffeur. When we were in the limousine, I tried again. "You did see him before the opera started, didn't you?"

"Yes, I saw him. And he was already in costume. So?"

My heart sank. I'd wanted her to say the same thing Gatti-Casazza had said, that Jimmy was *not* in costume, that Amato and I were mistaken. But now it looked as if Gatti-Casazza were the one who was mistaken. "Are you sure?"

"Of course I'm sure. Why?"

"Amato said the same thing. He said Jimmy was ready before the opera started."

"Well, that should settle it then. Jimmy Freeman was in costume and make-up before the curtains opened. I am glad we have solved this earth-shaking problem."

"But don't you remember, Emmy? Jimmy told Lieutenant O'Halloran he didn't put on his costume until after the first act had started.''

"Oh." She was silent a moment. "I must have missed that. Everyone was talking at once and I didn't hear everything. That *is* serious. Have you spoken to Jimmy about it?"

"Not yet." I dreaded the thought of it.

Emmy was nodding to herself. "It would explain a lot, wouldn't it?"

"It explains nothing!" I flared. "You know Jimmy wouldn't do such a dreadful thing."

"I know nothing of the sort," she retorted. "Gerry, I understand Jimmy is a pet of yours, but I have never thought he was the innocent young man he appears to be. There is no such thing as an innocent young man any more. Jimmy is smart enough to know that a lot of women find that boyish manner appealing—it appeals to you, doesn't it? I wouldn't take him at face value if I were you."

I glared at her. "How would you like to walk the rest of the way home?"

"I should loathe it. But face facts, Gerry. Nobody else benefited from Duchon's 'accident' as much as Jimmy. He was the first one I thought of when I heard what had happened."

I didn't answer right away. My fondness for Jimmy had blinded me to some dark side of his nature that I simply did not wish to see? What nonsense; I felt foolish even thinking it. Yet . . . "Do you really think he could have done it?"

"I really do," Emmy said quietly.

We rode in silence for a couple of blocks, and then Emmy asked me to take her to an uptown gallery where she was meeting Caruso. The gallery was auctioning off some eighteenth-century Flanders lace the tenor wanted to bid on. That was good news. If his mind was on precious lace, then he wouldn't be pestering me for a while. We delivered Emmy to the gallery door on upper Madison.

My next—and last—stop was the Belasco Theatre, on West Forty-fourth Street. There was no place to park, so I told the chauffeur to keep going around the block until he saw me come out. I went into the small lobby and hesitated; I thought David Belasco would probably be upstairs in his private rooms, but I heard voices coming from the auditorium. I pushed through the swinging doors to the back of the seating area.

The Belasco is quite a theatre; it impresses me all over again every time I go there. At the back of the auditorium stands a handsome screen of carved wood and crystal glass to protect the audience from drafts. The auditorium chairs are made of heavy wood and upholstered in a rich, dark leather; the back of each chair is embossed with an emblematic design of some sort, a different design for each chair. Over the proscenium opening hangs a large painting, and along the sides are murals and occasional tapestries. The paintings are all of symbolic figures—Tranquility, Grief, Music, Blind Love, and the like. Overhead the ceiling is made up of a number of rich stained-glass panels lighted from above; the panels feature the coats-of-arms of Shakespeare, Goethe, Racine, other writers. The Belasco Theatre is grand enough to be an opera house, although the seating capacity is a little small for opera—only about a thousand, I think.

A rehearsal was in progress. David Belasco was sitting in the seventh or eighth row, putting his actors through their paces. I sat down behind him and tapped him on the shoulder.

He turned, his face showing an annoyance that quickly turned into a welcoming smile when he saw who it was. (Nice.) "Gerry!" he said softly. "You have come to tell me you are going to act in one of my plays!"

"Not this time, I'm afraid," I said with mock regret. "But I would like a few moments of your time. I can see you are busy, but—"

"Say no more." He turned the rehearsal over to an assistant and invited me up to his rooms for tea. But I didn't want to keep him away from his rehearsal that long, so I suggested we talk where we were. We moved to the back of the auditorium, where our voices wouldn't disturb the actors, and Belasco remarked astutely, "Something is troubling you. The smile is as bright as ever, but today it hides something not very happy. Tell me."

"It's what happened at *Carmen*," I sighed. "You know the police think I put the ammonia in Duchon's throat spray. Either I or Jimmy Freeman—Lieutenant O'Halloran has made that quite clear. I am a *suspect*, David!"

He took off the glasses he'd started wearing lately and tucked them away in a pocket. "I know Lieutenant O'Halloran, Gerry, and the man is no fool. He won't arrest you for something you didn't do. Do you know what I think? I think he's fishing, just tossing out a line to see if he can get a nibble or two."

"Well, I wish he'd stop tossing it in my direction." I brooded for a moment. "What's bothering me is all those contradictory stories we told. I can't get it straight, all those different movements."

"I was backstage only ten minutes or so," Belasco said apologetically. "How can I help?"

"You were there during the intermission between Acts I and II, right after I threw my castanets at Duchon—correct?"

"Correct."

"You told Lieutenant O'Halloran you saw Scotti backstage then, didn't you?"

Belasco rubbed his temple with one finger. "I've been thinking about that. Scotti said he wasn't backstage then, didn't he? I could have been mistaken—perhaps I saw him out front. But I *thought* it was backstage where I caught a glimpse of him, and since I went backstage only after the first act, it would have had to be then. But now I'm not so sure."

"What was he doing when you saw him?"

He waved a hand gracefully. "Nothing in particular that I remember. It was just a glimpse."

"What about Morris? Pasquale Amato said he saw him backstage *before* the first act."

"Amato is mistaken. Morris was with me, remember. I would have known if he'd gone backstage then."

"He was with you all the time?"

"Yes."

"He didn't leave you at all? Not even for a minute?"

"Not even for a minute. Unless you want to count the time he went into the gentlemen's restroom."

I stared at him. "How long was he gone?"

He looked surprised, thought a minute, and then looked even more surprised. "Rather longer than he should have been, come to think of it."

"Long enough to slip backstage?"

"Possibly. Yes," he mused, "he would have had time."

"Before you ask," I said, "I do not think Morris Gest doctored the throat spray. I don't think that at all."

"Morris was very angry at Duchon," Belasco said. "Angrier than I've seen him in a long time. He felt Duchon had made a fool of him."

Belatedly I remembered David Belasco and his son-in-law were not exactly the best of friends. "Nevertheless," I said firmly, "if Morris did go backstage before the opera, it had to be for some reason other than putting ammonia in the spray bottle. That's just not his style, David. He'd be more likely to get even by arranging a public humiliation of some sort—he'd want people to know about it."

"But why would he have gone backstage then?"

"That's what I'd like to know. And why would he lie about it?"

"To avoid being suspected? To keep *me* from finding out? Lord knows what he was up to."

I sighed. "I'm going to have to ask him about it."

Belasco smiled—rather wickedly, I thought. "Let me take care of that for you."

"Gladly. You'll call me?"

"As soon as I find out something."

I let him go back to his rehearsal then. I went out and stood in front of the theatre entrance, waiting for my chauffeur. Jimmy Freeman had lied about when he put on his costume, and now it looked as if Morris Gest had lied about going backstage before the opera. Who else had lied? Scotti?

The chauffeur pulled up to the curb, and I sank gratefully into the back seat. I could feel the weariness working its way through my bones; who would have thought detective work was so exhausting? Scotti and I had planned to go to the theatre that evening—Ethel Barrymore in *The Shadow* at the Empire—but I was going to beg off. When I got home I wanted a bath, food, and sleep, in that order.

But what I wanted was going to have to wait. I was just taking off my shoes when Bella came in to say Lieutenant O'Halloran had just arrived.

Back on with the shoes. I found O'Halloran standing at the window, gazing down on the darkening street. "Good evening, Lieutenant," I said, and waited.

He took his time about turning to face me, and when he did I didn't like what I saw. His face was dark and drawn, angry. He spoke two words: "Philippe Duchon."

"You've talked to him? He's able to communicate?"

"No, Miss Farrar, he is not able to communicate. He never will communicate. Not ever. Duchon is dead."

The floor gave a sudden lurch beneath my feet. "Dead? But Dr. Curtis said—"

"He killed himself. He opened a vein in each wrist and bled to death. One of the hospital nurses found him this morning."

Something happened to my knees just then: they stopped working. I felt myself sinking toward the floor when O'Halloran grabbed my arm and got me seated on the sofa. *Phillippe Duchon had killed himself.* That's what he'd said.

"Do you have any smelling salts?" O'Halloran asked. "Shall I call the maid?"

"I'm not feeling faint, Lieutenant," I said as steadily as I could. "It's just that my legs suddenly turned to jelly."

He looked me straight in the eye, satisfied himself I wasn't going to have hysterics or pass out, and pulled up a chair to sit opposite me. "He left a note. Just one line, in French, and his signature. It translates, 'My life is already ended.' That's all."

"He didn't mention . . . ?"

"Any names? *Your* name? No. Only 'My life is already ended.' You know what struck me about that? You said just about the same thing, the last time I talked to you. You said whoever put the ammonia in the throat spray had virtually killed Duchon. You said his life was over."

I dropped my forehead into my hands. "Any singer would have told you the same thing, Lieutenant," I muttered.

"Ah, but any singer didn't. *You* did. Well, you were right. Did you know he would commit suicide? Or were you just hoping he would?"

If he'd thrown a bucket of ice water in my face, he couldn't have shocked me more. When I was sure my voice was under control, I stood up and said, "Get out of my home, Lieutenant O'Halloran. Get out right now."

He gave me a sarcastic smile and headed toward the door. But when he had the door open, he turned for one departing shot. "By the way, I spent an hour in the district attorney's office this afternoon. They were arguing about whether this was a case of manslaughter or not. Do you know what manslaughter is, Miss Farrar?"

What was he talking about? "What?"

"Manslaughter is causing someone else's death without meaning to. An accident, say, or simple negligence, or the result of some act committed without malice. Involuntary killing. One of our prosecutors is saying whoever doped the throat spray didn't intend for Duchon to die, and that makes it manslaughter."

"But . . . but Duchon's suicide was the direct result of his using that spray!"

"Exactly. And there was malice in the act of tampering with the spray—malice of the nastiest sort. There's no doubt in my own mind what we've got here. It's murder, Miss Farrar. Now I'm looking for a murderer."

He closed the door behind him. I went over to the window and watched until he left the building and got into a waiting motor car. He was barely visible in the near-dark, that bearer of tragic news. Philippe Duchon was dead—by his own hand, but another hand had helped.

Duchon was dead, and he'd gone to his death thinking I was responsible.

□ **12** □ I lay with my head back and my feet up on the sofa (not my sofa) and listened to my partner in detection, advisory capacity only, ranting and raving. I'd told Caruso about O'Halloran's visit the night before a good ten minutes ago and he hadn't stopped yelling yet.

"Non posso capirlo—I do not understand!" he protested for about the hundredth time. "Lieutenant O'Halloran is not that kind of man—he does not *bully*. He hints, he insinuates, but he does not *bully*."

"Well, he gave a good imitation of a bully last night," I said wearily. "He served warning on me, Rico. He thinks I did it."

"Ridicolo."

We were in Caruso's apartment in the Hotel Knickerbocker. I'd gone there to keep him from coming to my place; I had a performance that night and needed most of the day to myself, and here I could just get up and leave whenever I wanted. Caruso never took hints about leaving.

He'd already known about Duchon's suicide when I arrived that morning. The police had notified Gatti-Casazza, who'd taken on the chore of telephoning everyone else. He'd even called me, after Lieutenant O'Halloran had left. Caruso had been as shocked as I was, but not really surprised. The suicide was as understandable as it was deplorable; we could all imagine what Duchon must have been going through these last few days, knowing he would never sing or even talk again. Now when it was too late I regretted every harsh word I'd ever spoken to him.

Finally Caruso's indignation sputtered itself out. "Mario!" he bellowed. "Bring us coffee, please."

Mario, the perfect valet, had anticipated his employer and had the coffee pot and cups already set out on a tray. Mario was a nice-looking young man with a shock of thick black hair that kept falling into his eyes. As he poured out the coffee and handed me my cup, he murmured, "Do not worry, Signorina Geraldine. Lieutenant O'Halloran, he never puts so great a lady as you in the jailhouse."

So he'd been listening; I smiled at him anyway. "Thank you, Mario."

Caruso gulped his coffee and then sat down briskly at his writing table and took out some paper, all business. "Now, tell me what you learn yesterday."

I tried to get my thoughts in order. "The most important thing was that Jimmy Freeman lied about not getting into costume early," I said reluctantly. "Gatti-Casazza thinks he did *not* get into costume before the first act started, but he's the only one who says so. Three other people, including myself, saw him dressed before the performance began."

Caruso was busy scribbling away. "Mmm. That does not look good, no?"

"The fact that he got into costume so early might not mean anything in itself. But the fact that he lied about it—well, you're right, that does not look good."

"Do you talk to Jimmy?"

"Not yet. I want to wait until after tonight." Tonight was the performance of *Madame Sans-Gêne* that Jimmy was scheduled to sing.

"So. What else?"

"Well, Morris Gest may have lied about where he was right before the opera started. David Belasco is going to try to find out the truth—Rico, what *are* you writing?"

"Notes. A good detective always makes notes. So we wait to hear from Mr. Belasco? *Bene*. Now—do you ask Emmy Destinn about the note from Duchon?"

"She said she thought she gave it back to me, and I'm sure she was telling the truth. Neither of us was paying much attention at the time."

"Eh, Lieutenant O'Halloran probably just picks it up from your dressing table."

"Probably. But Rico, how did he get into my dressing room? I have the only key."

"Ahhhhh, that is right! I forget about that. You must ask the lieutenant how the note comes into his possession."

"I did ask him. He wouldn't tell me."

"Ask him again."

"Rico, you're just *beginning* to sound bossy."

He was busy reading through his "notes" and didn't

hear. "Mr. Gatti. I think I see him go into Duchon's dressing room, but—"

"But he denies it," I said. "Without even being asked, he denies it. He made a point of telling me twice he was never on the dressing-room level at all. How sure are you?"

"Not very. Backstage—so much confusion! I wish someone else is there to see also!"

"Yes, that would simplify matters considerably. Perhaps I should go back and ask everyone whether—Rico, doesn't all this strike you as slightly redundant? Surely Lieutenant O'Halloran is asking these same questions!"

"Of course he is asking these same questions," Caruso said smugly. "But is he getting the same answers? People do not talk to the police as openly as they talk to a friend."

"That makes me feel like a traitor," I complained.

"No, no—you must not feel that way," he told me in a surprisingly serious voice. "You must persevere—we must find the truth!" Then he switched back from that high-minded tone to his usual little-boy eagerness. "So, what else do you find out?"

I hesitated. "It's what I didn't find out," I finally said. "It's Scotti. Was he backstage between Acts I and II or not? He said no, Belasco said yes. But Belasco became uncertain when faced with an absolute denial, the way you are no longer sure about Gatti's going into Duchon's dressing room."

"It cannot be Scotti."

"Of course it can't."

We both sat in gloomy silence for a few moments. "So, then," Caruso asked, "what do we do?"

I made up my mind. "We ask him. Between the two of us, we ought to be able to convince him how important it is to tell the truth."

"*Eccellente!* I call him." He reached for the telephone.

"No, wait—let me." Scotti's apartment was directly under Caruso's, so I stood in the middle of the room and "called" the baritone. I began to sing, full voice, *Vissi d'arte* from *Tosca*.

I was only halfway through the aria when the knocking started; Mario opened the door and Scotti rushed in. "Gerry! You do not tell me you are coming here! Good morning, Rico. Do I interrupt, *cara mia*?"

"No, Toto, you do not interrupt," I smiled. "In fact, we wanted you up here."

"*Bene!* Is that coffee? Mario, one more cup, please!" But the valet as usual had known what would be wanted and was even then bringing in another cup.

When Scotti had poured his coffee and seated himself, Caruso and I exchanged an uneasy look; neither one of us wanted to broach the subject. Finally I did. I told Scotti as simply and as earnestly as I could how necessary it was for us to know where he had spent the interval between the first and second acts of last Friday's *Carmen*.

He stuttered and stammered a bit, but with Caruso's encouragement he eventually admitted that he had indeed come backstage after Act I. "But I do not put ammonia in the spray! Surely you do not think I do such a thing!"

"No, no—but what are you doing backstage, Toto?" Caruso asked. "Where do you go? Do you see anything?"

But instead of answering Caruso, Scotti turned his face to me. And suddenly I understood. I knew that look—oh, how I knew that look! I grabbed a silk cushion from the sofa and hurled it at his head. "Who was she, Toto?" I screamed. "Some little girl from the chorus? *Who was she?*"

Scotti was stammering something and Caruso started talking loudly in an attempt to play peacemaker and I was still screaming and Mario came running in to see what was the matter—so of course we all turned on poor Mario. The valet scuttled back out again, and the rest of us settled down some.

It had been a chorus singer after all. Scotti had been on his way to see me right after Act I but had been diverted—"only a little conversation, yes?" He wasn't even aware that at that very time I was throwing my castanets at Philippe Duchon and drawing blood; he learned of that only afterward. And no, he hadn't noticed anything else in particular going on. Some "little conversation" that must have been.

It wasn't the explanation I would have chosen, but it did account for Scotti's movements during a rather crucial period during Friday evening. Not that I ever suspected him of being the one who'd contaminated the throat spray, but it was one loose end that was now tied up. I believed Scotti's story; whenever he was engaged in one of his little "flirts," as the Italians call them, he was deaf and dumb and blind to everything else going on around him.

"If we could only pin down the time more precisely," I complained, "we might get a better idea of who could have done it. As it is now, the ammonia could have been put in the spray bottle any time after Emmy Destinn showed up backstage carrying her saddlebag with the ammonia in it. That was ten or fifteen minutes before Act I started, and Duchon didn't actually use the spray until right before his entrance during Act II. That's a big stretch of time."

"It sounds unplanned, does it not?" Scotti offered. "Who would know ahead of time Emmy so conveniently brings a bottle of ammonia with her that night?"

"Yes, it must have been a spur-of-the-moment thing," I agreed. "Emmy probably just dumped the bag somewhere while she was talking and someone saw it and thought, 'Well, it won't hurt to look.' And found the ammonia."

Caruso was back at his writing table, shuffling through his papers. "So. Now we remove one name from the list—Antonio Scotti."

"What list is that?" Scotti asked.

"Our list of suspects."

"You put my name on your list of suspects?"

"And my own," said Caruso. "And Gerry's."

Scotti held out a hand. "Let me see." He glanced at the piece of paper Caruso gave him. "Eh, we know we three are not guilty. Let us see, that leaves—Gatti-Casazza, Toscanini, Amato, Destinn, Gest, Freeman, Springer, Dr. Curtis, and Uncle Hummy." He lowered the paper. "Uncle Hummy?"

I shrugged. "He was there."

"Emmy and Pasquale," Caruso said decisively. "We remove their names too."

"Is that the way a good detective works, Rico?" I asked, amazed. "First, eliminate one's friends from the list of suspects?"

"You do not seriously suspect Emmy and Pasquale," Caruso said reprovingly. "You know you do not."

"Of course I don't, but that's no way to go about it—we wouldn't have any suspects left that way. Look, Rico," I said sarcastically, "there's only one person on that list who's not a close friend of ours. That's Osgood Springer. So why don't we just save time and decide *he's* the culprit and go after *him*?"

"Morris Gest is not my friend," Scotti said. "Not particularly."

"Well, he's mine, and if we're eliminating suspects on the basis of friendship, his name goes too." Then I noticed Caruso; he was sitting up straight, his face was lighted up. "Rico?"

He turned his beaming face toward me and said, "Osgood Springer!"

"Oh, for heaven's sake, Rico!" I exploded. "Couldn't you tell I was being sarcastic?" Scotti just laughed.

Caruso brushed my objection aside. "Gerry, I think you are right! Osgood Springer did it!"

"I didn't say Osgood Springer did it!" I cried in exasperation. "Oh, Rico—why don't you *listen*!"

Scotti was looking at the list again. "Jimmy Freeman is not my friend either. We leave his name on."

Scotti was being facetious, but his mention of Jimmy Freeman reminded me that the young singer was our prime suspect. Oh, how I hated that thought! Caruso explained to Scotti that Jimmy had lied about when he got into costume, and then said to me, "You are going to have to meet with him, Gerry. Find out the truth. He tells you if you ask him right, yes?"

"Why do I not meet with him instead?" Scotti asked in an overcasual manner. "We have man-to-man talk."

I had to smile at that. "Toto, do you really think Jimmy would confide in you? You know he wouldn't."

"But he tells Gerry," Caruso added. "If there is anybody in the whole big world he tells, it is Gerry."

Scotti glared at him, jumped to his feet, and announced, "Gerry, you do not meet with Jimmy Freeman. *I* do."

I went over to him. "Now, Toto—as long as you indulge in little tête-à-têtes with chorus singers, you have nothing to say about whom *I* choose to meet." He had no say in the matter under any circumstances, but why rub it in? "Tonight at *Madame Sans-Gêne* I'll arrange to meet Jimmy tomorrow. It's best this way, Toto."

"In a public place!" Scotti shouted. "You meet him in a public place! With hundreds and thousands of people around you! This Freeman, he may be dangerous!"

Why, he was worried about me! *That* was his objection to my meeting Jimmy! Without any preamble I put my arms around his neck and pulled his face down for a long, intense kiss that reassured both of us. I didn't want to worry Toto; he was too dear. We rested our heads on each other's shoulders and just stood there a while, feeling good.

But then I noticed Caruso was sketching away like a madman; nothing can kill a romantic moment faster than discovering Enrico Caruso is drawing a caricature of you. It wasn't his usual kind of caricature, it turned out. Our faces were recognizable without any exaggerations being drawn in. Scotti's nose was not elongated, and my teeth weren't showing at all. He'd caught our postures perfectly, with our heads on each other's shoulders. *But*—he'd drawn us both without any clothes on.

I tried not to laugh; that only encouraged him. "Shame on you, Rico!" I exclaimed. "Nobody must see that!" I reached for the drawing.

But Scotti whipped it away before I could tear it up. "Oh, I like this, Rico! I like it *assai molto*! May I keep it?"

"*Sí, certo*," the tenor said expansively.

I made a mental note to steal the drawing from Scotti the first chance I got. "Well, I'm going home now," I announced. "I've been here all morning, and I want to get some rest before I start vocalizing."

Scotti wanted to see me home, but I knew better than to let him come with me just then.

Jimmy Freeman's first and last performance in *Madame Sans-Gêne* was . . . satisfactory. He made no mistakes, neither vocally nor in his stage movements. But he didn't bring the audience to its feet either. The role itself simply wasn't good enough to create that kind of effect, and Jimmy wasn't seasoned enough a performer to make something more out of it. Pasquale Amato gave the role some personality when he sang it, but Amato had years of experience behind him. The overall performance of *Madame Sans-Gêne* was a rousing success, however, because I was marvelous. It's a soprano's opera; that's why I was singing it.

Jimmy was pleased with himself, however; he accepted everyone's congratulations with a glow on his cheek and a sparkle in his eye. I gave him a light kiss and made a dinner date with him for the following evening.

"Where?" he asked eagerly.

I was going to suggest Sherry's—but Sherry's was right across the street from Delmonico's, and I didn't want to remind Jimmy of that time he'd behaved so badly in the other restaurant. "You choose."

"What about Sherry's? I'll reserve a table."

Osgood Springer was watching all the fuss being made over his pupil with a wry smile on his lips. I left Jimmy to some new congratulators and motioned his vocal coach aside. "All right, so it wasn't a standard-setting performance," I said. "But you're not going to tell him that, are you, Mr. Springer?"

"There's no point," he shrugged. "James will never sing the role again."

"It wasn't a wasted effort, you know," I lectured him. "Jimmy has more experience now than he did twenty-four hours ago. And exposure—don't underestimate the value of exposure. The more the audiences hear him, the better off he'll be."

"Yes, I understand all that, Miss Farrar. But what now? What comes next?"

I had no answer for him.

The next evening while I was dressing for my dinner date with Jimmy, David Belasco telephoned. "Morris did slip backstage before the first act of *Carmen*," he told me, "while I thought he was in the gentlemen's restroom. But he won't tell me why."

"Well, well, isn't that interesting," I murmured.

"He may be seeing another woman," Belasco said darkly.

"At the Metropolitan? Where everybody knows him? And with you in the building? David, that would be the *last* reason he'd sneak backstage!"

He laughed. "Perhaps you're right. So far as I know, Morris has always been faithful to my daughter. But there's always a first time."

"Always? How depressing. But didn't Morris even give you a hint?"

"Nothing. The more I questioned him, the more nervous he became—but he just wouldn't say."

I thanked him for letting me know and hung up. I suppose I should have felt relieved that Jimmy was no longer the only suspect, but it was like trading in one friend for another.

About an hour later I arrived at Sherry's to find Jimmy had booked a private room; so much for Scotti's instructions to surround myself with hundreds and thousands of people. But I had no reason to fear Jimmy. *Nobody* had any reason to fear him, I was positive of that. Jimmy looked nervous and determined at the same time—oh dear, not a proposal, I hoped.

We dined on salmon in aspic and beef *à la périgourdine* and artichoke hearts and endive soufflé and we drank far too much champagne. We'd both relaxed considerably by the time the waiters brought in the apricot tart. Jimmy's eyes were glistening from the wine and maybe something else that I didn't *think* was indigestion and I was feeling giddy and rather boneless and we both laughed all the time. I decided I liked detective work.

When the waiters had brought us still another bottle of champagne (the third? the fourth?) and had discreetly withdrawn, Jimmy seized my hand and went through an elaborate throat-clearing process that I thought was hilarious. I laughed and laughed.

"Don't laugh," he laughed, "I have something serious to say." He hiccuped. "'Scuse me."

"You're 'scused." I had a rather bad case of the giggles. "How can you be serious at a time like this?"

He cleared his throat again ha ha. "I didn't feel I could say anything before ha ha," he laughed, "but things are ha ha different now."

"Tell me hee hee how things are different now hee hee," I giggled.

"Ha ha now I, *I* am a princ'pal singer too, ha, and more ha ha worthy of your hand ha!"

"Oh, you poor innocent lamb!" I sobbed.

"Don't cry. Don't laugh either ha ha. Jus' listen, ha."

"Somebody drank our wine hee hee."

Jimmy filled our glasses and lifted his in an unsteady toast. "To Geraldine Farrar—the mos' beaushiful woman inna worl'. Ha ha I meannit." He tossed off his glass; me, I couldn't seem to stop laughing. Fortified, Jimmy said in his best forthright manner, "Will you gerry me, Mary?"

That struck us both as uproarious and we went off into new gales of laughter. "I don't believe hee hee I've ever gerried anyone before," I hee-heed.

"Then ha don't you think it's ha ha time you gave it a try ha ha ha ha?"

"Hee hee why did you say you didn't get into costume early for *Carmen* hee hee when you did hee hee hee?"

" 'Cause Misser Springer tol' me to ha ha ha!"

"Mr. hee hee Springer?"

"You 'member ol' Ossie Springer, doncha? Ha ha you dint answer my queshion ha ha may I call you mine, Gerry?"

"Mine Gerry? That sounds like a funny name hee hee but you can call me Mine Gerry if you want to hee hee hee."

"Mine Gerry Farrar!" Jimmy sang—and slipped under the table.

I waited three or four days but he didn't come back up,

so I pressed the button that summoned the waiter. When he came in I said, "We have a small problem," and pointed to Jimmy sleeping peacefully under the table.

The staff at Sherry's was well used to dealing with such small problems. Fortunately Jimmy and I had arrived separately; the maître d' fetched both our chauffeurs, and the two of them managed to get Jimmy out through a side door I hadn't even known was there.

Once Jimmy was safely on his way home, my chauffeur asked me, "Are you all right, Miss Farrar?"

"Never better," I said, managing to swallow the *hee hee* in time, and climbed unsteadily into the limousine. "Number eighteen West Seventy-fourth Street," I told the chauffeur grandly, just as if the man hadn't been working for me the past four years.

I must have fallen asleep, because the next thing I was aware of was the chauffeur's hand on my shoulder and his voice saying, "We're home, Miss."

I declined his offer of assistance, because I didn't want it all over town the next day that Geraldine Farrar had arrived home so drunk she couldn't walk without help. I sailed into the building, trilled hello to the night doorman and one of the other residents standing there, and survived the elevator ride up without falling back to sleep.

But the whole business of locks and keys was beyond me, and one of the maids was sure to be up. I couldn't find the doorbell so I knocked at my own door, which was opened immediately—by Enrico Caruso.

"Where have you been?" he shouted. "Do you know what time it is? For hours I am waiting! You find out something, yes? Tell me what happens!"

"I think I'm engaged to Jimmy Freeman," I said, and collapsed into his arms.

☐ **13** ☐ Even when I do foolish things like stay up too late and eat too much and drink too much and flirt with intoxicated young men, I still can't sleep late the following morning. *The following morning*— are there three more depressing words in the English language? So at my usual hour I dragged myself out of bed and told Bella to run a hot bath. But first she helped me navigate the hundred miles between my bedroom and the dining room; I sank down at the table.

And found I had a guest. Across from me Caruso was heartily attacking a steak with two fried eggs on top of it. My stomach turned over at the smell. "Juice," I told Bella. "Grapefruit, tomato, orange, even *lemon* if we have it." I asked Caruso if he'd been there all night.

"Certainly not!" He sounded scandalized. "I take care of you last night and now I come back to see how you are. How are you?"

"My head feels twice its normal size and my stomach's queasy and my arms and legs seem to be made out of rubber. Other than that, I'm fine, thank you. Why don't you eat that in the kitchen?"

"Here is satisfactory, *grazie*. I think perhaps you do not feel so wonderful this morning so I bring you a little something." He stuck two fat fingers into his waistcoat pocket and drew out a small paper envelope, which he unfolded to reveal a mound of white crystals. He poured me a glass of water from the pitcher on the table and dumped in the medicine, which immediately started to bubble furiously. "Good for the head and the stomach. Does nothing, *sfortunamente*, for rubber arms and legs."

I waited until the noise of the bubbling had subsided to a tolerable level and drank down Caruso's hangover remedy. Not that I had a hangover, you understand; I just wasn't feeling too well. And after drinking the cure, I was feeling even worse. "I think I'm sicker," I said. Just then Bella brought me a big glass of tomato juice with something added, and that helped.

"Mr. Freeman telephoned earlier," Bella said, "while

you were still asleep. He said he'd call back later." I
thanked her and waved her away.

Caruso polished off his steak and eggs and poured us
both some coffee. "You are feeling better, yes? Now you
tell me about your tête-à-tête with Jimmy?"

"What day is it?"

"Thursday. Why?"

I groaned. "I'm singing *Butterfly* Saturday afternoon.
I'll never make it."

"Now, Gerry, you must pull yourself up with the boot-
straps. We have nice long talk—"

"Oh, Rico, I haven't even had my bath yet." I stood
up, with effort. "I'm going to go soak for a while and then
we'll talk."

He pushed back from the table. "We talk *while* you
soak—I come with you."

"You'll do no such thing!"

"I sit on nice chair in hallway and talk to you through
bathroom door—which you leave open a little, yes?"

Well, that sounded all right. I let him pick out his own
nice chair while I went into the bathroom. Bella had
poured bath salts into the water, but the scent that was
normally so pleasing for some reason seemed sickeningly
sweet just then. But when I got into the tub, it felt *soooo*
good that I didn't mind the smell. After a while I started
feeling better; I could even feel my bones again.

"So?" Caruso said impatiently from the hallway. "Do
you ask Jimmy why he tells lies about getting into costume
early?"

"I asked him."

"And?"

I would have preferred a little time to think about what
it meant first. "He said Osgood Springer told him to."

There was a brief silence, and then a whoop that made
my head ring. "Osgood Spring-er!" Caruso sang, insert-
ing a little cadenza between the *Spring* and the *er*. "You
were right, Gerry! Osgood Springer—he is our man!"

"I never said Osgood Springer was guilty!" I snapped.
"Why *do* you persist in saying that?"

"But it fits, Gerry, it fits! Jimmy Freeman does everything his Mr. Springer tells him, no? Osgood Springer is behind it all!''

Just then Bella came and tapped at the bathroom door. ''Mr. Freeman is on the telephone, Miss Farrar.''

Oh dear—I wasn't ready to talk to him yet. ''Tell him I'm in the bath and I'll call him back.''

When she'd gone, Caruso asked, ''What are you going to tell him?''

''The truth. That we both had a little too much to drink last night and I'm not thinking about marriage just now.''

''Ah, poor Jimmy! Another broken heart you leave behind you! Callous Gerry!'' he laughed.

''I am not callous,'' I protested. ''Things just got a little out of hand, that's all.''

Bella was back. ''A Mr. Springer is here to see you.''

I could hear Caruso gasp. His favorite suspect, right there in the next room! ''I can't see him now,'' I objected.

''But I can,'' Caruso said eagerly. ''Show him back, please. *Che fortuna!* Now we can ask him questions! Where is another chair . . . ?'' I could hear him moving something—and then there was a light crash, as of glass breaking. ''Oh, *scusi, scusi*—I buy new one!''

New one *what*? ''Rico—''

''Shh! He comes.'' He greeted Mr. Springer and offered him a chair, and explained that he and I were talking through the bathroom door.

Springer adjusted to the arrangement immediately. ''I come to offer my best wishes, Miss Farrar. James tells me you and he are to be married?'' Yes, definitely a question mark at the end of that sentence; he didn't quite believe it.

That made things easier. ''I'm afraid there's been a little misunderstanding, Mr. Springer. We'd been drinking champagne all evening and perhaps I didn't make myself as clear as I should have. But I have no plans for marriage right now.''

''Ah, I was afraid it would be something like that,'' he sighed.

Afraid? He wanted me to marry Jimmy? Well, being married to a star certainly wouldn't hurt his pupil's career any. Or perhaps he just meant he was afraid Jimmy was going to be hurt. "He thinks I said yes, then?"

"He is definitely under that impression, Miss Farrar. I cautioned him not to say anything until he'd spoken to you again, but you know what young men in love are like. James does plan to call on you this morning." A small laugh. "As soon as he is able to walk."

"This is all most unfortunate, Mr. Springer. But don't say anything to Jimmy, will you? Telling him is my duty."

He agreed. Then a silence developed, a rather uncomfortable one. Caruso, who'd been so eager to question Jimmy's mentor, didn't seem able to think of anything to say. Springer was starting to make those sounds people make when they're preparing to leave when a familiar voice shouted *"Where is she?"*

Scotti! And he sounded angry. Had he heard . . . ?

He had. "Come out of there *subito* and explain yourself! What do you think you do, Miss Geraldine Farrar? You dangle me on the string and then marry *little boy*? Come out!"

For a moment there I thought he was going to come bursting right into the bathroom, but I'd made it clear to him years ago that the one place in the world where a person was entitled to absolute privacy was the bathroom. "Toto, it's all a mistake," I called out. "Do calm down. I'm not marrying anybody."

"Not anybody?!" he roared.

"I mean I'm not marrying Jimmy Freeman. How did you hear about it anyway? Just relax, Toto—I'll be out shortly."

Caruso was talking to him in Italian and then Springer was working on him in English, and between the two of them they eventually persuaded Scotti there was no need to declare war on either me or Jimmy Freeman. I heard another chair being moved into place. It must be getting crowded out there in the hallway; ah well, the bathwater was beginning to cool anyway.

"Gerry," Scotti said in a more reasonable voice, "are you mad at Rico?"

"At Rico? No, why?"

"Oh, pieces of broken vase—all over the floor here."

I'd stepped out of the tub and was starting to dry myself when Bella tapped at the door again. "Miss Farrar, someone from *The New York Times* is calling on the telephone. He wants to know if it's true you are marrying James Freeman."

That set Scotti off again. "Tell him *no* it is not true!" he bellowed. "*Per la vita mia!* Now the newspapers! Eh, what next?"

"Find out where he got his information!" I called after Bella.

"I think I can tell you that," Osgood Springer said. "James was so excited this morning that he started telephoning everyone he knew with the good news. I have no doubt they too told other people and . . . I finally persuaded James to stop, but by then the word was already out."

So Jimmy liked to kiss and tell, but in the end he still obeyed Mr. Springer. I covered my body with dusting powder and slipped into a robe, a lovely silk Oriental kimono, a gift from an admirer who'd been impressed by my *Madame Butterfly*. *Madame Butterfly*—Saturday afternoon. I was beginning to think I might make it after all.

I heard a low murmur from the hallway, and then Caruso said, in a surprisingly small voice, "You have another visitor, Gerry—I think you come out now?"

Guess who. I opened the door and said, "Hello, Lieutenant." O'Halloran was standing facing the bathroom door; Caruso, Springer, and Scotti were seated in a row along the wall. Caruso looked anxious, Springer looked out of place, and Scotti looked like Mt. Etna. I could hear the telephone ringing. "An official visit, Lieutenant? Or have you taken to making social calls?"

He grinned crookedly, his ever-present derby dangling from one hand. "Well, Miss Farrar, it's like this. When my two favorite suspects announce they're getting married, it seems only fitting for me to drop by and offer my congratulations."

Scotti jumped to his feet. "They do *not* marry! *Misericordia!*"

Springer rose more slowly, looking shaken. "Your two favorite *suspects*?"

Caruso placed himself between me and the police detective. "Lieutenant O'Halloran, that is not nice, saying things like that," he scolded. "Are you not ashamed?"

"No," O'Halloran answered casually. "Miss Farrar, are you and Mr. Freeman getting married?"

"No, Lieutenant, we're not. The whole thing's a mistake."

"Of one kind or another," he nodded.

Now what did he mean by that? Bella appeared at the end of the hallway, now so crowded with chairs and people that she couldn't get through. "Miss Farrar!" she called. "Miss Destinn is on the telephone and she wants to know if it's true that—"

"Tell her no, it's not true," I said. "And from now on, Bella, just take the names of whoever calls and say I'll call back later."

I was ushering everyone out of the crowded hallway when we all heard a young voice singing out, "Gerry! Where are you, my darling Gerry?"

"Enter the hero," Osgood Springer said dryly. I shushed Scotti's growl and went to meet my unintended intended.

"Gerry! There you are!" Jimmy Freeman shouted, and threw both arms around me—only to look over my shoulder into the furious face of Antonio Scotti. Jimmy released me and manfully faced his rival. "Mr. Scotti, I must ask you not to call on my fiancée again unless I am present." Then before Scotti could answer, Jimmy noticed the others. "Mr. Springer, what are you doing here? Uh, hello, Mr. Caruso. And Lieutenant O'Halloran—is something wrong?"

O'Halloran cocked an eyebrow at him. "Miss Farrar is your fiancée?" All the time the telephone kept ringing, ringing.

I had to do something fast. "If you would all care to take a seat . . . ? I must speak with Jimmy privately and I'll rejoin you shortly." Scotti was the first to object; I placed my fingers over his mouth. "Please, Toto. I won't be long."

He acquiesced as graciously as could be expected under the circumstances. I took Jimmy by the arm and steered him toward the music room, dreading what I had to do. The direct approach would probably be kinder in the long run; so I closed the door, faced him, and told him.

He did not take it well. He didn't cry, but he looked as if he wanted to. I gave him a little hug. "Jimmy, it's not you, you understand. It's just that I don't want to be married to anybody, at least not right now. I'm flattered to death that you asked me, and I can't tell you how sorry I am about this misunderstanding. I'm very fond of you—you know that, don't you?"

"No," he snuffled, "I don't know that. I don't exactly feel overwhelmed with love right now."

I kept talking to him and eventually he accepted it. "You're still part of my life, Jimmy," I said. "We're not saying goodbye."

"I suppose," he said with a sigh of resignation, "that deep down I never really believed you'd marry me. But I want you to know I'm not giving up! I'm going to keep trying!"

Ah, the resilience of youth! I gave him a quick kiss and said, "Now I've got to get dressed. You go on out with the others—I'll be there in a few minutes."

I hoped he and Scotti would be polite to each other. What a morning! There was only one person in my apartment right then that I really wanted to see, and that was Osgood Springer. My next step was obviously to find out why he'd told Jimmy to lie about getting into his *Carmen* costume early. But there was no chance of talking to him in private with that mob in my parlor! I'd just have to arrange something later.

But when I'd dressed and gone into the parlor, the mob had been reduced to one solitary figure. "I sent the others away," Lieutenant O'Halloran said laconically. I suppose you can do things like that when you're a police official. "Do you know what conspiracy is, Miss Farrar?" he said.

For some reason I felt confident his attack-techniques

weren't going to work that day. "Of course I know what conspiracy is, Lieutenant," I said, seating myself casually in an armchair. "It's an unlawful agreement between two singers to dispose of a third. That's what you have in mind, isn't it?"

"Is that what happened?"

The telephone was ringing; I ignored it. "Lieutenant, tell me the truth. Do you honestly think that Jimmy Freeman and I, either separately or together, are responsible for Philippe Duchon's death? Is that what you honestly think?"

He gave a very human sigh. "I doubt if Freeman could carry off something that tricky. And from what I hear, you're capable of taking care of yourself without having to resort to pouring ammonia into somebody's throat spray. But you're the only suspects I've got. Duchon himself thought *you* were the one who did him in—"

"Don't remind me."

"—and Freeman is the one who stands to gain the most from the other man's death. He—"

"But it wasn't an intentional killing, was it? The ammonia was only meant to disable. Did the district attorney's office ever decide between manslaughter and murder?"

He nodded. "It's murder. Duchon's suicide was the direct consequence of an act of destructive malice, the D.A. decided. But if it wasn't one of you two who did it, then who? Which brings up another matter. The word I get is that you've been asking questions—all sorts of interesting questions. You wouldn't be doing my job for me, would you, Miss Farrar?"

It was getting impossible to keep any secrets at all. "What do you mean?" I asked innocently.

"I think you know what I mean. Your friends might tell you things they aren't willing to tell the police. Has that happened? Do you have anything you want to tell me?"

I thought of Osgood Springer, of Morris Gest, and even of Jimmy. It wouldn't do to run to this overly suspicious policeman with every hint or stray thought that happened to pass through my head. When I knew something definite, I would go to him. "No, I don't have anything to tell you."

He stood up to leave. "I'm going to tell you the same thing I told Mr. Caruso. Leave the detective work to the police. We know how to investigate, you don't. Leave it alone, Miss Farrar."

I gave him my startled-ingenue look. "Why, I wouldn't have it any other way, Lieutenant."

The expression on his face said he didn't believe me for one minute, but he left without further comment. At last, I was alone for the first time that day! I stretched my arms over my head in pure pleasure.

My harried-looking maid came in and handed me two pieces of paper. "This one," Bella said, "is a list of the people who telephoned. And this one," a folded note, "was left for you by the gentleman with the scar." She ran a finger along her jawline to demonstrate.

I read the note first.

Dear Miss Farrar,
   I apologize for intruding on your time, but it is essential that I speak to you without delay. I will meet you at any time and at any place you designate. You can reach me by calling James' telephone number. Please do not disappoint me.

                                        Very truly yours,
                                        Osgood Springer

Well, well. So the vocal coach wanted to talk to me as much as I wanted to talk to him. This was working out nicely.

I looked at the list of people who had telephoned. Well, well again: The grapevine had been busy that morning. In addition to Emmy Destinn and *The New York Times,* there'd been calls from Pasquale Amato, Morris Gest, Toscanini (twice), David Belasco, Gatti-Casazza, other singers (including a *seconda donna* who was trying to cultivate my friendship), other newspapers, and a couple of people whose names I didn't recognize. Even Mildredandphoebe had called. The President of the United States did not call, but he was about the only one.

I put off telephoning Osgood Springer for the time being because I hadn't yet figured out a way to approach him. I needed to put it all out of my mind for a while, to clear away the cobwebs.

There was always one reliable way to do that. I went into the music room and started practicing my scales.

Star of India, the sign read. Thought to be the largest star sapphire in the world.

"Impressive," Osgood Springer said. I agreed. Someone jostled against us, eager to get a look at the prize piece in the Morgan collection of gems.

I'd chosen the American Museum of Natural History for our meeting because it was public, because it was a place where we were unlikely to run into anyone from the Metropolitan Opera, and because it was only a few blocks around the corner and up Central Park West from where I lived. I paused to look at a rubellite from the mountains of China that had been used as an idol's eye in India.

The Star of India was a big drawing card; there were too many people around for a private conversation. Springer and I wandered away toward the hall of fossil mammals.

Inside was a whole series of skeletons of animals that were now extinct. Two young men were earnestly examining a display of skulls set in an alcove of one wall. Springer and I found a bench facing a reconstructed saber-toothed tiger and sat down. I'd been planning to lead into the question of Jimmy's *Carmen* costume gradually, but my companion saved me the trouble. "James told me you asked him why he'd lied about getting into costume early the night of Philippe Duchon's misfortune," he plunged in.

"Did I put it like that?" I didn't think I had. "He said you told him to."

"I did," he said with a catch in his voice, "in a futile attempt to avoid the very thing that has happened. You heard Lieutenant O'Halloran this morning—he said you and James were his 'two favorite suspects.' "

"Mm, I think that's just part of the lieutenant's technique. He accuses you of something and then watches the expression on your face. He made it fairly plain after you had all left that he wasn't convinced either Jimmy or I was the culprit he was looking for."

"Truly?" Springer was surprised. "That's very interesting." He lapsed into silence.

"You thought Jimmy would be suspected?" I prompted.

"It seemed likely. No one else stood to benefit so directly from Duchon's removal. An ounce of precaution . . . there was so much confusion backstage that night, I didn't think anyone would notice his getting dressed so early." He gave me a wry smile. "I hadn't counted on your remembering."

"I'm not the only one who remembered. Mr. Springer, why *did* Jimmy get into costume so early?"

He was silent a moment, as if making up his mind. "Because I was fairly certain he'd be singing that night."

A mild shock ran through me. Was I hearing a confession? The two young men had left the skulls display and were working their way around to our saber-toothed tiger. Five more people came into the hall together, all of them talking loudly. I stood up and gestured for Springer to follow.

The North Pacific hall was relatively uncrowded. Along one wall was a mural called *Dancing To Cure the Sick*, showing Indians of the Tlingit tribe in some sort of shamanistic ceremony. I had never heard of Tlingit Indians. "Did you say you knew Jimmy would be singing that night? Before . . . ?"

"I said I was fairly certain he would be," Springer answered. "I was upstairs on the dressing-room level before the performance started, and I could hear Duchon warming up. Then right in the middle of a vibrato passage he started coughing—big, racking coughs, alarming to listen to. I hurried to his dressing room . . . and Miss Farrar, I saw him spitting up blood."

"Oh, no! You mean there really was something wrong with his throat? I thought it was all . . . ."

"In his mind? So did I. But it wasn't."

"Oh, the poor man—but wait, Duchon had consulted Dr. Curtis. He said nothing was wrong."

Springer shook his head. "The throat is such a delicate instrument. So many things can go wrong. Even the best of doctors can overlook something."

My hand crept to my own throat. Dr. Curtis had once performed a throat operation on *me*. We stopped to look at a display of Indian clothing; how very small those people were. "Poor Duchon—spitting blood right before a performance. What did he do?"

"He used Caruso's spray—"

"The spray? Was it all right then?"

"Perfectly all right—no ill effects at all. After a few minutes he was warming up again. But I hunted up James and told him to get into costume and make-up right away. He did, and he didn't even ask why."

The ever-obedient student. Suddenly I wondered if Gatti-Casazza had known his new baritone had been spitting blood. If he had, and he'd allowed Duchon to go on anyway—well, that certainly wouldn't endear him to other singers. Perhaps that was why he was so adamant about not being on the dressing-room level that night. I asked Osgood Springer if he'd seen Gatti there.

He closed his eyes to think. "I may have. I can't be sure." He opened his eyes and started to finger the scar on his jaw. "Are you going to tell Lieutenant O'Halloran about this? About my instructing James to say he didn't get into costume early?"

"I can't think of any reason why I should. If he asks me, I'll tell him the truth. But I won't bring the subject up."

"Thank you." He dropped his hand down from his face. "It was totally innocent on both James's part and my own. Perhaps *naïve* is a better word. I thought I was avoiding trouble." He laughed shortly.

"Mr. Springer, where was that bottle of spray the last time you saw it?"

"Why, in Duchon's dressing room, I suppose. The one he had later was Caruso's, wasn't it? The one Uncle Hummy picked up by mistake?"

"Yes, but that wasn't the dangerous one. Someone must have taken Duchon's spray out of his dressing room to put the ammonia in it. Then Duchon missed it and sent Uncle Hummy to look. Uncle Hummy spotted Caruso's spray and made the natural mistake of thinking that was the one he'd been sent to look for."

Springer raised his eyebrows. "So Duchon then had another bottle of safe spray."

"But it didn't stay safe, did it? Our villain must have substituted Duchon's original spray for that one when Duchon wasn't looking—only now it had ammonia in it."

"And in the meantime Caruso had sent back to his hotel for still another bottle of spray—"

"Confusing the matter even further," I said. "But when the police got there, there were only two bottles—the one with the ammonia and Caruso's second bottle. I wonder what happened to the other one."

"It was probably thrown away long ago."

Not that it mattered. Only one of those three bottles was important, and it had done its deadly job.

□ **14** □ *Geraldine Farrar Denies Marriage Plans*, the small headline declared starkly.

Newspaper people amaze me, they really do. It's incredible how they can tease a story out of absolutely nothing at all. If I had announced my engagement, well, that would have had some news value. But here I was getting all sorts of free publicity because I had *not* announced my engagement! My name was splashed through all the morning papers, all of them hinting I was some sort of exotic *femme fatale* irresistible to innocent young men.

I didn't mind.

When I'd returned home from the Museum of Natural History the day before, Caruso had been waiting for me, demanding a "report" on whatever I'd found out. I told him about Springer's seeing Duchon coughing blood, and how that had prompted him to tell Jimmy Freeman to get into costume early. Caruso seemed disappointed. He wanted Osgood Springer to be the villain.

I flipped through the rest of the newspapers. Conan Doyle had accused the Germans of abusing wounded prisoners. One-fourth the population of Belgium was dependent upon American bounty, which was feeding 175,000 a day in Brussels alone. The *Lusitania* was to sail under the Union Jack. Still no news of Prague; Emmy Destinn would be unhappy about that. I wondered what it must feel like, never knowing what was going on in your own country.

There was one article headlined *Should Women Vote in New York?* I didn't even bother to read that one; men would never willingly give up the whip hand. New spring fashions—oh dear, puff sleeves were back! Well, that was something Emmy *would* be happy about.

And then I saw something on the entertainment page of the *Times* that chilled me down to the marrow of my bones: a small advertisement announcing that Emma Calvé was appearing at the Palace Theatre. Emma Calvé! In a vaudeville house! It was Emma Calvé who'd sung in the first opera I ever saw, that production of *Carmen* in Boston that convinced me I was destined to be an opera singer. Emma Calvé, my inspiration and my idol! Now I was the one who was singing *Carmen* while she was playing the Palace along with the jugglers and the comedians and the trained-dog acts and Lord knows what else. The thought gave me no pleasure, no pleasure at all.

I swore to myself right then and there that at the first sign my voice was beginning to go, at the *very* first sign, I would retire. No prolonging of a dying career for me, no singing in vaudeville houses or saloons or town halls in little places nobody ever heard of. When I made my exit, I wanted it to be a graceful one, full of taste and discretion. Abdicate while you're still queen, that's the way to go.

I thrust the papers aside in irritation. I'd already put in several hours in the music room, but the practicing wasn't good because my mind had been on other things. There were two things I had to do today, and I didn't want to do either one of them. I had to try to pin Morris Gest down as to why he'd sneaked backstage right before *Carmen*. And I had to cheer up Jimmy Freeman. He'd made a fool of himself again when he told everyone I was going to marry him, and now he was feeling depressed.

It was beginning to look as if Morris Gest was the only real suspect left. I counted out Jimmy, Osgood Springer, Caruso, and myself, of course. Emmy Destinn hated Duchon, but he was no real threat to her. He *was* a threat to Scotti and Amato, by being in a position to take their roles away from them; but both Scotti and Amato had dispatched rival baritones before without having to dump ammonia into their spray bottles. They simply outsang them. Duchon was a bigger threat to Gatti-Casazza, who clearly was worried about losing his job to him. Very well, a question mark by Gatti's name, absurd though that was. Toscanini wasn't backstage long enough to do any damage. Dr. Curtis had no reason for wanting Duchon out of the way. And David Belasco hadn't even met him.

So that left Morris, seething with resentment over the way Duchon had cheated him and fearful of losing his reputation as a tough operator it didn't pay to cross. But that sneaky, underhanded way of getting even just didn't sound like Morris; a full-page advertisement in the newspaper denouncing Duchon as a duplicitous double-dealer—yes, that was more Morris's style. But not ammonia in the throat spray when nobody was looking.

My plan was to drop in at Morris's office unannounced, but when I got there his secretary told me he was at Carnegie Hall arranging a concert. My chauffeur let me out at the corner of Seventh Avenue and Fifty-seventh Street and drove away to look for a place to park. I found Morris coming out of one of the business offices in the concert hall.

His rubbery face broke into a smile when he saw me. "Ah, Gerry, what luck! I was planning to call you in a day or two. I got a proposition for you, darling. How about taking over that concert schedule I set up for Philippe Duchon? It would be a nice gesture on your part."

And it would mean some money for you. "I don't want to talk about that now, Morris. But there is something I want to ask you. In private." I opened one of the doors to the main auditorium; that huge place was dark and empty and quiet—no rehearsal in progress, thank goodness. "In here."

Morris propped the door open so we'd get some light from the hall and sat down beside me in the last row. I casually mentioned my chauffeur would be coming in as soon as he parked the limousine—and then realized what I was doing. I was *protecting* myself! From Morris! Good heavens.

Plunge in. "Morris, I want you to tell me why you went backstage right before *Carmen* started. And why you told David Belasco you were in the gentlemen's restroom. I want the truth, Morris."

He grunted. "Everybody's full of questions these days. Why do you want to know?"

"*Morris.* Tell me."

"Oh, all right, I suppose it won't make any difference now. I went back to see Caruso. I want to take over the management of his affairs. Not his bookings—his regular agents could still handle that. But Caruso needs a personal manager, if he'd just realize it. And it might as well be me."

"You wanted to talk to him about a thing like that while he was getting ready for a performance?"

"I just wanted to plant the idea. We'd have talked about it later."

"Rico didn't say anything to me about that."

"I never saw him! I stopped to break up an argument and it took longer than I thought it would and—well, there just wasn't time."

"What argument? Who?"

"Dr. Curtis and Philippe Duchon. Duchon fought with everybody, didn't he?"

"Dr. Curtis! What were they arguing about?"

"Curtis's fee. He said Duchon had consulted him about his throat and then refused to pay his bill. Duchon said Dr. Curtis hadn't done anything and didn't deserve to be paid. I don't think Curtis cared about the money at all—he just hated that highhanded way Duchon had of treating people. I wasn't any too fond of it myself, as you know."

"Is that all it was? Why didn't you want David to know about it?"

Morris sighed. "I didn't want him knowing I was trying to drum up more business. The Old Man says I spend too much time at work as it is and I ought to cut back. He says I'm neglecting my family."

Oh my—such a simple explanation, and it so had the ring of truth to it! "Well," I said, "I don't think anyone so addicted to work as David Belasco has the right to tell you to ease up. Good luck with Caruso. And Morris—thank you for telling me."

He laughed. "The cat's outta the bag anyway. Lieutenant O'Halloran made me tell him yesterday."

So the lieutenant had been there first. "Does David know now?"

"Yes. He's furious, of course."

My chauffeur showed up just then, so I left Morris to cope with his father-in-law problem the best he could. Our little talk had lifted one burden but added another. I was delighted at no longer having to think of Morris as my one real suspect, but I was also at something of a loss because now I had *no* suspects.

I couldn't seriously suspect Dr. Curtis, in spite of what Morris had just told me. Philippe Duchon had been spitting up blood right before he saw Dr. Curtis—who had told him earlier that nothing was wrong with his throat. I was willing to bet that was how the argument started. But it was absurd to think of crotchety, outspoken Dr. Holbrook Curtis deliberately damaging the throat of a patient who owed him money. There was no way that could happen.

But it did sort of round things out. Now *everybody* had a reason for disliking Philippe Duchon.

I was expecting Jimmy Freeman at six; we'd talk a little and then go out to dinner. If Jimmy were seen in public with me so soon after the engagement fiasco, perhaps he'd feel a little less foolish. The telephone kept ringing at regular intervals; it was always Caruso. I'd told Bella to say I was out whenever he called for the next couple of days. The man was becoming a nuisance.

While I was waiting for Jimmy, I worked on a song I was writing as a birthday gift for my godchild, the daughter of a long-time fan. That was one of the nicest things about the gerryflappers; even when they married and started their families, they remained loyal fans. I was godmother to four little Geraldines and one small Gerald, and I kept careful track of their birthdays so I could send them something. The gerryflappers were always giving *me* things— some fine sewing, miniature paintings they'd done themselves, personal things like that. Last year one of them gave me the measles.

The song was coming along nicely. The little girl I was writing it for would be five in April. It's never too early to start a child singing; I can't remember a time in my own life when I was not singing. I owe so much to the kind of childhood my mother gave me. In case you haven't noticed, the primary occupation of little girls is sitting still. *Stop fidgeting, behave yourself, act like a lady, don't, don't, don't*—that's what little girls hear the most. But my mother *never* said those words to me. She said *Go! Do! Sing!*

Jimmy arrived right on time, looking sheepish and a

little disconsolate. I suggested that after dinner we drop in at the Metropolitan for a couple of acts of *Aïda;* Pasquale Amato was making his first appearance after recovering from his illness and I wanted to wish him well. Emmy Destinn was singing, but Caruso, fortunately, was not. I'd had enough of Caruso for a while.

Jimmy was far from his usual peppy self. I had to work on him; only when I began flirting openly did he start to respond. When at last he laughed, I felt we were getting somewhere. We dined at the Waldorf, and over dinner Jimmy mentioned that Osgood Springer had told him about our little meeting at the museum the day before. "He said you were very understanding."

"Mm. Didn't you wonder why he wanted you to get into costume so early? For *Carmen*?"

"No, not really. Mr. Springer just said for me to get ready. He didn't say why."

"And you just did it. Why?"

"Why what? Why did I get into costume?"

"Why do you do everything Mr. Springer tells you to? Don't you ever question him?"

"Never. I owe him everything, Gerry. I wouldn't be singing at the Metropolitan at all if it weren't for Osgood Springer. Besides, he never tells me to do anything that isn't good for me."

"You owe him *everything*? Oh, really, Jimmy! He's your vocal coach, that's all. How could you owe him everything?"

"Well, he did give up all his other students in order to concentrate on my career. That's a pretty big sacrifice, I'd say."

I put down my fork. "I didn't know that."

Jimmy nodded. "He's put all his eggs in one basket, so to speak, and I'm the basket. I think he sees my career as a substitute for the one he had to give up when he had his accident. He does everything for me, Gerry. He rehearses me every day, he negotiates my contracts, he fights with Gatti-Casazza for me—he does more for me than my own father ever did. I even live in a suite of rooms in his house. I owe him, more than I'll ever be able to pay."

That certainly put a different cast on things. Jimmy's career was Springer's *life*—would the vocal coach destroy another singer to protect it? Could he have lied to me about seeing Duchon spit blood? Suddenly a terrible truth occurred to me: *Everybody could be lying.* I'd not really questioned anything anyone had told me. Foolish, foolish! How many lies had I accepted as truth? I couldn't tell who was lying and who wasn't.

Morris Gest, for instance. He could have lied about why he'd gone backstage. How could anyone check up on him? Could he have gone back to argue with Duchon one more time, spotted the ammonia in Emmy's medicine bag, and then lost his head? He could have given in to one irrational moment, his desire to get even with Duchon overriding everything else.

Or Gatti-Casazza—I still didn't know if he was lying about not going into Duchon's dressing room. Oh, there was no end to it! Scotti could have lied, Toscanini could have lied. You could even make out a good case against Emmy Destinn. After all, she was the one who'd brought the ammonia backstage; the only other person who knew she'd have it with her was Dr. Curtis. Dr. Curtis?

I had to face the fact that all my so-called "investigating" had left me in a state of abysmal ignorance. Once I started doubting one person's word, then I ended up doubting everybody's. That's what I should have done right from the start—not believe anybody.

"You're very quiet," Jimmy smiled.

We finished dinner and got to the opera house in time for Act II of *Aïda*. Pasquale Amato was in fine form; you'd never have known he'd been sick. Emmy Destinn was weighed down by about a ton of stage jewelry—the most richly ornamented slave girl in opera, no doubt.

During the intermission we went backstage; I found Amato and gave him a big hug and a kiss. Jimmy gracefully congratulated the other baritone on his performance in a role Jimmy would have liked to be singing himself. Growing up, maybe?

"You just miss Rico," Amato told me. "He says he tries to telephone you all day."

"I've been out all day," I lied. "Is he still here?"

"No, he goes home to bed. Scotti keeps him up all last night playing cards and he is tired. You know how it is."

I knew. All-night card games were nothing unusual for Scotti, but they were for Caruso. Lucky for me he was tired and had gone home early.

Since we were already backstage, I decided to do something I'd never done before. With Jimmy in tow, I headed for the star dressing room to see Emmy Destinn.

"Gerry!" she exclaimed in surprise. "This is the first time you've ever come backstage during one of my operas! But of course—you came to see Amato, did you not? Tell me something, did you hear any flat notes in *Ritorna vincitor*?"

Now, since *Ritorna vincitor* is the soprano aria that comes in the first act and we had missed the first act entirely, I was able to say truthfully that I hadn't heard any flat notes. "Did you, Jimmy?" He shook his head, straight-faced.

Emmy sniffed. "Toscanini says I flatted at the end."

"Toscanini is crazy."

"Oh, I know that," she answered in utter seriousness, "but he still has perfect pitch."

I noticed Emmy didn't have much to say to Jimmy; in fact, I caught her shooting an uneasy glance at him once. Then I remembered that on the day I'd taken her to my dressmaker, she'd expressed the opinion that Jimmy wasn't nearly as innocent as he appeared to be. Before the atmosphere could grow uncomfortable, I spoke a hasty goodbye and dragged Jimmy away.

We stayed through Act III and then slipped away. At my place I had a little trouble persuading Jimmy I didn't want him to come in; but still he went away whistling, no longer depressed. At least *that* part of the day's efforts had gone well.

On the whole, I don't like to sing matinees. But when the opera is *Madame Butterfly*, I'll sing it at eight o'clock in the morning if I have to.

While I don't entertain any particularly warm feelings

for Puccini himself, I adore his music; of all the composers whose work I've sung, his is best suited to my voice and personal singing style. And that's important—oh, I can't tell you how important that is! Some singers will sing anything, any role they're asked to sing whether it fits their voices or not. But not I. One reason my career has progressed so steadily is that I have one gift most other singers do not: I know my limitations.

I think of myself as a singing actress; I always try to choose roles that will display my voice at its best while giving me plenty of opportunity to indulge my thespian skills (which are considerable, if I do say so myself). I've never hesitated to abandon a role once I decided it was not right for me. Once, in Berlin, I learned the role of Leonora in *Il Trovatore*. I spent months studying with my vocal coach and weeks in rehearsal—and then after all that work, I sang the role exactly once. At the time I'd felt like a cricket chirping away through the thunderous chords and ponderous orchestration of Verdi's score. The German critics, usually so kind, had nothing but harsh words for my performance—and I had to admit they were right. I never sang Leonora again.

But it's possible to learn from mistakes like Leonora, and in time I did develop the ability to look at a score and hear in my head how the music would sound sung in my voice. That ability kept me from making several bad mistakes—but sometimes it was hard. Years ago Richard Strauss approached me in Berlin; he was not happy, he said, with the soprano singing the lead in his new opera then playing in Dresden. The opera was *Salome*, and would Fraulein Farrar consider singing the role when the opera moved to Berlin?

So, at Strauss's invitation, I attended a performance of *Salome* in Dresden—and saw the problem immediately. The title role was being sung by a muscular, meat-and-potatoes soprano who looked like an escaped Valkyrie from a Richard Wagner opus. Naturally the composer wanted someone slimmer and more attractive in the role of the seductive, sexually obsessed young girl who demanded (and got) the head of John the Baptist on a platter. ''So I have come to the most beautiful soprano in Europe for help," Strauss had said flatteringly.

But as I listened, and later when I was reading the score, all sorts of warning bells were going off in my mind. It was an exciting role, but it wasn't right for my voice. I could make Salome *look* good, but I couldn't make her sound right. So even though it almost killed me, I turned down the role.

So whom did Strauss get to sing the role in Berlin? Emmy Destinn! Hefty Emmy, looking every bit as Valkyrie-ish as the Dresden soprano she replaced. Vocally, she *was* right for the role—but that's as far as it went. Her Dance of the Seven Veils, for instance, had to be seen to be believed. Emmy alternately lumbered about the stage like a distraught elephant and posed statuesquely, discreetly dropping a bedsheet-sized veil now and then. It was undoubtedly the most chaste striptease ever to be performed on any stage, anywhere, at any time.

Speaking of Emmy, she was Covent Garden's favorite Madame Butterfly at the time the Metropolitan first decided to stage Puccini's Oriental opera. That was in 1907, and Emmy hadn't yet worked up the courage to cross the Atlantic and try her fortune in America. So I became the Metropolitan Opera's first Butterfly—and you can be sure I wasted no time in establishing ownership of the role. When Emmy finally did come to New York, Gatti-Casazza was quick to notice that when she sang Butterfly the house was half empty; but when I sang the role, the house sold out quickly and they even paid to stand in the back and listen. Emmy hadn't sung the role for some time now. So let her keep *Salome* and *La Fanciulla del West; Madame Butterfly* was *mine*.

Not that it had been easy—far from it! Puccini had come from Italy to supervise that first production, and he'd made life miserable for all of us. Caruso and Scotti were in the cast with me, and Scotti was the only one the composer didn't criticize constantly. Puccini didn't like *anything;* he whined and complained and objected to this and disapproved of that. The chorus was no good, Caruso was lazy, my voice didn't carry (I was singing half-voice in rehearsal, for heaven's sake!). Puccini almost drove the poor conductor crazy (not Toscanini; he and Gatti hadn't left La Scala for the Metropolitan yet).

Puccini and I just weren't attuned at all. For one thing, he considered himself quite a ladies' man. I, however, found his charm utterly resistible; I even mentioned to a few people that the only reason he wore such a luxuriant mustache was to hide the fact that he had rabbit teeth. Puccini heard about it and retaliated by criticizing my singing.

But the composer changed his tune quickly enough once he heard and saw the audience's response to our production, and more specifically, to *me*. They *loved* me. And not only that first-night audience; the general public made a sort of pet of my Butterfly. For instance, I'd shaved my eyebrows for the role—and unintentionally set the pencil-line style that actresses and debutantes aped for years.

So Puccini had started telling interviewers that I was exactly right for the role, that I was the most charming Butterfly ever to sing his opera, and on and on. What a hypocrite! He'd gradually come to understand that every time I sang one of his operas, his royalties took a dramatic leap upward. I'd made a lot of money for Puccini over the years.

And I was going to make some more for him at the Saturday matinee. Caruso was not singing *Butterfly* this season, although Scotti still was. It's not a particularly gratifying opera for a tenor (for a soprano, it's *magnificent*). But the real reason Caruso wasn't singing was money. Caruso sold out the house every time he sang, I sold out the house every time I sang. Gatti-Casazza figured he was losing money whenever we sang together, so he split us up as often as he could. I was lucky to have Caruso for *Carmen*, I suppose.

But right then I didn't miss him at all. Caruso had actually shown up at my place that morning wanting a "report"—on the day of a performance! I threw him out.

The first person I saw backstage Saturday afternoon was a man who looked vaguely familiar. He also looked terribly out of place, so I marched myself up to him and demanded to know who he was. He said he was Sergeant somebody of the police and showed me some impressively official-looking identification. Lieutenant O'Halloran had stationed him there—"to watch for the old man you folks call Uncle Hummy" was the way he put it.

"Uncle Hummy?" I said. "Why are you watching for him?"

"He's dropped out of sight, Miss Farrar. Nobody's seen him since the night Mr. Duchon used that ammonia spray on his throat."

I thought back. It was true; I hadn't seen Uncle Hummy since the *Carmen* performance. Since he was always careful to stay out of the way when he *was* there, I hadn't even missed him. "Are you sure?" I asked Sergeant Whatsisname. "He could be here now, out of sight somewhere. I know he sometimes spends the night here."

"No, ma'am, he's not here now. We found the place he sleeps when he stays overnight—upstairs in the wardrobe department. He hasn't been here once since *Carmen*, we're sure of that. And nobody knows where he lives."

"Surely Lieutenant O'Halloran doesn't suspect Uncle Hummy?"

"He just wants to ask him some questions, ma'am."

Oh my—I wondered what all that meant. Uncle Hummy? I hurried up to my dressing room, where Bella was waiting for me to unlock the door. Inside, I'd barely had time to get my hat and coat off before who should come bursting in but my least favorite tenor of the moment.

"Gerry!" Caruso cried. "You hear? Uncle Hummy, he is missing!"

"I heard."

"Do you not see what this means? Uncle Hummy did it! And now he goes into hiding!"

"It doesn't mean anything of the sort," I snapped. "Maybe he's ill. Maybe he's been here without the police's knowing."

Caruso shook his head vehemently. "Uncle Hummy never gets ill. And the police, they watch for him every night since *Carmen*. He must be guilty—why else does he hide?"

"Oh, I don't know," I said irritably, "perhaps he saw something and he's afraid. Get out, Rico—I have to warm up."

"Plenty of time for the warming up. We never suspect Uncle Hummy before—"

"And we're not going to suspect him now. Rico, you're making a pest of yourself! I've had enough of your badgering me! I want you out of here—*now*."

"But—"

"Out! Out, *out*, OUT!"

He got out. I did some deep-breathing exercises to calm myself down. If ever I went into the detective business again, it would *not* be with Enrico Caruso as my partner.

The truth was, I wished I'd never started this. After all my prying and asking of impertinent questions, I was right back where I'd started. I had no proof of anything, just suspicions—and they weren't any too reliable. And Caruso had lost what little perspective he'd had; look how quick he'd been to suspect poor old Uncle Hummy, just because we didn't know whom else to point the finger at!

Scotti stuck his head through the open door. "Dinner afterwards, *carissima*?"

"Sorry, Toto," I answered absently, "I have a prior engagement."

He stepped into the dressing room, glowering so darkly that Bella actually shrank back from him a little. "A prior engagement?" he roared. "With little Jimmy Freeman, no doubt!"

Oh, I didn't have time for this! "No, with Gatti-Casazza, if you must know."

That stopped him. "Gatti? Now I must worry about Gatti too?"

"Worry about whomever you want, but please do it in your own dressing room, Toto." He was gone before I'd finished the sentence.

Toscanini was next. I'd just finished putting on my costume when he waltzed in and demanded to know what I'd said to Scotti. "He is in bad mood and it is your fault."

"Oh, go away," I said crossly. "Everybody's pestering me to death today."

Toscanini gave me an elaborately sarcastic bow. "But *certo*, Miss High-and-Mighty Prima Donna. One must do nothing to disturb the *star*." He left before I could throw something at him.

The omens were not favorable for a great matinee.

But as I stood in the wings waiting to make my entrance, I put all those other matters out of my mind. I listened to Scotti singing, and became aware once more of how *likable* the man was on stage. He had the capacity to make audiences love him no matter what character he was singing. That was why he made such a compelling Scarpia in *Tosca*. Scarpia is one of the blackest villains ever to tread the operatic boards, but Scotti always made him evilly attractive—much more exciting than the one-dimensional interpretation usually given the part. Scotti's role in *Butterfly* was a sympathetic one; so by the time he'd finished his scene, I'd completely forgiven him for acting like a jealous lover.

It was time. Butterfly's entrance is a difficult one; I have to go on followed by a women's chorus and cross a narrow little arched bridge, singing away all the while. All of us have to look like delicate, fragile porcelain dolls, taking these tiny little steps, moving in graceful unison. We all mentally hold our breath until the bridge is successfully negotiated, and that day it went flawlessly. I've sung *Butterfly* about fifty times so far, and I've never been able to figure out why the entrance goes perfectly one performance and then falls to pieces the next. It's a mystery.

Since this was one of Toscanini's sarcastic days, I half expected some hanky-panky from the Maestro; but he did his job with his usual professional verve. I finished the love duet with the tenor, and the Act I curtain closed to enthusiastic applause as well as squeals and screams from the gerryflappers.

I headed straight for Scotti's dressing room. He was sitting at his dressing table, staring glumly into the mirror. I went up behind him and put my hands on his shoulders.

"It's a business dinner, Toto," I said. "There's something I must talk to Gatti about."

His slow, big smile filled the mirror; he placed his hands over mine, not doubting my word at all. That was all right, then.

In my own dressing room I was refreshing my make-up when Caruso popped in again, grinning from ear to ear. "A *beautiful* Butterfly, Gerry—exquisite! Simply exquisite! And you are right about Uncle Hummy. I am foolish man to suspect Uncle Hummy."

"Oh, I'm glad you agree," I said in relief. "We must be careful not to jump to conclusions."

He nodded. "It has to be Osgood Springer after all," he said as he left. I'd rejoiced too soon.

Back downstairs and into Act II. That afternoon was one of those performances that just kept getting better as we went along. By the time of Butterfly's suicide at the end of the opera, I could swear I heard a few people sobbing in the audience. I just *love* it when that happens!

Gatti-Casazza loved it too, as he told me over dinner at the Ritz. "Not a single empty seat today!" he exulted. "In spite of the weather, everyone shows up."

It had been raining all day, the gray gloomy kind of rain that makes people want to stay in bed and sleep until it goes away. I waited until Gatti started to get that drowsy look that comes whenever he's had enough to eat; I'd decided my best approach was a nice, straightforward lie. "The night Duchon was injured," I said, "remember that? You did go into his dressing room. Caruso wasn't the only one to see you." I hoped he wouldn't ask who else had been watching.

It took him a moment to realize what I was saying. *"Che dice?"*

"I said you were seen. Going into Duchon's dressing room. Two witnesses, Gatti. Yet over and over again you've denied being there."

"You are accusing me . . . ?"

"Only of not telling the whole truth. I'm trying to find out what happened. You *were* there, weren't you? You might as well tell me why."

He looked at me a long time and then sighed. "I go to see Duchon because he asked me to. No, Duchon did not *ask*—he *summoned*. Then when I hear what happens later, I think it is best not to involve myself. I lie, and now you find me out. I am sorry, Gerry."

"Why be sorry?" I muttered. "Everybody else lied too. What did Duchon want to see you about?"

"Toscanini. Duchon claimed he was not satisfied with, ah, the quality of conducting at the Metropolitan. *Cielo!* He said Toscanini is careless and imprecise, and he wanted me to watch him carefully that night."

"Careless? Imprecise?" I couldn't believe what I was hearing. "*Toscanini?!*"

"Absurd, of course. It was just more trouble-making— the Frenchman thrived on it, I do believe."

"What did you tell him?"

Gatti pulled at his beard. "I fear I lost my temper. We had an argument—no shouting, but some unpleasant name-calling on both sides. You see why I do not want anyone to know I was there? If the police know . . ."

"Yes, I see. Does Toscanini know Duchon was complaining about his conducting?"

Gatti frowned. "I think he must. Toscanini—eh, he is not acting like himself. You know he wants me to resign with him? He says we leave La Scala together, and now we must leave the Metropolitan together."

"I know he's been thinking of leaving, but he's threatened to walk out before. He's serious about wanting you to go with him?"

"As a protest to the Metropolitan's board of directors," he nodded. "It is their policy of retrenchment, you see. Toscanini thinks if we both resign, the board will come to its senses."

"And hire you both back?"

Gatti threw up his hands. "Who knows? But I cannot resign! My duty is to the opera house, not to one man— even if that man is Toscanini. He is angry with the board, he was angry with Duchon, and now he is angry with me."

"Then it really is serious."

"Very serious. He is *violently* angry, Gerry. It shames me to say this, but I have even wondered if it was not *he* who put the ammonia in Duchon's spray bottle."

There it was—that ugly suspiciousness that kept creeping in no matter how much you wanted to keep it away. Emmy Destinn suspected Jimmy Freeman. Caruso suspected Osgood Springer. I tended to suspect Morris Gest. And now here was Gatti-Casazza suspecting his old friend Toscanini. "Did you know Duchon was spitting up blood before the performance started?"

"No!"

"While he was warming up. You didn't see any signs?"

"He had not yet started warming up when I was there. Oh, if I had known—if I had known, I would have substituted Freeman immediately and none of this would have happened! Duchon would still be alive!"

"*Would* you have taken Duchon out?" I asked. "If you'd known about the blood, I mean. Would you really?"

He stared at me. "Of course I would! You think I let a singer go on who is spitting blood? Is that what you think?"

"Well, uh . . ."

He threw his napkin down on the table in disgust. "You are like all the rest! None of you, you never credit me with any decent behavior! Everything that goes wrong, you blame me! You make me into a monster. Gerry, listen to me—*I am not a monster*. I resent this. I resent it very much."

A strange feeling crept over me that took me a moment to identify because I feel it so seldom. Then I had it: It was guilt. Gatti-Casazza was absolutely right; we did all tend to blame him for everything that happened, and to ascribe base motives to everything he did. The man in charge is such a convenient scapegoat. I felt like an idiot.

"I feel like an idiot," I told him. "I didn't think, Gatti, and I'm sorry. Of course you wouldn't have let Duchon sing if you'd known—and it was wrong of me to imply that you would have. I apologize, and I'll never say or even think a thing like that again."

Gatti stared at me absolutely dumbfounded, and it wasn't

hard to guess why. It was the first time in our long association that I had ever apologized to him for anything.

We'd finished our dinner, and Gatti had to get back to the opera house. It was *The Magic Flute* that night, and something was always going wrong with that one, he said. Gatti and I parted friends, better friends than we were before, I think.

When I got home, Bella met me at the door. "Mr. Caruso was here," she whispered uneasily, "but I wouldn't let him in. Then Mr. Scotti came, and I did let *him* in. He's here now. Did I do right?"

"You did exactly right," I told her, and sent her to bed, where she'd be out of the way.

❑ 15 ❑

At the crack of dawn the next day, Caruso showed up in the hallway outside my apartment door with his valet, Mario. Mario was loaded down with a collapsible chair, an ashtray, a thermos jug of coffee, one pillow, and three newspapers. Once he had the tenor settled comfortably, Mario rang the bell and told the startled maid that Signor Caruso was fully prepared to camp in the hallway indefinitely, until Miss Farrar saw fit to grant him entrance. He, Mario, would keep his employer supplied with all the necessities of life for as long as was necessary.

I kept him waiting an hour, while I bathed and had breakfast. Then, when I couldn't put it off any longer, I let him in.

First he grumbled at me for keeping him waiting so long. Next he sent Mario into the kitchen with instructions to flirt with whomever he found there. Then he seated himself in the middle of my best sofa and demanded that I "report."

"Rico, it's a good thing we're friends," I told him. "Otherwise I would probably have killed you by now. I can't stop everything and 'report' whenever you get fidgety. Wait for me to contact *you*."

"But you are so *slow*, Gerry," Caruso complained. "The killer, he gets farther away every day, no? We must move with dispatch!"

"I haven't been idling away my time, you know," I snapped. Who was he to call me *slow*? But I did make an effort to remember what I'd learned since the last time I talked to him.

I told Caruso that Morris Gest had indeed gone backstage before *Carmen* and he'd found Duchon embroiled in an argument with Dr. Curtis. I told him Osgood Springer had given up all his other students to concentrate on Jimmy Freeman's career. I told him Gatti-Casazza had also been backstage during the crucial time, and that he too had quarreled with Duchon. I told him Toscanini might not be back next season.

That last piece of information Caruso dealt with by

refusing to believe it. "Never!" he said emphatically. "Toscanini *never* leaves the Metropolitan. He is part of the institution, no? The Metropolitan is *home*. Toscanini stays here forever."

"Gatti doesn't think so. And I'm afraid he might be right."

Just then we had a visitor. Bella showed in Pasquale Amato, who wasted no time on amenities. "They tell me at the Knickerbocker that you come here," he said to Caruso accusingly. "I know what you two are up to! Gerry, you should know better."

I agreed. "But sometimes circumstances force you to do what you'd rather not do. Sit down, Pasquale. Have you had breakfast?"

But he wouldn't be diverted. "Rico, you are impossible—I wash my hands of you. But Gerry, the man you seek—he is dangerous, no? What if he begins to think you suspect him?"

"I've been very careful always to leave the impression that I did *not* suspect anyone." That was true.

"Nevertheless, you should not go hunting a criminal." He looked exasperated with both of us. "*Per giunta*, what do you learn? Do you now know who hated Philippe Duchon enough to destroy him? Of course not! What do you know?"

"Well," I sighed, "not a whole lot. It all seems to come down to Uncle Hummy."

"It does?" Caruso asked wonderingly.

"Of course it does. The old man must have seen something that frightened him off. Why else would he stay away from the opera house so long?"

"He might be dead," Amato said heavily.

Caruso and I exchanged an anguished look; neither of us had thought of that. I asked, "Would an accidental killer kill again, this time deliberately, to hide his first crime? I know nothing about these things. But until and unless Uncle Hummy turns up dead, we have to go on the assumption that he is alive somewhere and can tell us something we don't know."

"Alive *somewhere*," Amato stressed.

"Lieutenant O'Halloran," Caruso said, "he looks high and low, and he cannot find one person who has even *heard* of Uncle Hummy."

"How did you know that?" I said. "O'Halloran surely didn't tell you."

Caruso grinned smugly. "I ask the sergeant who waits backstage."

Amato got a strange look on his face. "I just think of something. Does anyone call him Uncle Hummy besides us? 'Uncle Hummy,' it is our nickname for him at the opera house, yes? But when the police ask about Uncle Hummy *outside* the opera house—"

"Nobody knows whom they're talking about!" I cried. "No wonder they couldn't find him!"

"Pasquale, you are good detective," Caruso said admiringly. "That name 'Uncle Hummy'—where does it come from?"

No one knew; both the nickname and the man who bore it antedated all three of us. I'd never once heard the old man humming, so it couldn't be that. "This makes a difference," I said excitedly. "Now we know what to do!"

"We do?" the two men said together.

"We do," I repeated firmly, reaching for the telephone. "What we do is mobilize the gerryflappers."

"The *gerryflappers?*" two voices said.

"Don't you see, they can find Uncle Hummy for us."

Caruso and Amato exchanged a look. "Gerry," said the latter, "how can the girls find him when the police cannot?"

"You'll see. Just wait a minute." I got the leader of the gerryflappers on the telephone and asked her to come over immediately. Then I called downstairs and instructed the doorman to let them in when they got there. *They*, plural, because Mildred never went anywhere without Phoebe.

"I repeat," Amato said patiently, "how can the girls succeed where the police fail?"

"Because the girls are going to have something to help them the police don't have," I told him. I went over to my writing desk and took out a couple of dozen sheets of foolscap. "Come here, Rico." He came. "Sit down. Now draw."

Caruso's face lit up like a spotlight when he understood. "Pictures! Pictures of Uncle Hummy—that is what the girls have! *Ella mi confonde*, Gerry! What a good idea!"

Even Amato was nodding in reluctant approval. Caruso fell to sketching with enthusiasm. No two of his drawings were exactly alike, but all were recognizably Uncle Hummy. He'd finished thirteen by the time Mildredandphoebe got there.

Phoebe was visibly awed at being in the company of three opera stars at the same time, but Mildred took it in stride. "What do you want us to do, Miss Farrar?" she asked briskly.

I explained. "I want you to round up as many of the other girls as you can and start a search for Uncle Hummy. He'll undoubtedly be in one of the Italian neighborhoods in town, and you'll have pictures to show around. Don't call him 'Uncle Hummy' when you ask about him. He'll be known by another name to his neighbors and family—I wonder if he has any family? Anyway, if you find him, don't say anything to him. We don't want to scare him off. Come back and tell *me* where he is. Do you have any questions?"

"Just one," said Mildred. "Who's Uncle Hummy?"

I stared at her a moment, and then both Amato and I laughed. Of course the girls wouldn't know who Uncle Hummy was. Uncle Hummy was part of our backstage life; Mildredandphoebe were part of the audience. I let Amato explain as I went over to check on Caruso's progress. "One thing," Amato remarked. "Those immigrant neighborhoods—are they safe places for young ladies to go alone?"

"We'll go in pairs," Mildred said.

"In twos," Phoebe explained further.

"In threes," I said, "and only during the daytime. If you have any brothers or gentlemen friends you can take with you, so much the better. But find him."

"We'll find him," Mildred said. "Don't worry, Miss Farrar."

"Don't worry," Phoebe echoed.

Caruso had finished the last drawing. "This is Uncle Hummy," he said, giving the sketches to the two girls. "An old man, you see. He smiles a lot, big teeth."

I touched Mildred on the shoulder. "I know, with so many people involved, discretion is going to be difficult. But it truly is important that Uncle Hummy not take fright and go looking for another hiding place."

"We'll be careful," Mildred said. "We'll say he's a relative we're trying to find."

"We'll be careful." Guess who said that.

Caruso was back at the desk, making another sketch. I asked him what that one was for. "For you and for me, *cara* Gerry. We go look too."

"Not today we don't. Don't you remember, Rico? We're meeting David Belasco this afternoon."

He struck his forehead with the palm of his hand. "*Per dio!* I forget." He held out the drawing hopefully to Amato, but at the baritone's look he quickly handed the paper to Mildredandphoebe. "Now be careful," he scolded them in a fatherly way, "and say nothing to Uncle Hummy if you find him!"

"Not a word," Mildred promised, and the two girls left to organize their search.

"Fans!" Amato was shaking his head. "We are using *fans* to do police work!"

I rather liked that *we*. "They might surprise you, Pasquale. They're bright girls, and full of energy—Lieutenant O'Halloran could use a few like them."

"Lieutenant O'Halloran!" Caruso exclaimed, aghast. "I forget all about him! What if he finds out what we do?"

"Why, he'll probably put you in jail and lock the door and throw away the key," I said gleefully, enjoying Caruso's discomfort. "That's what he promised to do, isn't it?"

"Gerry," Amato said in mock reproachfulness, "do not tease Rico. Great detectives must be treated with respect."

"But great detectives must not be afraid of the police, isn't that so?"

"True, true. Eh, Rico, you must practice unshrinking fortitude from now on."

Caruso decided he didn't like the tone the conversation was taking on and left in a huff. Ten minutes later he was back, a bit red in the face; he'd forgotten Mario. (So had I.) But then they left for good, and I invited Amato to stay for lunch on condition that we talk about anything in the world except matters pertaining to or stemming from the unexpected advent and abrupt departure of Philippe Duchon. He heartily agreed.

At three in the afternoon I met Caruso and David Belasco in one of the rehearsal halls at the Met. Some time ago I'd asked Belasco to coach me on my acting in the final duet from *Carmen*, but he'd said it wouldn't do much good unless both singers took part. So Caruso had grumblingly consented to try to do something about our stiff and unconvincing acting in the duet. There was only one more scheduled performance of *Carmen* before the season ended, and I did so want to get it right *once*.

Caruso had brought his own accompanist. Quickly we were deep into the duet, Belasco stopping us every time he saw something he thought we could do better. It wasn't going very well; Caruso would do what Belasco told him the first time we'd try it and then forget about it the next. I accused him of being uncooperative.

"Gerry, you know French is difficult language for me," he complained. "I have to think about the words as much as I think of the music. And then to remember *stop here, turn there*—it is too much!"

"It's not too much," I snarled. "You're not concentrating."

"Let's try this," Belasco said in his soft voice. "Mr. Caruso, you grab her hair. Gerry, fall to the floor and reach up with both hands and take hold of his wrist. Then Mr. Caruso, you start backing across the stage—it will look to the audience as if you're dragging her by the hair."

Caruso was appalled. "It is too complicated!"

"No, it isn't. Just try it."

We tried it—and tried it and tried it and tried it. Caruso finally got the action right, but he had trouble coordinating it with the music. I yelled at him to stop thinking about what the gerryflappers were doing and he yelled back that I should be thinking of nothing *but* what the gerryflappers were doing and the accompanist jumped up from the piano and wanted to know *what* the gerryflappers were doing and David Belasco had to stamp his feet on the floor to get our attention.

The whole session went like that. By the time we finished, Caruso and I were barely speaking to each other. He marched out in a huff again, the second time that day; his accompanist hurried after him.

Belasco patted perspiration from his forehead with a folded white handkerchief. ''I'm afraid our rehearsal wasn't a total success.''

''We're still a long way from perfect,'' I admitted, ''but we'll be better than we were. Thank you, David—both for your help and for your patience.''

''Is there trouble between you and Mr. Caruso?''

''Not yet,'' I said darkly, ''but there's going to be if he doesn't mend his ways.''

''Unfortunate. By the way, I have a message for you from Morris. He says Dr. Curtis couldn't have done it—he's afraid he left the wrong impression. Does that make any sense?''

''It makes a lot of sense,'' I smiled. Morris Gest didn't want me thinking that *he* thought Dr. Curtis's argument with Philippe Duchon had led to the doctor's contaminating the spray. I was glad to have the message for one very good reason: Would the real culprit worry about incriminating other people? I didn't want Morris to be the guilty one.

I thanked Belasco again and we both left. When I got home, Bella handed me a note from Mildredandphoebe. They'd had no luck in locating Uncle Hummy, but they'd try again tomorrow.

Three days later, and still no Uncle Hummy. By now Mildredandphoebe had a small army of fans out looking; Caruso had had to make quite a few more drawings. At least it kept him busy for a while. The rest of the time he spent pestering me. Three days of it.

He kept telling me to think of something to do. I kept telling him I *had* thought of something to do and we could only wait while it was being done. He told me to think of something else. I told him to go take a swim in the Hudson. Fortunately Scotti and Amato seemed to agree between them to take turns acting as a buffer; otherwise Caruso and I would have torn each other's eyes out long ago.

Then came the season's final performance of *Carmen*. Backstage, the man Lieutenant O'Halloran had stationed there was still standing watch, still waiting for Uncle Hummy. Surely they didn't still believe he was coming back? I caught Gatti-Casazza's arm as he hurried past. "How much longer is that man going to be here?" I asked him.

"I wish I knew," Gatti answered. "I ask him, but he does not know. He just does what his lieutenant tells him. He is not in your way, is he?"

"Oh no, he's no bother. It's just that seeing him here every time I come in . . ."

"I understand. I too wish he would go away. The police, they find nothing. We will never know who destroyed Philippe Duchon's life."

"Don't be too sure of that," I smiled, but refused to say more when he pressed me.

I was just starting up the stairs to the dressing rooms when Caruso came blustering in, making his usual noisy entrance. What kind of performance would we have that night? I decided it was worth one more attempt, and called to him. "Rico, will you try? Will you remember what David Belasco told us and try?"

"I always try," he said grandly. "And I may even remember."

"You *may*. If you feel like it?"

"*Per dio*, why not? There are *two* of us on the stage, no?"

"Then why must I do the acting for both of us?" I snarled.

"You do the acting for *everybody*!" he roared.

Scotti appeared silently from nowhere and led me away up the stairs; Amato appeared equally silently from the same place and led Caruso away *from* the stairs. "That man is impossible," I complained to Scotti as I went into my dressing room.

"He is a *terrible* man," he agreed earnestly. "You are patient woman to put up with him."

"Oh, stop humoring me—I'm in no mood for it."

I was mad and I stayed mad, all the time I was getting into costume and make-up and warming up. I was mad back down the stairs and mad while I was waiting in the wings. Then my cue came and I made my entrance and started to sing—and, funny thing, I forgot about being mad.

We got through the first act without mishap, and almost made it through the second. Caruso and I had avoided each other during intermission, the second act started, Amato came on in his black wig and droopy mustache and sang that blasted *Toreador Song*, and then shortly after that Caruso made his entrance.

I must say a word here about saliva. It's an unpleasant subject, I know, but it's one of those very real problems singers have to worry about. Singing opera makes all sorts of demands on the human body, and sometimes saliva accumulates in the mouth as a result of all the *pushing* you have to do to get the sound out. That's why the first few rows of the audience sometimes see one singer spraying another—which makes love duets particularly hazardous. Often there's simply no time to swallow, if you're in the middle of a tricky passage or a continuous line.

Enrico Caruso had worked out his own solution to the saliva problem. Over the years he'd developed the absolutely disgusting habit of turning his back to the audience and *spitting*—right there on the stage, where anyone could step in it! He didn't do it often, but the fact that he did it at all I found downright nauseating. And he did it during the second act of *Carmen*. We were locked into what was supposed to be a passionate embrace—when he spit right over my shoulder on to the stage floor.

I slapped his face.

The audience thought it was part of the action; Carmen changes mood a lot in that act. But Caruso knew. And I wanted him to know. "How *dare* you?" I hissed at him under cover of the music.

"You go too far!" he hissed back.

I went too far? I had a thing or two I wanted to tell him, but right then I had to go back to singing of Carmen's undying love for Don José. David Belasco had suggested that at the end of Act II Caruso pick me up and carry me off the stage. Well, he did, in a way; he slung me over his shoulder like a sack of flour and barreled his way into the wings before I knew what was happening.

"I'll kill him!" I screamed when the curtain was closed. "Where is he? I'll kill him!"

"Now, Gerry," Amato said worriedly, holding on to both my arms. "Wait until after the opera—*then* kill him."

I'd seen Scotti grab Caruso and hustle him away before I could get to him. All right, if Scotti wanted to change camps, let him. I'd wait until the opera was over and kill *both* of them.

I was changing my costume when Toscanini barged into my dressing room, looking scandalized. "What do you think you do?" he demanded. "Never before do I see such unprofessional conduct! The opera stage is no place for your personal quarrels!"

"Talk to that devil Caruso," I muttered.

"I intend to do just that, but right now I am talking to you. Sometimes you overstep yourself, *Queen Geraldine*," he said, heavy on the sarcasm.

"For heaven's sake, he spit over my shoulder! Didn't you see?"

"I see, and he is wrong to spit—but you do not *strike* him for it!" He went on haranguing me until I screamed at him to leave me alone, and he did.

Toscanini must have lectured Caruso as well, for Act III was remarkably uneventful. Caruso and I both kept our distance, circling each other warily. At one point in the act he was to seize my wrist, and I noticed he was careful not to hurt me when he did. So I was careful not to scratch him when I pulled away.

When the curtain closed on the third act, Caruso turned to me in front of everybody backstage and spread his arms. "Can we not be friends, Gerry? Please?"

I wanted to tell him to go gargle with razor blades, but everybody was listening and it wouldn't do to appear ungracious. So I forced myself to walk into his embrace and said, "Of course we're friends, Rico."

Caruso sighed as all the onlookers applauded. "*Bene, bene.* Only one more act, Gerry—we make it a good one, yes? I try."

It was a nice gesture, I suppose, but I didn't trust him. He'd "try" as long as he remembered to.

"*What is* going on?" Emmy Destinn's voice said from behind me. "From out front you two look as if you want to throttle each other, yet here you are billing and cooing like a couple of lovebirds. *What* is going on?"

I turned—and was absolutely *appalled*. Emmy was wearing the gown my dressmaker had made for her . . . but she'd ruined it! She'd added spangles and flowers and *feathers*—she even had feathers sprouting out of the tiara she wore! Emmy looked like a vaudeville performer! "What have you done to that dress?" I cried, not even trying to hide my disapproval.

She glanced down at herself. "I have compensated for its notable lack of imagination. Why?"

"You've *ruined* it, Emmy—don't you see? You've taken a perfectly lovely gown and turned it into a clown costume!"

"Gerry!" Caruso said sharply. "Do not listen to her, Emmy, she is out of sorts tonight. You look beautiful."

Emmy was standing there with her mouth open. I knew I was taking my anger at Caruso out on her, but I couldn't stop. "You've completely destroyed the gown's lines, Emmy! A simple, flattering, dignified dress—and look what you've done to it!"

She got a look in her eye I didn't much care for. "I will not say what I am thinking right now," Emmy said. "I will wait until you have calmed down, and *then* I will say it." She turned on her heel and charged off, scattering chorus singers right and left.

"That woman has no taste whatsoever," I muttered.

"Why you do that to Emmy?" Caruso raged. "Always, you make fun of the way Emmy looks! She never makes fun of you! You are jealous of her!"

I? Jealous of *Emmy Destinn*? I threw back my head and laughed at the utter absurdity of it! "You're out of your mind, Rico!" *I* was the one who sold out the house every time I sang, *I* was the one who had more male attention than I knew what to do with, *I* was the one who had a hard core of fans who worshipped everything I did! And *I* was not afraid to look at myself in a mirror sideways! "Emmy is the *last* person I'd be jealous of!"

"You are jealous," Caruso persisted stubbornly. "Ever since Puccini chooses Emmy to sing *La Fanciulla del West* instead of you—"

I flew at him. A pair of arms encircled my waist from behind and I felt myself lifted and carried toward the dressing-room stairs. "Gerry, Gerry, Gerry," Scotti whispered in my ear. "That can wait. Amato is dressed and ready, but you—you have not even started to change! We must hurry, yes?" He urged me up the stairs.

"Did you hear what he said? He said I was jealous of Emmy!"

"I hear, I hear."

"What's she doing here anyway? Why does she keep coming to *Carmen*?"

"She likes it."

"Oh, and maybe she wants the role for herself? Ha! She'll never get it. She doesn't have the bottom notes!"

"Of course she doesn't," Scotti murmured.

I sank down on the chair in front of my dressing table, suddenly depleted of energy, weary of the whole business. I looked at myself in the mirror: sad eyes, droopy mouth. "Rico is driving me crazy, Toto. He's deviling me to death."

"I know. Something must be done. It is all this 'detective' work—I think you both must stop. I and Amato, we talk to Caruso tomorrow."

I nodded; it was probably best. "Thank you."

Act IV, with its big final duet—that's all that was left. I put on my fancy Act IV costume; I'd always liked the fact that in the last act Carmen looks like a million dollars while Don José comes on dressed in rags. I repaired my make-up, fixed my hair, and picked up my fan. I was ready.

The last act of *Carmen* opens with a processional, a fast-moving spectacle in which the chorus does all the vocal work. Then I sang my brief duet with Amato, everyone else drifted off to attend the bullfight, and suddenly I was alone on the stage with Caruso.

Now I know this next part can't be true, and I'm not even going to try to explain it. But as Caruso advanced toward me, I could have sworn I saw horns pushing up through his thinning hair and a tail with a spatulate tip twitching behind him. I sang the opening words of the final duet—*C'est toi?* And instead of the answering *C'est moi,* it sounded to me as if what Caruso actually sang was *Report, Gerry!* Nobody else remembers hearing it, but that's what it sounded like to me.

Almost immediately he grabbed me by the arm—we hadn't rehearsed that!—and this time he wasn't careful not to hurt me. So I cracked him across the jaw with my fan and heard a surprised murmur from the audience. Caruso grabbed my other arm, and I stepped on his foot; he pushed me away. In the middle of all this I became aware we were singing the duet with more intensity than we'd ever managed before, but somehow that seemed of secondary importance right then.

We came to the part where David Belasco had directed Caruso to drag me across the stage by the hair and I was hoping the tenor wouldn't remember it. No such luck. He pushed me to the floor and grabbed my hair and started pulling—and I mean *really* pulling! It was the only time I've ever regretted not wearing a wig for *Carmen.* I dropped my fan and used both hands to hold on to his arm, but he still managed to *pull my hair.* When we got to the place where he was supposed to let go, he simply turned around and started dragging me back the other way!

I scrambled to my feet and knocked his arm away; then I started beating at his chest with both fists, not paying much attention to what I was singing. He twirled me around and pinned my arms to my side, with one arm around my waist and the other across my chest.

I bit his hand.

I caught one glimpse of Toscanini's horrified face from the podium; it was probably the first time in his life he didn't know what to do. But the audience was murmuring its approval of all this fiery "acting" they were watching. Caruso shoved me away so hard that I stumbled, while he sang of how we should go away together and be lovers again. I sang back I wasn't going anywhere with him and kicked him in the shins. He sang that if he couldn't have me, no one could—and made a grab at my arm. I twisted away and I heard this horrible *ripping* sound and felt cool air against my arm and realized I had just lost part of my costume.

It must have been the sight of Caruso standing there holding the sleeve of my dress in his hand that finally made the audience realize that what they were watching on the stage was *real*. In the quarrel between Carmen and Don José, the outcome is ordained: He kills her. Carmen's death marks the end of the opera. But when Caruso came at me with his stage knife, I was so furious with him that—incredible as it seems now—I *snatched* the knife out of his hand and thrust it *hard* against his stomach! *Take that, you devil!*

A loud gasp went up from the audience. Caruso was so surprised he forgot to sing his line. "Fall down, you idiot!" I hissed. "You're dead!" I kicked out and tripped him; and when someone of Caruso's girth and weight hits the floor, everybody in the house feels it.

But a tenor who has been unexpectedly "killed" is in no condition to sing his final lines, the lines that close the opera. So I sang them. *"C'est moi qui lui ai tué!"* I sang, changing the French to fit the new circumstances. *"Ah! José, mon José, adoré!"* The curtain closed.

There was an absolutely stunned silence from out front.

But backstage was anything but quiet; what the audience didn't know was that behind the closed curtain Caruso and I were rolling around pummeling each other, wrestling on the floor like a couple of schoolboys. A hundred voices were screaming and a thousand hands were pulling at us, but that didn't stop us; we kept right on fighting.

Pasquale Amato finally put an end to it. I'd never realized how strong Amato was, but somehow he wedged his body in between Caruso and me and forcibly pushed the two of us apart. Then there were about a million people separating us, and the fight was over.

Scotti helped me up, looking endearingly worried. "Are you all right, Gerry? Shall I call Dr. Curtis?"

"Whatever for?" I smiled at him. "I don't need a doctor." In fact, I felt *marvelous*.

"What have you done?" Gatti-Casazza screamed at me. "He is supposed to kill *you*, you are not supposed to kill *him*! What have you done?"

"I changed it," I said mildly.

"This is terrible!" Gatti moaned. "How will we ever live it down?" Toscanini came running up and stopped at Gatti's elbow and stared at me, his eyes round and his mouth open, not saying a word. "How can you do such a thing?" Gatti went on. "Do you lose your mind?"

"Curtain call!" someone was crying. "Places for the curtain call!"

Toscanini kept staring at me, wordless.

The crowd had thinned out a little and I could see Caruso again, listening as Amato talked earnestly into his ear. The expression on Caruso's face told the whole story; he looked absolutely horrified. It had finally sunk in on him what he had done. He had been seen fighting, in public, with a *woman*! Horrors! Shame! Disgrace! He looked overwhelmed with embarrassment. "Oh, Gerry," he managed to choke out, "Gerry, I am, oh, I do, you, oh . . ." He whirled and dashed out through the stage door, still in costume, with no overcoat.

Toscanini was now shaking his head while he stared at me. And stared.

"Curtain call! Please!" The voice was growing frantic.

Amato hurried out in front of the curtain, took a quick bow, and hurried back. Caruso was gone, and Toscanini refused to take a curtain call. So I went out by myself—rumpled, sleeveless, battered and bruised—but *the winner*!

The people in the audience were actually stamping their feet while they cheered. Oh, it was a glorious moment! I took only one curtain call—but it lasted fifteen minutes. I looked out at those laughing faces and laughed with them; the gerryflappers weren't the only ones chanting "Ger*ee*" that night.

When the hubbub at last began to die down, I went backstage and immediately caught sight of David Belasco advancing toward me. Oh dear! I should have known he'd come to see how his new stage directions had worked out! What could I say to him? He was probably ready to kill me.

I couldn't have been more wrong. The man was *beaming;* I'd never seen such a big smile on his face before. "Gerry, that was magnificent!" he cried. "The most exciting theatre I've seen in ten years! I think I like your ending more than the regular one!" He turned to Gatti-Casazza. "I say, Mr. Gatti, I don't suppose you could—"

"*No!*" Gatti roared. "Do not even think it! Disgraceful, perfectly disgraceful! Oh, what will the board say?"

"Nevertheless," Belasco whispered in my ear, "you were *superb*." He lifted my hand and kissed it.

Scotti whispered in my other ear. "I think this is good time to leave."

He was right. I worked my way through the backstage visitors, more of them than usual tonight and all of them full of questions. I hurried upstairs to change and came down to find Scotti waiting for me by the stage door.

The last thing I saw before I left was Toscanini, standing by the door and watching me go, his mouth still open, still unable to say a word.

□ **16** □ Morris Gest was the first to arrive the next morning, a stack of newspapers under each arm. "The Old Man called last night and told me what you'd done," he grinned. "Ah, Gerry, Gerry! If only the rest of my clients had the nose for publicity that you have!"

"What do they say?" I asked, reaching for the newspapers.

"What don't they say? From one extreme to the other. One of them is running a polite announcement of what they call 'an altercation arising from artistic differences' or some such fanciness. But another one is carrying a blow-by-blow description, right down to the knockout punch! Here, read them."

I read them. I read them, and I relished every word. This was even better than not announcing my engagement! Every paper in New York had something about my fight with Caruso; and whether the tone was polite or scandalized or gleeful or simply puzzled, not one of the newspapers made Caruso out to be the hero. Tee-hee.

The telephone was ringing. I'd already warned Bella that this was going to be one of *those* days and simply to take messages unless it sounded important. One other thing I'd done before Morris got there; I'd sent one of the other maids with a note to Emmy Destinn.

Dearest Emmy,

I'm certain you have understood by now that my unforgivably bad manners last night were not caused by any animosity toward you but were instead the result of a little war I was then waging with a certain tenor we both know. Dear Emmy, please come to lunch and allow me to apologize properly. I would come to you but I fear you might shut the door in my face—and with justification! Although my behavior was inexcusable, I hope you'll find it in your heart to excuse it anyway. Please come, around noon.

Penitently,
Geraldine Farrar

The sooner I patched things up with Emmy the better; I didn't want Caruso spreading the rumor that I was jealous of her. Not that anyone would believe such a ridiculous notion, but still . . .

"With luck, we can keep this going for a week," Morris Gest said, rereading one of the newspaper articles. "I talked to the Met's publicist this morning—he loves you, darling. You've made him very happy."

"Delighted to hear it. What's he planning?"

"Follow-up stories—causes of the fight, that sort of thing. He'll need to talk to you."

And then, while we were still reading, the flowers arrived—baskets and baskets and baskets of them, containing everything from exotic purple-tipped white orchids to delicate little violets. There were lilies—orange tiger lilies, white calla lilies, and those pale pink Japanese lilies with red spots on the petals. There were blue China asters, creamy white magnolias, velvety purple pansies with yellow throats, scarlet-striped amaryllis, bronze Dutch tulips, Boston yellow daisies, sweet-smelling narcissus, five varieties of rose, irises, camellias, birds of paradise, sweet peas, lilies of the valley, and two potted ferns—all grown in hothouses and therefore all terribly expensive. By the time the two deliverymen had brought them all in, there was barely room left to walk.

Morris stood in the midst of all that floral abundance and asked in amazement, "Who sent them?"

"Caruso," I said, reading one of the cards. "This is the softening-up stage. He thinks."

Morris discovered a wreath with *Forgive me, Gerry* spelled out in rosebuds. "He must have rousted the florist out in the middle of the night to get this one done."

The maid I'd sent with my note to Emmy came back, and gasped when she saw the roomful of flowers. She handed me an envelope and moved among the baskets, ooh-ing and ah-ing. The note in the envelope contained neither salutation nor signature.

I think it would have been more fitting for you to wait meekly outside my door; nevertheless, I will

*come, if only to prove that I am a nicer person than
you are. Please have both a good explanation and
an excellent lunch prepared.*

She wasn't going to make it easy for me, but she was
coming. Ah well, I'd serve up a little humble pie for
lunch. A little wouldn't hurt me.

Bella squeezed between two baskets of lilies and said,
"Excuse me, Miss Farrar, but Mr. Gatti-Casazza is on the
telephone—he says it's urgent."

"Very well, I'll take it."

Gatti may have told my maid it was urgent, but he took
his time getting to the point. He hemmed and hawed and
inquired after my physical well-being, and finally got around
to saying what he'd called about. "I am thinking about
scheduling one additional performance," he said in an
overly casual voice, "a benefit for the Emergency Fund,
you know."

"Additional performance of what?" I asked, as if I
didn't know.

"Ah, hem, of *Carmen,* as a matter of fact. The season
ends soon, so I am thinking of scheduling it right away,
yes?"

"To take advantage of all the free publicity I've generated? Why, what a surprise! Last night you were ready to
have me boiled in oil."

"Last night is over," he said tightly. "Today, I try to
make plans. One more *Carmen.* A *benefit,*" he stressed.

To which I was expected to donate my services. "You
know, Gatti, this just might be a good time to discuss my
new contract."

Dead silence.

"I'll let you talk to my manager," I said sweetly, and
called Morris.

When he understood what was afoot, Morris grinned
from ear to ear. "See? It's working for you already,
darling. Maybe you should plan a nice little stage brawl
once every season." He picked up the telephone. "Good
morning, Mr. Gatti. Perhaps now we can have our little
talk?"

I left him to it and called Bella and one of the other maids to try to rearrange the flower baskets so as to allow more walking room. We managed to get one pathway running through the middle of the room, but now it was a little hard to find the furniture.

Morris hung up the telephone, but it rang again immediately. He answered, and then covered the part you talk into with his hand and said, "Jimmy Freeman." I shook my head. The two maids and I stood there and listened as Morris wove an impromptu fantasy about how I couldn't come to the telephone because I was soaking in a special medicinal bath designed to alleviate pain and stress following unusual physical exertion. It's a good thing Morris Gest had no criminal tendencies; he could talk anybody into believing anything.

Finally he finished with Jimmy and stood up to leave. "I'm gonna run down to the opera house," he said. "Gatti is ready to negotiate." He gave me a quick kiss on the forehead, made an exaggerated lunge toward the maids (who fled giggling), and waved a cheerful goodbye as he left.

I got in about an hour's work in the music room, ignoring the ringing telephone as best I could, before I was interrupted by the arrival of my two favorite baritones. Scotti, unfortunately, was unbearably solicitous, treating me like some frail, battered blossom until I ordered him to stop (he of all people should know better!). Amato, on the other hand, was practicality itself.

"This argument with Caruso—it must end," Amato said to me. "You cannot work together if it goes on."

"What argument?" I smiled. "I'm not mad at anybody." Not any more.

"Good, Gerry, I hope you say that. You and Rico are friends for too long for something like this to drive you apart, no? You do not know how bad he feels."

"He is miserable," Scotti put in. "Miserable, embarrassed, ashamed. He is horrified by what happens, and he humbly begs your forgiveness. He is so humiliated that all the way up here he hides his face—"

"All the way up here? He's here?"

"Out in the hallway," Amato said, "waiting to learn if you will see him. Let him come in, Gerry. Do not punish him further—he makes us all unhappy! Allow him to make his apologies."

I didn't mind. "Oh, very well," I said in a resigned tone. "You may bring him in."

Well, it was all I could do to keep from bursting out laughing when Caruso came in. I have never seen another human being look so *contrite* as Caruso looked at that moment! He stood cringing inside the doorway, his big black eyes filled with tears as he kept turning his hat around nervously in his hands. He put his weight first on one foot and then on the other, trying to work up the nerve to come further into the room. I eyed him stonily, waiting for him to speak first.

Finally he did. "Gerry!" he burst out. "Can you forgive me? I am a pig! I go a little crazy, yes? Say you forgive me, or I go all the way crazy! I am desolate! Do not hate me—I cannot stand it if you hate me!"

I allowed myself a small smile. Now that I'd gotten the resentment out of my system, Caruso no longer seemed to have horns and a tail. The monster who had deviled me so much was gone; he was just Rico again. "How do I know it won't happen again?"

His eyes overflowed and the tears ran down his cheeks as he dramatically slapped one big hand over his heart. "Never! Never again does it happen! On my mother's grave, I swear I never fight with you again! Not for any reason in the world!"

Now that was a promise I intended holding him to. Suddenly I just couldn't keep up the pretense any longer; it wasn't fair for Caruso to suffer so while I was having such a grand time. I opened my arms. "Come here, Rico."

With a cry he dashed toward me, knocking over a basket of roses on the way. He swept me up in a big bear hug and was laughing and crying and kissing me, and I was laughing and not crying and kissing back. Amato did a little jig among the spilled roses.

"That is enough kissing, I think," Scotti said.

At length we all settled down. "We have something we

must talk about,'' Amato said, like a chairman presiding at a meeting. "Gerry, this investigating you do—it is the cause of the trouble between you and Caruso, yes? Tell me, is it worth it? Is it not better to forget the whole thing?''

"Perhaps so," I conceded, "but remember, Pasquale, I was not just amusing myself. The police suspect me of having put the ammonia in Duchon's spray. And Jimmy Freeman—they suspect him too."

"Ah, but have you been arrested?" Amato smiled. "Or Jimmy? You are not in jail, you are both free. This danger from the police, it does not still exist."

"It might," Caruso said uncertainly.

Scotti shook his head. "The police, they arrest no one. They never find the culprit. Not ever. It is hard, but we must get used to the idea."

We were all silent a moment, and then Amato said, "So, Gerry—do you agree to stop your investigation?"

"Yes, if Rico will also agree."

Caruso scowled; he hated to give up on it. But ultimately he yielded. "It is not right," he complained. "A man who destroys another man should not go free."

I felt the same way myself. It was no longer a matter of self-protection; I wanted to find the man responsible. But I'd given my word, and I'd stick by it.

Someone was at the door. The maid admitted Emmy Destinn, who came charging straight in. "I have not decided whether I want lunch or the apology first." She looked around her. "What is this? Do you open your own flower shop, Gerry?"

"Good heavens!" I said. "Is it noon already?"

"So nice to feel welcome," she said, searching for a place to sit.

"No, I didn't mean that—I just meant the morning has slipped away so fast. Of course you're welcome. I invited you, didn't I?"

Emmy had found a chair behind one of the potted ferns. She parted the fronds and peered out at the four of us. "I did not know it was to be a luncheon party."

"It's not," I told her. "The men are just leaving."

"But Gerry," Caruso protested, "I plan to take you to nice restaurant for big fancy lunch!"

"I had the same idea myself," Scotti said wryly, "but you may come too, Rico."

"You have made up your differences?" Emmy asked Caruso. He nodded happily.

"Why do we not all go out to eat?" Amato asked. "The five of us?"

"Thank you, but Emmy and I are staying in for lunch," I said politely but firmly. "We have things to talk about."

"Well, now, a moment please, let us not be hasty," Emmy said. "Gerry, what are you planning to serve?"

I gaped at her. "You want to know the *menu*? To decide whether we stay here or go out?"

"That is correct," she said imperturbably. "What do you have planned? Some sort of salad, I suppose."

I did have a salad planned, as a matter of fact, but obviously this was not the time to persuade Emmy to start on a diet. I floundered for something to say while the three men argued amiably over where we were all going for lunch.

Emmy picked up one of the newspapers Morris Gest had brought and started leafing through it. "Still no news of Prague!" she complained. "I begin to think I must go there myself, to find out what transpires!"

"You do not mean that," Amato said uneasily. "Go to Prague? Now?"

"She is not serious, Pasquale," Scotti said.

"Yes, she is," Emmy said. "I am seriously thinking about going, as soon as the season is over."

"Do *not* think about it," Amato ordered. "Emmy, you could be killed. You do not go visiting in war countries! *Ridicolo*." The rest of us chimed agreement.

Emmy sighed. "I know. If the newspapers would just print *something* once in a while—"

She was interrupted by an urgent hammering at the door. The maid admitted Mildredandphoebe, who came rushing in wide-eyed and breathless. "Miss Farrar," they gasped together.

They looked so distraught I was alarmed. "Here, sit

down—oh, where are the chairs? My goodness, what's the matter?''

"We found him," Mildred panted. "Uncle Hummy—we know where he is."

"Are you sure you can do this?" Caruso asked dubiously.

"Of course I'm sure," I answered impatiently. "I always drive myself on the chauffeur's day off. Get in— we're wasting time." In the last four years Caruso had owned five motor cars and never learned to drive any of them; so naturally he had trouble believing I could operate such a mysterious machine.

"You promised me lunch," Emmy complained.

"Emmy, I'll buy you *ten* lunches—but not now! Please get in."

Everyone piled in. Scotti sat up front with me, while Amato, Emmy and Caruso squeezed into the back seat. That meant Mildredandphoebe had to sit on the men's laps. Amato and Mildred adjusted easily to their enforced intimacy, but Phoebe looked scared to death perched there on Caruso's knee.

"Where are we going?" I asked.

"Mulberry Street," Mildred said. "Just head downtown— I'll give you directions."

The last time I'd driven down Broadway, the street had been icy and treacherous. But today was clear, and New York had the look of a city that was just remembering there was a season called spring. There was an unusually high number of motor cars in the streets, and I'm afraid I gave one of them a little scratch. At least that's what that yelling mob in my back seat said, only they called it a gash. Some people always exaggerate.

"Mildred, how did you find Uncle Hummy?" I asked. "I mean, is he trying to hide?"

"We weren't the ones who found him, Miss Farrar. It was Mary Perkins—short girl, curly red hair? She told Phoebe and Phoebe told me and I told you. All we know is an address."

"Bless Mary Perkins," I said, trying to remember her.

"Mildred, I want you to spread the word. I'm giving a party for everyone who helped."

Squeals of pleasure from the back seat.

"Do I imagine it?" Amato asked. "I think I remember Geraldine Farrar makes a solemn promise to end her investigation, to do no more detective work."

"Really?" Emmy said. "How sensible."

"Yes, but no one seems to remember that except me. You *do* promise, Gerry, no?"

"Eh, but that is before," Caruso answered for me. "Before these fine American girls come in with answer we are waiting for." Phoebe suddenly whooped and then giggled nervously.

"Rico, leave Phoebe alone," I said. "As for my promise, Pasquale, are you seriously suggesting we just drop everything now—now when we have an address for Uncle Hummy?"

"We can tell Lieutenant O'Halloran," Amato said. "Let him go to Mulberry Street, yes?"

"But what if it turns out that Uncle Hummy saw nothing, knows nothing? Then it will look as if we're trying to put the blame on a poor helpless old man. No, we have to go ourselves."

"It is chasing the wild goose," Amato objected.

"If you think that, then why did you come along?"

Scotti turned around and smiled toward the back seat. "Give up, Pasquale."

Mulberry Street was in a part of town where I'd never been, that teeming section of the Lower East Side known as Little Italy. I turned on to Canal Street; but when we reached Mulberry, the street was so crowded I didn't even try to go in. I found a place on Mott Street to leave the limousine, and we walked back, only a block.

It was like entering a city within a city. The street was full of people yelling good-naturedly to one another and to other people leaning out of the windows of the ugly tenement buildings that made up the neighborhood. The fire escapes were mostly covered with drying laundry; some were being used to store what looked like chests and crates and even pieces of furniture.

Both sides of the street were lined with pushcarts filled with fruits, vegetables, fish, olives, old clothing, firewood; and horsedrawn wagons were used as movable stores, from the backs of which their owners sold chairs, flour, blankets, baskets, heaven knows what else. One man sat on a barrel underneath a pipe frame from which pair after pair of men's shoes were hanging, all exactly alike. The people themselves were poorly dressed, some even in rags; but they were colorful, lively, and *noisy.*

A tear appeared in Caruso's eye. "Just like home."

The sudden appearance of seven well-dressed strangers did not go unnoticed on Mulberry Street; we were the immediate object of curious stares and that kind of under-the-voice mumbling that makes you start to feel just a little bit uneasy. One young man with a huge mustache shouted something at us but I couldn't make out what he said; I think he was speaking Sicilian. A sudden odor of cooking onions and garlic assaulted us and my stomach contracted in protest. I think I heard Emmy murmur *Lunch.*

"Do you notice?" Amato said. "These buildings, they have no numbers!"

It was true. We passed a narrow doorway that proudly proclaimed itself the entrance to the *Banca Italiana,* but there wasn't a number to be seen. We were looking for number eighty-four Mulberry Street, but it was clear we'd never find it just by looking. Amato went up to a man sitting in a chair on the sidewalk before a store that displayed religious icons in the window and asked where number eighty-four was.

"Who is it you look for?" the man asked.

"We do not know the name," Amato said, "only the number. Eighty-four."

"I know nothing of numbers. If you tell me the name, I tell you where he lives."

"Uncle Hummy?" Caruso said hopefully.

"I do not know your uncle, signore."

Amato threw up his hands and walked on, the rest of us trailing after him. Finally we found a woman selling bread out of a basket almost as big as she was who told us she thought number eighty-four was "down there" somewhere, pointing in the direction opposite to the way we'd been heading. So we turned back and tried the other way.

"Look," said Scotti. "Look how they watch Rico."

I'd already noticed. We were still drawing stares, but most of them were directed at Caruso. Caruso and Scotti and Amato were all from Naples, but only Caruso *looked* Italian. Amato had the appearance of one from a more northern country, while Scotti looked as if he could have come from any country in continental Europe—as did Emmy too, in a way. Mildredandphoebe and I probably looked every bit as American as we were. But the people of Mulberry Street recognized Caruso as one of their own.

Moreover, they recognized him as a celebrity. The jaunty way he wore his hat, the spring in his step—his whole demeanor bespoke a man sure of his welcome wherever he went. It was only a matter of time until someone realized it was the great Caruso who was walking through their neighborhood, and if we didn't find number eighty-four soon we might never get there. Why had that girl given Phoebe a house number? Why didn't she just say next door to Dino's barbershop or upstairs over the meat-seller?

"There!" Emmy cried. "On that canopy!"

Sure enough, there it was—an eight and a four, prominently displayed on a storefront canopy. The store was a tobacconist's, and a quick look inside told us Uncle Hummy wasn't there. In one of the rooms over the shop, then.

"There's another door right next to the entrance," Mildred said. "It must lead upstairs."

Unfortunately, at the doorstep we encountered an obstacle in the form of three boys about seventeen or eighteen who were lounging there and showing no inclination to move. When Scotti asked them please to let us through, one of them casually took out a wicked-looking knife and began cleaning his fingernails while another asked us insolently why we wanted to go in.

"We wish to visit someone who lives here," Scotti said pleasantly, trying not to look at the knife.

"What if we say we don't want you to go in?" The boy took a step toward Scotti. It was a challenge of some sort. I never dreamed seventeen-year-old boys could be so menacing! These three were obviously bored and looking for trouble. I could have screamed in frustration; to get this close and—

And then it happened. "Caruso!" a male voice boomed. "*È Caruso!* Enrico Caruso!"

There was a heartbeat of stunned silence, and then something like an electric shock ran through the crowd in the street. Soon every one of those opera-loving Italians was shouting *Caruso! Caruso!* as the mob surged toward our frightened tenor. Before we knew what was happening they swooped down on him and swirled around him and swept him up and away. A couple of dozen pairs of hands half-helped, half-forced Caruso up on to one of the wagons in the street, as everyone screamed for him to sing, sing, sing!

Caruso looked helplessly toward us. Both Scotti and Amato pantomimed extravagantly that he should sing for them—it was the distraction we needed. Caruso gulped, took a deep breath, and launched into *Questa o quella* from *Rigoletto*.

The three young toughs who'd been barring our way forgot all about us and pushed their way into the mob surrounding Caruso's wagon. Scotti opened the door and we crowded inside together at the foot of a rickety-looking stairway.

"*Ascoltatemi*," Amato said. "I just think of something. If Uncle Hummy is not home but he hears Caruso sing, he will come to listen, no?"

"He might be out there in that crowd right now," Emmy said. "That is where we should look."

"We'd better split up," I said. "The girls and I will go upstairs and—"

"Right," Emmy interrupted, already on her way back out. Scotti and Amato followed her.

Mildredandphoebe and I picked our way carefully up the stairs. I was thinking we'd just have to knock on every door we saw, but the building was so small it wasn't necessary. There were only two doors on the second floor, and one of them bore a sign that indicated the inhabitant was someone named Falgione who would write your let-

ters for you for a fee. I knocked on the other door. There
was no answer; I tried the knob, but the door was locked.
Outside, Caruso had switched to *La Bohème* and was
starting on *Che gelida manina*.

"Let me try," Phoebe offered. She reached to her hair
and pulled out a hairpin and bent over the lock. I didn't
hear a click but the door suddenly swung open an inch or
two.

Mildred and I stared at her. "Phoebe!" her friend exclaimed. "Where did you learn to do that?"

Phoebe blushed. "Well, uh, I'm always forgetting my
key and, uh, you know."

What unexpected talents these girls had. I felt a brief
pang about entering a man's home like that, but this was
no time to grow fainthearted. I pushed the door open.

The first thing I saw inside was myself—that is, a
picture of myself in my *Carmen* costume; it was a newspaper
photo that Uncle Hummy had cut out and fastened to the
wall. For this was Uncle Hummy's room, there could be
no doubt about that. Every inch of wall space was covered
with pictures cut from newspapers, and every one of them
had something to do with opera.

"Did you ever see anything like this?" Mildred gasped.

I counted about two dozen pictures of me, and a couple
of dozen more of Caruso. There were photos of Scotti and
Amato and Emmy, and a few pictures that showed stage
settings. I think the faces of just about all the Met's singers
adorned Uncle Hummy's walls—Bori, Martinelli, Botta,
de Luca, Alda, Hempel, everybody. There were five or six
pictures of Toscanini, a few of Puccini, and I even spotted
one of Gatti-Casazza.

"And I thought I was a fan!" Mildred exclaimed. "Look
at all this stuff on the floor! There's barely room to walk."

The "stuff" was piles of opera programs, posters,
newspaper clippings—Uncle Hummy probably couldn't af-
ford to buy scrapbooks, but he kept everything he cut out
anyway. In one corner was a stack of opera scores, a few
of which I had given him. There was so much paper in that
room there was barely space left for the necessities of life:
a narrow cot, a battered chest of drawers with a washbasin

on it, and a wobbly wooden table pulled up next to the cot; there wasn't even a chair to sit on. On the table were a pair of scissors and a pot of glue, and Uncle Hummy's few clothes were hanging from nails on the back of the door. That was the way he lived.

"Look," said Phoebe. "Here's a program from 1891—*Die Meistersinger*."

"I'll bet he has a program for every production the Metropolitan has ever put on," Mildred said. "Is that possible, Miss Farrar?"

"I suppose it is," I said. "The Met opened in the early 1880s yes, Uncle Hummy would have been about forty then, or a little older. It's quite possible."

"So what do we do now? Wait for him here?"

Outside, Caruso was singing *Di quella pira* from *Il Trovatore;* someone was accompanying him on an accordion. "I don't know about you, but I feel uncomfortable here," I said, "invading his privacy like this. I tell you what—you two wait for him downstairs by the door. I'll go help the others search the crowd. If Uncle Hummy comes, each of you just grab an arm and hold on. He's a frail old man, he won't resist you. Phoebe, do you think you could lock that door with your hairpin?"

She could. We went back downstairs and outside, and my two favorite gerryflappers took up positions like sentries on either side of the door. I caught sight of Amato, who looked a question at me. *No,* I shook my head. *Not here.*

Caruso had just finished his aria and the crowd was applauding wildly and yelling *Bravo! Bravo!* I waited until the noise died down a little and then called out, *"Pagliacci!"* The cry was immediately taken up by the crowd—*Pagliacci, Pagliacci!* Caruso didn't know he was the bait, but we had to keep him singing until we'd had time to make a good search.

He sang. The crowd had more than doubled from the time I went into Uncle Hummy's building, and it wasn't easy moving around. And I couldn't see very far, because no matter where I went somebody taller always seemed to be standing directly in front of me. But I was used to crowds; hordes of strangers were always pressing up against me after a performance—sometimes cutting off a lock of my hair, sometimes tearing away a piece of my clothing (I wasn't too fond of *that* part of it!). So there I was, pushing my way through a mob of people I didn't know, looking everywhere for Uncle Hummy.

Caruso finished his *Pagliacci* aria and I heard Scotti's voice cry out *Aïda!*—and the tenor started again. Thank God Caruso had a lot of staying power. I bumped into Emmy once; she was looking rumpled and cross. But I was learning how to use my elbows to make myself a passageway, and plowed on.

Surely he was here somewhere! I couldn't believe that Uncle Hummy would run away and abandon his fantastic collection of opera memorabilia—which was all he had to show for his life, when you came down to it. And if he was anywhere in the neighborhood, he'd *have* to come to this particular block of Mulberry Street once the word about Caruso spread. Uncle Hummy could no more resist Caruso's singing than Caruso could resist Italian cooking.

Then I saw him. Standing out at the edge of the crowd, wearing the coat Caruso had bought him, a peddler's tray suspended from a strap around his neck. His mouth was open and his eyes were closed, a look of sheer ecstasy on his face, oblivious to everything else in the world except the sound of Caruso's voice.

"Uncle Hummy?" I said. "Uncle Hummy, I want you to come with me."

It took him a moment to realize he was being spoken to, but then he looked at me and his face registered surprise, pleasure, and puzzlement—in that order. He glanced at Caruso and then back at me. "Miz Zherry? Is trouble?"

"No trouble," I smiled. "Not now, now that we've found you. Come with me, Uncle Hummy—I want to talk to you."

Just by talking while Caruso sang we were attracting disapproving stares and angry mutters. Fortunately we also attracted the attention of both Scotti and Emmy, who came shouldering through the crowd from opposite directions. "Uncle Hummy!" Scotti cried. "We look everywhere for you!'' Which did nothing at all to reassure the uneasy old man. ''Do you—''

''*Silenzio!*'' someone commanded us.

I motioned the others into a doorway. ''I'll take Uncle Hummy to the limousine,'' I said, speaking as low as I could. ''Toto, you're going to have to find Amato and the two of you rescue Caruso from this crowd. Emmy, will you collect Mildredandphoebe?'' I pointed down toward the corner of the street. ''I'll wait there with the limousine.''

''Going?'' Uncle Hummy asked shakily.

''There's nothing to be afraid of,'' Emmy said reassuringly. ''Just go along now, Uncle Hummy. Don't worry.''

I took the old man by the arm and led him away while the other two went to round up the rest of our party. Personally, I was delighted to get away from Mulberry Street. We'd been there for over an hour; and while Caruso had been given a hero's welcome, not one single person had recognized *me*.

Neither Uncle Hummy nor I spoke on the way to Mott Street, but once we were in the limousine I couldn't wait any longer. ''Uncle Hummy, the night Philippe Duchon was hurt—did you see something? Did you see someone with Duchon's throat spray?''

A look of terrible anxiety came over the old man's face. He dropped his eyes without speaking and began fiddling nervously with the contents of the peddler's tray in his lap—some candles, about a dozen small boxes of matches, a few bunches of sachet. Hardly enough to keep him in newspapers.

''Uncle Hummy? What is it—are you afraid?''

A barely perceptible nod.

''Oh, you mustn't be afraid!'' I cried. ''We won't let anything happen to you, I promise you that. Do you understand? We'll take care of you.''

He hesitated, but then shook his head.

''Uncle Hummy, do you know that the police suspect *me*?''

He looked up, alarmed; that meant something to him. I reminded him that Duchon himself had accused me, right before he collapsed on stage, and the police were equally suspicious. Tears welled up in the old man's eyes, and finally he choked out, "Saw him. Take spray."

"Saw whom? Who was it?"

He shook his head helplessly. "Name."

"You don't know his name?" That was odd; Uncle Hummy knew everybody at the Metropolitan, I thought. Unless possibly . . . "Uncle Hummy, what did he look like? Was there anything different about him, anything unusual?"

Shakily, he drew one finger along the line of his jaw.

A scar.

Silently I nodded, and didn't press him further. There was no need; I had my answer. I sat quietly for a moment, trying to assimilate it. Then I started up the motor.

By the time I got to the corner I'd indicated, Emmy was already there with the two girls. I couldn't see the men, but there was a lot of angry shouting going on further up Mulberry Street.

"That crowd's getting ugly," Mildred said as she got into the limousine. "They don't want to let Mr. Caruso go."

"Ugly," Phoebe echoed. Both girls stared long and hard at Uncle Hummy, the elusive object of their long search.

"Here they come," said Emmy.

Amato and Scotti were shoving their way through the surly crowd, with Caruso between them. *"Basta!"* Amato shouted, and pushed away a belligerent-looking young man. I hoped there wouldn't be a fight. Caruso was pale and a bit shaken, as he had every right to be.

Emmy had the door of the back seat open for them. Scotti squeezed in front with Uncle Hummy and me and the other two piled in the back. "Go!" Amato cried.

But I couldn't; there were people all around the limousine, and even *on* the limousine. A woman leaned over and shouted something at me through the windscreen, and I could hear fists banging on the roof. Uncle Hummy looked scared to death, and I didn't feel much braver. "What do I do?" I asked Scotti.

"Go, start, drive," he said tightly. "They get out of the way."

So of course that was the time the limousine decided to get temperamental; and instead of the gradual acceleration I had in mind, we jerked forward in a series of ear-splitting backfires. But it did the trick; the good people of Mulberry Street jumped back in alarm, and I was able to drive away. It wasn't a smooth getaway, but get away we did. There was one huge sigh as eight people let out the breaths they'd been holding.

"I'm hungry," Emmy said.

□ **17** □ It was my first time in a police station, and it wasn't a place I cared to visit again in the immediately foreseeable future. The atmosphere was depressing; the place was a focal point for crime, after all. Everyone there had some connection with wrongdoers. As did we.

Caruso, however, was feeling his oats; he was the only one of us who'd ever been in a police station before and so he appointed himself our guide and instructor. The man had been impossible ever since I told the others that Osgood Springer was the one Uncle Hummy had seen with Duchon's spray bottle. "I am right!" he'd cried. "I say all the time it is Mr. Springer! I figure it out, no?"

It did no good whatsoever to tell him that he hadn't figured out a thing, that he'd merely made a wild guess. He simply would not listen; he was determined to take credit for solving the mystery and that was that. He went on and on about it until even good-natured Scotti began to get irritated with him.

We'd dropped Mildredandphoebe off; they'd done their job and there was no need to subject them to a police interrogation. I owed those girls more than I could say, and I planned to repay them in every way I could think of. But I was going to have to postpone thinking about that for a while, because we weren't quite finished yet. Because of Uncle Hummy.

The minute he saw the police station he'd started to cry. He'd kept crying even as we went in, turning to me once and saying something that sounded like, "You promise." While we were explaining to Lieutenant O'Halloran how we'd found Uncle Hummy and what he'd seen, the old man went right on crying. I tried to get him to tell me why he was crying but he wouldn't.

Lieutenant O'Halloran looked as if he wanted to cry himself. It couldn't have pleased him, learning that a group of girls had succeeded where his police force had failed. He bellowed at us that we should have given *him* the sketches Caruso made of Uncle Hummy, and Caruso bellowed back that the lieutenant was just put out because

he hadn't thought of the idea himself. O'Halloran asked
sarcastically if Caruso thought the police kept an artist on
the payroll, and Caruso said why not? It sounded like a
good idea to him.

In frustration the police detective started yelling at me,
since I was the one who'd had the idea of sending the
gerryflappers out with the sketches in the first place. Emmy
looked at me and rolled her eyes, Scotti sprang to my
defense, and Amato tried to reason with the lieutenant. I
just waited until he'd sputtered himself out.

"Why is he crying?" O'Halloran asked, pointing to
Uncle Hummy.

"He's afraid," I said. "Of Osgood Springer, I suppose.
I don't know why else he'd be crying." I told the lieuten-
ant everything I had learned during my period of snooping;
I couldn't tell how much of it he already knew.

"You five wait here," the lieutenant instructed us, and
hauled Uncle Hummy off to another room.

So the five highest-paid singers on the Metropolitan
Opera's roster sat twiddling their thumbs while the police
interrogated Uncle Hummy. Scotti and Amato tried to talk
about Osgood Springer and how desperately he must have
wanted Jimmy Freeman to succeed, but Caruso kept turning the talk back to his own "detecting abilities." We sat
and stared at the walls for a while, but that didn't help.
Emmy's stomach growled.

Eventually Lieutenant O'Halloran came back. "Well,
we finally found out your Uncle Hummy's real name. It's
Umberto."

"Is that his first name or his last name?" Emmy asked.

"Both. Umberto Umberto. And it's not Osgood Springer
he's afraid of, it's the police. It seems Mr. Umberto was in
trouble with the police some years back, through no fault
of his own. There was an unpleasant incident involving a
very young girl—you understand? She tentatively identi-
fied Uncle Hummy, but it turned out to be another man
who looked like him. The girl was frightened and simply
made a mistake, and Uncle Hummy was released immediately. But the experience so disturbed him that he's been
terrified of the police ever since. That's why he was crying."

"Poor old man," I murmured. I made a mental note to buy him a Victrola when this was all over.

"He's all right now," O'Halloran said. "We reassured him we just needed his help and there'd be no trouble at all for him. He says he saw the man with the scar on his jaw taking a spray bottle into Duchon's dressing room."

"What do you do about Osgood Springer?" Amato asked.

"I've sent a man to bring him in. Once Uncle Hummy identifies him in person, we'll place him under arrest and try to get a confession." He paused. "To tell you the truth, this is a tremendous load off my mind. I was beginning to fear we weren't going to find whoever was responsible."

I decided to ask a question I'd asked before without getting an answer. "Lieutenant, the note Duchon wrote me on the night all that happened—the one asking me to stand while he was singing his aria? Will you tell me now where you got it?"

He shrugged. "I found it on the floor of your dressing room."

"But I keep my dressing room locked. And I have the only key."

Unexpectedly he grinned at me. "Any policeman who can't pick a lock isn't worth his salt. It was easy, believe me."

I thought of Phoebe and her hairpin and believed him. "You searched my dressing room without my permission?"

O'Halloran started to shrug off my protest but then changed his mind. "Miss Farrar, I owe you an apology. Not for suspecting you—that's part of my job. But I shouldn't have yelled at you a little while ago. Your idea worked, and you have helped us. So I want to thank you."

For some reason I couldn't put my finger on, I felt uncomfortable. "Perhaps you'd better save your thanks, Lieutenant—until you have the villain locked up in a cell."

They all stared at me. "What is wrong, Gerry?" Scotti asked.

"I don't know," I said uneasily.

We knew soon enough. The man O'Halloran had sent to fetch Osgood Springer came back without him. "He's not at home," the man said. "His housekeeper said he'd gone to the opera house—some sort of last-minute rehearsal. You know how big that place is, Lieutenant. I thought I'd better get some help."

"A last-minute rehearsal?" Emmy said. "What opera?"

"The housekeeper said *Bore Us Good Enough,* sounded like."

I stood up. "Shall we go, Lieutenant?" Jimmy Freeman sang a small role in *Boris Godunoff,* a Russian giant of an opera that no conductor at the Met would touch except Toscanini. And where Jimmy Freeman was, Osgood Springer could not be far behind.

Two or three uniformed policemen in the station house were watching us as we left. One of them called, "Hey, Mr. Caruso—you gonna ask Miss Farrar for a rematch?"

Caruso turned beet red and hurried out through the door to the sound of laughter. I didn't join in; we were on our way to find a man responsible for another man's death, and this was no time for levity.

The *Boris* rehearsal had just ended when we got there. The orchestra musicians were packing up to leave, and most of the singers were still there. Then I saw something that made my heart sink: Toscanini and Gatti-Casazza were communicating through an intermediary. Gatti would say something to one of his assistants, and the assistant would run over to Toscanini. The Maestro would listen and answer, and the assistant would run back to Gatti. The two old friends had reached the point where they were no longer speaking to each other at all.

But that was not my concern now. The immediate problem was finding Osgood Springer and getting Uncle Hummy to identify him. Lieutenant O'Halloran had brought four men with him who immediately started looking for Springer; the lieutenant himself remained on the stage with Uncle Hummy. Emmy Destinn announced that if she was going to starve to death, she might as well do it on the stage of the Metropolitan Opera, and asked a stagehand to bring her a chair. Caruso announced that sitting down was an excellent idea and asked the stagehand to bring a chair for him too—and, as an afterthought, one for me as well. At that point the stagehand just shrugged and started dragging on chairs for anyone who felt like sitting.

Scotti, Caruso, Amato, Emmy, and I—we sat scattered about the stage, far from the orderly semicircle we'd made when Lieutenant O'Halloran first questioned us after that fateful performance of *Carmen*. Gatti-Casazza came up on the stage and asked the lieutenant what was going on. O'Halloran told him, and Gatti's face registered first shock and then relief. Shock at the impending arrest, relief that the man the police were looking for was not a member of the Metropolitan Opera Company.

Toscanini must have been watching because he immediately came on the stage too; but instead of approaching O'Halloran, who was still talking to Gatti, he came over to where Scotti and I were sitting and asked us. "They're looking for Osgood Springer," I said. "Uncle Hummy saw him taking a spray bottle into Philippe Duchon's dressing room."

"Ah." Toscanini thought a moment. "How do they know it is the right one?"

"Lieutenant O'Halloran seems satisfied it is."

Toscanini drew up a chair and sat down. Nobody wanted to miss the finale.

"Lieutenant O'Halloran, I understand you're looking for me?" Osgood Springer came on the stage, followed by Jimmy Freeman and one of O'Halloran's men.

Instead of answering him, O'Halloran turned to Uncle Hummy. "Is that the one?"

Uncle Hummy nodded uneasily. "Go now?"

O'Halloran gestured to his man. "Take him back to the station house. Keep him there till I get back." The man took Uncle Hummy by the arm and led him away.

"Lieutenant, what's going on?" Jimmy Freeman asked. "Is something the matter?"

"Something is very much the matter," O'Halloran said. "Mr. Springer, Uncle Hummy saw you taking the spray bottle into Duchon's dressing room."

Jimmy gasped, and Springer turned ghost-white. The latter recovered quickly, though. "He's mistaken."

"Is he?" O'Halloran asked.

"I tell you he is. Are you going to take that old man's word against mine?"

"I think he's telling the truth, yes. You put the ammonia in that spray bottle, and you did it because you thought your pupil here would never get his chance as long as Duchon was around. You did it—you're the one who put Duchon out of commission. That makes you responsible for his death. You're under arrest, Mr. Springer."

Jimmy immediately started protesting—loudly, angrily; he looked terribly frightened. Springer was weaving unsteadily on his feet, and Amato rushed over with a chair. The accused man sank down, looking as if he were going to pass out.

I didn't like this. I didn't like anything about it.

"You rummaged through the medicine bag Miss Destinn had put down somewhere looking for whatever was there, and you found the ammonia," O'Halloran went on. "Then you waited until no one was looking and took Duchon's spray bottle, emptied out the contents and poured in the ammonia, and put the bottle back in Duchon's dressing room. Then you told Freeman here to get into costume. You knew he'd be going on that night. Nobody else knew yet—but you knew. Isn't that the way it happened?"

"You're wrong, Lieutenant!" Jimmy cried hotly, his voice higher than I'd ever heard it. "You've made a mistake, a terrible mistake! He couldn't—"

"He could, and he did. What was it, Mr. Springer? Were you hoping to have the career through Freeman that you never had for yourself? You've made Freeman your surrogate, your substitute in your search for success—and you'd do anything to make sure he got ahead, wouldn't you? *Wouldn't you?*"

"This is insane!" Jimmy shouted. "Mr. Springer has never hurt anyone! Oh, Lieutenant, you're wrong, wrong!"

"James." Springer laid a restraining hand on his protégé's arm. "It's no use. Don't say any more. Yes, Lieutenant, I would do anything to assure James's success. *Anything.*"

"Mr. Springer!" Jimmy cried.

"Hush, James, say no more. Accept it." Jimmy turned away in anguish, and for a long time no one said anything.

Scotti whispered, "That is easy. I do not think evildoers confess so quickly."

"There's something not quite right here," I whispered back.

"We should not be here. It is . . . too personal, yes?"

"I, too, wish to be elsewhere," Toscanini whispered. But not one of us could get up and leave.

Caruso, however, was not in the least intimidated by the anguish we'd just witnessed. He walked over and planted himself squarely in front of Springer. "Mr. Springer, you do a shameful thing! Shameful, shameful! A great singer is dead because of what you do."

"Yes," Springer said tonelessly. "I . . . I never intended that to happen."

Lieutenant O'Halloran said, "Did you plan it ahead of it time, or what?"

"Ah, no, no I didn't. I acted on impulse. Yes. Impulse."

"Shameful!" Caruso repeated. "You know, Mr. Springer, I suspect you all along!"

"Did you really, Mr. Caruso," Springer said dryly.

"Ask anyone! Ask Gerry, ask Amato—"

Gatti-Casazza interrupted. "Congratulations, Lieutenant O'Halloran, and my sincerest thanks. You do a fine job. We are all grateful to you, I am sure."

O'Halloran shrugged. "Thank Miss Farrar. She found the eyewitness I needed."

Springer turned in his chair and looked at me. He looked me straight in the eye, without flinching; it was very disconcerting. Scotti put an arm around my shoulders.

O'Halloran tapped Springer on the shoulder. "Come along—we're finished here."

"Wait." I stood up. I didn't know what I was going to do, but I did know this wasn't right and I had to do something. Take the bull by the horns? I went over to Jimmy Freeman, who was sobbing silently, his back turned to Springer. "Jimmy? Jimmy, are you going to let this happen?"

His reddened eyes looked at me in surprise. "Wh-what?"

"Are you going to let Mr. Springer go to prison for something you did?"

There was this deathly silence for about three seconds, and then *everyone* started talking. "What *he* did?" Lieutenant O'Halloran said in surprise. "What are you talking about?"

"Gerry, are you feeling all right?" asked Emmy, always practical.

"Do I hear you right?" Scotti asked. "*Jimmy?*"

"*Che cosa dite?*" Toscanini wondered.

"*Che dite?*" Gatti-Casazza echoed.

"You do not understand, Gerry," Caruso explained patiently. "It is Mr. Springer who is guilty, not Jimmy."

"*Quiet!*" Amato roared, *fortissimo*. When everyone obeyed, he said, "Gerry—an explanation, please?"

Springer broke away from Lieutenant O'Halloran and headed straight for me. "Keep out of this," he hissed.

I turned on him. "Mr. Springer, you just said you'd do *anything* to assure Jimmy's success. Does that include taking the blame for a crime you didn't commit? Do you know what will happen to you?"

"You don't know what you're talking about," Springer said angrily.

Jimmy looked at me, his anguish evident to everyone. "Gerry—I'm no criminal!"

I put my hands on his shoulders. "I know you're no criminal, Jimmy. But even the best of people can slip when the temptation is too great. The temptation *and* the opportunity." *Be a man, Jimmy,* I prayed silently. "Remember when you told me how much you owed Mr. Springer? How he did everything for you, how he gave up all his other students for you? Are you going to let him give up his freedom too?"

"Don't listen to her, James," Springer snapped.

"I think you had better listen to her, James," Lieutenant O'Halloran said, coming up to us. "If I've got the wrong man, I want to know it. Do you have something to tell me?"

Guilt, fear, remorse, anxiety, uncertainty—Jimmy's face

reflected each of them in turn. By then almost everyone on the stage understood what had really happened; it only remained for Jimmy to admit it. Finally he crumpled into a chair and buried his face in his hands so he wouldn't have to look at anybody. He mumbled, "Mr. Springer didn't do it. I did."

"James!" Springer's cry held all the heartbreak in the world; with Jimmy's admission of guilt, the vocal coach saw the dreams of a lifetime crumbling before his very eyes.

"No no no no no no," Caruso instructed Jimmy. "*You* do not do it. It is Mr. Springer."

O'Halloran waved him away. "All right, Freeman, let's hear the rest of it. It was the medicine bag that gave you the idea?" Jimmy nodded. "So you saw the chance to get rid of Duchon for good—"

"No!" Jimmy cried. "It wasn't like that! I thought it would just make him sick for a while. Once when I was singing in Chicago, one of the other singers got sick from breathing ammonia fumes. He missed two performances. So I thought if Duchon sprayed the ammonia directly into his throat he might, oh, he might be out for the rest of the season. Just long enough to give me a decent chance. I thought everyone would believe it was just another one of those accidents that kept happening to him . . . I didn't know it would destroy his voice! I never dreamed that would happen!"

I for one believed him; it was just the sort of mistake Jimmy would make. Lieutenant O'Halloran seemed to believe him too. "So where does Mr. Springer come in? Why was he taking the bottle into Duchon's dressing room?" Jimmy just shook his head; he couldn't say any more. O'Halloran turned to Springer. "Mr. Springer? You might as well tell me. It's all up now anyway."

Springer smiled sadly. "Yes, it is, isn't it? Very well, what does it matter? I came upon James holding the spray bottle. He'd already put the ammonia in, but I didn't know that yet. James told me Duchon had forgotten his spray bottle, so I said I'd take it to him. Since I didn't know what was in the bottle, I didn't take any particular pains to avoid being seen—I was just returning a spray bottle, that was all. That was when the old man must have seen me.''

"But later?" O'Halloran prompted. "Later you figured out what had happened—after Duchon was taken to the hospital and Dr. Curtis said it was ammonia in the spray."

Springer grunted. "It was pretty obvious, wasn't it?"

"So you went to Freeman and you told him—"

"No. We never spoke of it. Not once."

Murmurs of surprise ran across the stage. *"Non credo niente,"* Toscanini muttered. Gatti sank silently onto the nearest chair.

"It's true," Springer said. "I think James knew all along that I knew, but there was a sort of tacit understanding between us. We would proceed as usual, and not make trouble for ourselves if we could avoid it."

I cleared my throat. "Mr. Springer, you didn't tell Jimmy to get into costume early, did you? That was his own idea."

Springer nodded. "I wondered at the time why he was getting dressed—but of course that made sense later too. It was his eagerness. He knew he'd be singing in Duchon's place."

"When we were in the museum," I went on, "you told me you saw Duchon spitting blood before the performance began. Was that true?"

Springer gave a loud snort. "No, it wasn't true. Duchon was healthy as a horse. He would have lived to be a hundred."

"So our talk in the museum was—"

"Lies, Miss Farrar. Lies to protect other lies. By then the question of why James had gotten into costume early had become something of an issue. I had to provide a believable reason for his doing so."

"You did," I said wryly. "I believed you. Didn't it bother you, Mr. Springer, how quick Jimmy was to put the blame on you? When he said *you* had told him to lie about getting into costume?"

"That was a temporizing measure. He told me about it immediately."

O'Halloran said, "I thought you never talked about it."

"We never talked about the act itself," Springer explained. "We did talk about protecting ourselves."

"You're making excuses for him," I murmured. Springer didn't answer.

"This makes you an accomplice, you know," O'Halloran said to Springer.

"I know. What does it matter now?"

"Only one thing left," O'Halloran growled. "Miss Farrar—how in the world did you know it was Freeman instead of Springer?"

"Yes, Gerry," Scotti said, "how do you know?"

"I didn't *know*," I protested. "It just seemed to me all along that what happened to Duchon was mostly a nasty trick that got out of hand, something that was far more serious in its consequences than was intended. Mr. Springer has been in the business of training the voice for—how long, Mr. Springer? Twenty years?"

"Twenty-four."

"Twenty-four years—that's a long time. It seemed inconceivable that a man so experienced in matters concerning the human vocal mechanism wouldn't know the effects on the voice box of something as strong as ammonia." I paused. "So many things can damage the vocal cords—we have to be careful all the time. Mr. Springer just isn't naïve enough to think there'd be no permanent damage."

"And I am," Jimmy said bitterly. "I see."

"Lieutenant O'Halloran," Springer spoke quickly, "James made a mistake—a stupid mistake, granted, but it was a mistake. He did not intend to ruin a man's career. He certainly did not intend that man's death. There was no murder in his heart. Will this be taken into consideration?"

"I'm fairly sure it will," O'Halloran said. "I'll say so myself, at the trial."

Jimmy stood up slowly and sort of gave himself a little shake. "Thank you, Lieutenant. I'll appreciate your help, although I'm not certain I deserve such consideration. I am responsible for Philippe Duchon's death. No one else. Just me."

So there it was. Jimmy Freeman was a decent young

man who had done one indecent thing in his life. And now he was going to pay for it.

It had finally begun to sink in on Caruso what had happened. "It is Jimmy?" he asked disbelievingly. "It is not Mr. Springer?"

Lieutenant O'Halloran gestured to a couple of his men, who each took Jimmy and Springer by an arm and started leading them off the stage. Jimmy stopped and turned to me. "I'm sorry, Gerry," he said. And then they were gone.

"Not the man I came here to arrest," O'Halloran said, looking after Jimmy. "That was a close one. If there weren't so many meddlers muddying the waters . . ." he trailed off. The lieutenant stared a moment first at me and then at Caruso and then at me again. "Oh, what's the use!" he muttered, and stalked off.

"It is not Mr. Springer?" Caruso asked me.

"Interesting," Scotti said. "You send Jimmy to jail and he apologizes to *you*. What does he apologize for?"

"I think for not being the sort of person I wanted him to be," I said. "But if I hadn't said anything, he would have spoken up on his own, eventually. He couldn't let Mr. Springer take his punishment for him."

"It is not Mr. Springer?" Caruso asked Gatti-Casazza.

Emmy had a funny look in her eye. "You surprise me, Gerry. Jimmy has always been such a favorite of yours, I would have thought—well, I'd have thought you'd be more likely to help conceal what he did than reveal it."

That hurt my feelings. "Really? Do you really think I'd do that?"

"The thought occurred to me. You've been championing his career for so long—why *did* you do it?"

"Because," I sputtered, "because it was the right thing to do!"

"Well, good for you," she smiled. "You do surprise me—but good for you."

Now that was grossly unfair of her; I frequently do things because they are right. "I didn't like doing it, you know."

"I know," she said sympathetically. Scotti gave me a little hug.

"Such a waste," Toscanini murmured, shaking his head. "That fine voice—locked up in a prison. A great waste, no?" We all agreed it was indeed a great waste.

Gatti-Casazza got up heavily from the chair where he'd been sitting silently for so long. "A member of the Metropolitan Opera Company in prison! I do not think . . . it does not . . . ah, such a promising young singer, lost, lost! *Cielo!* What a pity."

"A great pity," Toscanini agreed.

Gatti and Toscanini looked at each other quickly. *People draw together in times of misfortune,* I reminded myself and held my breath. Toscanini raised one hand a little, Gatti opened his mouth as if to speak—and for a moment I thought they were going to make up their differences then and there. But both men abruptly turned on their heels and marched off in opposite directions.

"No reconciliation," Scotti moaned. *"Mi rincresce."* I was sorry too.

"It is not Mr. Springer?" Caruso asked Amato.

"No, Rico, it is not Mr. Springer."

"It is not Mr. Springer," the tenor said leadenly, accepting Amato's word for it. "All the time—all the time, I think it is Mr. Springer."

"We know, Rico," Amato smiled.

"But it is Jimmy!" Caruso threw up his hands. *"Per dio!* Who would think young Jimmy can do such a terrible thing?" He turned and glared at me. *"You* think so! You think so, and you do not tell me!"

"Oh, Rico, I suspected almost everybody at one time or another," I said lightly. "I was even wondering about nyself at one point. The one person I never suspected was 'ou."

That made him feel better, a little. Amato said, "You .now what you need, Rico? You need a nice dish of pasta. With clam sauce, perhaps?"

Caruso grinned his old familiar wicked grin and wagged one finger under his friend's nose. "Eh, you think I do not know what you do, yes? You try to distract me with talk of food. But I am too clever for you, Pasquale—I understand you! Besides, I have pasta and clam sauce last night.''

Amato laughed and said, ''What about the rest of you? We go to the Café Martin, yes?''

''Hungry?'' Scotti asked me. ''Emmy, the Café Martin?'' She didn't hear him; she appeared abstracted.

How the men could think of restaurants at a time like this was beyond me. ''I couldn't eat anything, Toto,'' I said. ''In fact, I feel a little sick. I think I'll just go on home.''

He smiled in a kindly manner, understanding. ''Gerry. It is not good, being alone right now. You go home, you brood, you make yourself more unhappy. No, you come with us. You eat a little something, you feel better, yes? You come.''

Food, the universal solace. Maybe he was right; anything to put off thinking about Jimmy Freeman a little longer. ''You go on with the others,'' I told Scotti. ''Emmy and I'll catch up with you in a moment.'' The three men sauntered off the stage, the grim little scene we'd just witnessed already behind them.

I had to say her name twice before she heard me. ''Sorry,'' Emmy said, ''I was thinking about something else.''

''You were right all along,'' I told her. ''About Jimmy Freeman.''

She waved a hand. ''A guess. The same way Rico guessed Mr. Springer.''

''But your guess was right.'' We were both silent a moment, and then I roused myself and said, ''The men seem to have decided on the Café Martin. Is that all right with you?''

''I think I'll go home.''

That surprised me. ''You don't want something to eat after all?''

''No, I mean all the way home. Home to Prague, when the season's over.''

I was appalled. ''Oh, Emmy, you can't mean that! You can't travel through a war zone!''

"Prague is home. My house is there, and my friends."
She sighed. "I miss my cats. It is *home*."

I stared. "You're willing to get shot at because you *miss your cats*?"

She sniffed. "It's more than that. What if it was your country that was a battleground? Wouldn't you worry about it?"

"Of course I'd worry about it. But I don't know that I'd go there."

She shook her head. "I have to see for myself. I'll stay only a month, maybe less. Nothing will happen to me—you'll see."

I thought she was crazy and said so. But then, it was just one more evidence of the difference between us; she had her way, I had mine. "Emmy—shake hands."

She looked surprised. "Why?"

"I don't know. I just feel like shaking hands."

She shrugged and indulged me. We shook hands, and then went our separate ways.

❏ EPILOGUE ❏

Toscanini left the Metropolitan Opera in 1915 and never went back; he and Gatti-Casazza did not speak for seventeen years. Caruso married and settled down. Geraldine Farrar also tried matrimony but didn't like it much; she divorced her actor husband after a couple of years. Emmy Destinn spent the war years a virtual house-prisoner in Prague; the Austrians would not allow her to return to America. Pasquale Amato eventually turned his talents to teaching, joining the music faculty of Tulane University. Antonio Scotti continued the perennial bachelor, amiable, charming, and always in love—with Geraldine Farrar most of the time, with somebody or other the rest of the time.

But when they were all together, they made *glorious* music.

About the Author

BARBARA PAUL formerly taught at the University of Pittsburgh, but now devotes herself to writing full-time. Her mystery novels include *The Fourth Wall, Liars and Tyrants and People Who Turn Blue, First Gravedigger, Your Eyelids Are Growing Heavy, The Renewable Virgin,* and *A Cadenza for Caruso* (available in a Signet edition). She has also written science fiction: *An Exercise for Madmen, Pillars of Salt, Bibblings,* and *Under the Canopy*.

SUPER SLEUTHS

(0451)

☐ **ACCIDENTAL CRIMES by John Hutton.** It was the perfect place for murder... a lonely road through a desolate moorland. And in the killer's twisted mind, they'd been the perfect victims: young and pretty, hitchhiking alone after dark..." A dazzling psychological thriller..." —*Publishers Weekly* (137884—$3.50)†

☐ **NIGHTCAP by J.C.S. Smith.** Someone had taken Lombardo's reputation for drop-dead chic too literally—but to have gotten up to the penthouse without using the locked elevators, the killer would have to be deadlier and far more cunning than the subway rats Jacoby was used to chasing... (137736—$2.95)*

☐ **THE GREAT DIAMOND ROBBERY by John Minahan.** There were twelve diamonds, famous and flawless. And three suspects, all no-name, Class B hoods. There had to be a Mr. or Ms. Big, pulling the tangle of strings that leads Rawlings all the way to England... and a spooky aging beauty with a family secret that makes the Godfather's look tame... (135717—$3.50)*

☐ **JUNKYARD DOG by Robert Campbell.** Is the debris from a blown-up Chicago clinic the perfect cover-up for murder? When an anti-abortion demonstration ends with a bomb blast that kills a pretty young girl and an old woman, precinct captain Flannery takes it personally. But when the killer goes after Flannery's lady, he gets as mean as a junkyard dog—on the scent of dirty politics mixed with passion and revenge, a very deadly combination.... (143965—$2.95)

☐ **THE 600 POUND GORILLA by Robert Campbell.** It becomes a jungle out there when Chicago politicians get tangled up in monkey business—and the result is murder. When the boiler in the local zoo goes kaput, Chicago's favorite gorilla, Baby, gets transferred to a local hot spot. But things heat up when two customers are found beaten to death and everyone thinks Baby went bananas. But precinct captain Jimmy Flannery is about to risk his life to prove it's murder... (147103—$2.95)

*Prices slightly higher in Canada
†Not available in Canada

There's an epidemic with 27 million victims. And no visible symptoms.

It's an epidemic of people who can't read.

Believe it or not, 27 million Americans are functionally illiterate, about one adult in five.

The solution to this problem is you... when you join the fight against illiteracy. So call the Coalition for Literacy at toll-free **1-800-228-8813** and volunteer.

Volunteer Against Illiteracy. The only degree you need is a degree of caring.